D0497944

Praise for *The Museum of Abandoned Secrets* (translated by Nina Murray)

"*The Museum of Abandoned Secrets* is a magnum opus in which everything that the armory of literature can provide is mobilized against the forces of darkness: strong emotions, the power of pathos, the most compelling images . . . A novel of power—and a powerful novel."

—Deutschlandradio

"Violence and fear lie in the bones of generations of Ukrainians, and what power do the ostracized dead have over the living? Oksana Zabuzhko writes about this heavy subject as lightly and freshly as the main female character talks."

—*WDR*

"This book is a spectacular intellectual success. It is driven by the belief that intellectual and political freedom is the only thing worth fighting for, apart from love, of course . . . With *The Museum of Abandoned Secrets*, Oksana Zabuzhko has written both herself and Ukraine into the scabby heart of Europe."

—*Berliner Zeitung*

ALSO BY OKSANA ZABUZHKO

Fieldwork in Ukrainian Sex (translated by Halyna Hryn)

The Museum of Abandoned Secrets (translated by Nina Murray)

YOUR AD COULD GO HERE

OKSANA ZABUZHKO

EDITED BY NINA MURRAY

AMAZON **CROSSING**

Text copyright © 2017 by Oksana Zabuzhko
Translation copyright "Oh Sister, My Sister" © 2020 by Halyna Hryn
Translation copyright "Girls" © 2005 by Askold Melnyczuk
Translation copyright "The Tale of the Guelder Rose Flute" © 2020 by Halyna Hryn and Nina Murray
Translation copyright "I, Milena" © 1998 by Marco Carynnyk & Marta Horban
Translation copyright "An Album for Gustav" © 2017 by Nina Murray
Translation copyright "Your Ad Could Go Here" © 2020 by Halyna Hryn
Translation copyright "The Tennis Instructor" © 2020 by Halyna Hryn
Translation copyright "No Entry to the Performance Hall after the Third Bell" © 2020 by Halyna Hryn

Previously published as *Pislya tretioho dzvinka vhid do zaly zaboronyayetsia* by Komora Publishing House in Kyiv, Ukraine, in 2017. Translated from Ukrainian by Halyna Hryn, Askold Melnyczuk, Nina Murray, Marco Carynnyk, and Marta Horban. Edited by Nina Murray. First published as a collection in English by Amazon Crossing in 2020.

"Girls," translated by Askold Melnyczuk, was first published in *Words Without Borders*, April 2005.

"I, Milena," translated by Marco Carynnyk and Marta Horban, was originally included in *Two Lands, New Visions: Stories from Canada and Ukraine*, eds. Janice Kulyk Keefer and Solomea Pavlychko, Coteau Books, 1998.

"An Album for Gustav," translated by Nina Murray, was first published in *Berlin Quarterly*, Winter 2017.

Published by Amazon Crossing, Seattle
www.apub.com

Amazon, the Amazon logo, and Amazon Crossing are trademarks of Amazon.com, Inc., or its affiliates.

ISBN-13: 9781542019422 (hardcover)
ISBN-10: 1542019427 (hardcover)

ISBN-13: 9781542022521 (paperback)
ISBN-10: 1542022525 (paperback)

Cover design by David Drummond
First edition

CONTENTS

I   1

"Oh Sister, My Sister," translated by Halyna Hryn   3

"Girls," translated by Askold Melnyczuk   15

"The Tale of the Guelder Rose Flute," translated by
Halyna Hryn and Nina Murray   49

II   109

"I, Milena," translated by Marco Carynnyk and Marta
Horban, edited with additional translation by Nina Murray   111

"An Album for Gustav," translated by Nina Murray   145

"Your Ad Could Go Here," translated by Halyna Hryn   173

III   183

"The Tennis Instructor," translated by Halyna Hryn   185

"No Entry to the Performance Hall after the Third Bell,"
translated by Halyna Hryn   197

I

OH SISTER, MY SISTER

TRANSLATED BY HALYNA HRYN

You should have had a sister—say four, no, five years younger. Disembodied female names circled above your entire childhood, switching places with each other, calling out to each other—you didn't know how to connect them, and you didn't dare give them to your dolls: they were not dolls' names, not borrowed from living people, but rather from somewhere beyond. It was as if someone was trying to reach you through the moan of a name that bobbed up, unbeckoned, settled into your inner ear for a long, long time (all these names moaned, the one repeated most often was Ivánna)—someone wanted to be named. In second grade you had to transfer to a new school, and that was the first time you thought of a change of place as liberation, as breaking into a sphere where you could correct your own biography into that which should have been: you told your new classmates that you had a little sister, Ivánka, who didn't go to school yet, and thus inadvertently did what your parents lacked the courage to do: you summoned to life a girl's fair-haired head of fluffy curls lit up by sunshine. Later they would have inevitably turned darker, just as yours had. But your little lie was discovered, and once your daily verbal singing-brook dried up, its small current being the only place where Ivánka could move (you'd tell your desk mate in the morning, yawning wearily, "Ivánka was so cranky yesterday, wouldn't fall asleep—we stayed up playing until ten")—the fair-haired head of fluffy curls was also extinguished, forever falling out of that dimension where people grow and change.

Thus she was killed for the second time.

Because in fact you *did* have a sister. She had gills and a curled-up short tail instead of feet—like a small crayfish or a seahorse. A tadpole of a girl with a broad forehead like everyone else in your family. Her eyes, probably, had not opened yet, because actually, there wasn't anything to look at: it was dark all around her. And moist. And warm. Her cells wanted one thing: to divide, unstoppably and constantly—inside, where she was, it must feel the way it does when your body is racked by involuntary shivers, yet without that panic of weakness that generally besets us at such times, because we have already learned that the body must be obedient. But in there, when the soul is only beginning to grow a body, the persistent tremor of quickly multiplying cells must feel like an incessant, quivering joy of arrival, of being carried, swiftly and assuredly, through a dark tunnel toward the light. And that's why you could not shake the idea of fear—the first and last fear felt by your sister in this world, of whom there remained, like clothes on the shore left by someone who drowned, only the distant echo of a name (*Ivánna*, or perhaps another -*anna*) and an uncertain visage of a four-year-old girl's fair fluffy curls lit up by the sun, of the fear that came from the outside, that tossed and tumbled that entire whale in which she blissfully rocked like a tiny Jonah—a terrifying push, a noiseless infrasound of a sliding avalanche, and the surrounding darkness suddenly no longer a bubbly refuge, but pumping danger with such deadly intensity that the girl-tadpole thrashed in panic and would have screamed, but she had no lungs yet for screaming, was only the thin petal of endoderm that vibrated wildly, in vain—it was too soon, too soon!—while all around fear persisted, pure fear, formless and omnipotent; she thrashed about in its very nexus, blindly poking in all directions looking for a safe haven, because she still had to build up her tiny body, her frail arms, her skinny limp legs with tiny curled-out feet, like a frog's. Behind that fear something else was swiftly raising itself, something like a large lid designed for pressing down on a quashed tiny hot lump that didn't even have a voice yet, nor any way of giving a sign down that tunnel to let them know she was there—I'm here already, right over here, just let me build up my body a bit more! . . . You, of course, knew nothing about such things then; you were five and must have been swaddling your doll in the living room on the couch, when you suddenly heard muted choked noises from the kitchen, where your parents sat talking after dinner, barking noises—noises made with a woman's voice you did not recognize, because how could you know back then that a woman's voice could produce them?—and a second later your mother's cry sliced the air; yes, it was Mother's, but what a different, sinister, inner deep-well cry—it would be branded into your memory for the rest of your life:

"Bastards! Animals! Damn them!"

Whispers, Father's hushed persuading voice—like shuffling on an audiotape. You burst into the kitchen, and the sight (close up!) hit you between the eyes—your mother's wet, red face, strands of hair plastered onto her forehead, and that was all that was bestowed on you from that episode: your role of an observer, a helpless witness that stands to the side with her hands occupied by a doll, or a stack of books.

The books—there was another distinct memory, from before that night—you couldn't remember how much earlier—when men you did not know filled your apartment without taking off their coats, which instantly made the space feel cramped, and, with their backs to your parents, began digging through the bookcases and Daddy's desk while Mom and Dad sat on the couch and said nothing, only whispering to each other from time to time. After some time (one hour, two? three?) you got bored sitting around like that and snuck away to your corner to fill your lap with books, *Ukrainian Folk Riddles* on top, in hardback with a dreamy little boy on the blue cover. You asked if you could be excused to go—at least on the balcony if you were not allowed out-side—which was a rather rational thing to do for a five-year-old; you did seem to be about the only person in that one-act play to behave rationally, because, for example, your dad, whom they intercepted at the entrance to the building as he was returning from the institute, so he was the one to ring the doorbell and it ended up looking like *he* was the one who brought the men with him, when his wife opened the door, could only muster, completely shocked, "Natalia, look who joined me . . . ," as if indeed these were guests dropping by for a cup of tea, and it's not even hard to imagine how your mother, who was younger than you are now, your slender and warm mom, who always smelled nice, could, letting the man into the hallway, stutter out in reply, "Nice to meet you." And it was only then that they presented their IDs. (When many years later, in another building, they stopped you just like that, in the hallway, you, without skipping a beat, as if you'd been waiting for them these twenty years, demanded to see their identity papers, although, if you really think about it, what the hell did you need them for?—but, perhaps, the whole point was that back then, when you were five years old, nobody identified themselves to you, nobody said, "Darka, please meet Mr. So-and-So," nobody felt any need to explain anything to you, to make those men face you and explain who they were. In fact, the faces they have are those stiff folding ID cards with fine print on the left flap, which you wouldn't have had time to read anyway because as soon as they open it, they instantly make that all-powerful piece of cardboard disappear again, smooth as magicians, as you were able to ascertain for yourself twenty years later.) At first it was only their backs, grey-coated backs without the slightest interest in your existence, but in the presence of which it was nonetheless forbidden to leave the apartment or move around it as you wished—even tiptoeing to the toilet occurred under their supervision—and only once did something almost like a face shoot out of that grey blockading density at you, and it didn't really look at you because its eyelids were lowered—and that was exactly when you were standing there with your armful of books, topped by the *Ukrainian Folk Riddles* in hardcover with the drawing of the little blue boy lost in thought, with a finger on his forehead, and you asked your mother if you could at least go out to the balcony if you weren't allowed to go outside; that's when this almost-a-face said in Russian, "Let's have a look at your books, *dyevochka*," in a voice that also didn't really have room for you, contained no indication, in fact, that it was addressing *you*. And you were not *dyevochka*, your name was Darka, so you stood there, surprised, on the caramel-colored parquet floor still sticky from the varnish (renovations just finished!) with your armful of books, staring, chin up at that almost-a-face, until your mom, your slender and warm mom, who always smelled so nice and who had been quietly rocking your baby sister inside her for three months already, wrapped her arms around you, made a violet-scented woolen cocoon of her sweater sleeves around you as if trying to absorb you back inside of her, where in fact there was no more room for you, and said, with a gentle breath into your ear, "Why don't you go show that nice man what you've been reading." Yes, why don't you go and tell him all about it, or maybe even stand up tall there and recite a little poem for the guests, why don't you—your mother's instinct gave her the perfect strategy to domesticate the nice man, translate him into a familiar language, like that monster mutt who once chased you in a park and you got so scared, and ran, and cried, and tripped, falling to the sound of your own screams into the grass, while Mother, who had already calmed the dog down, laughed and brought him over to you: Look, silly, the doggy just wanted to play with you—the dog stood by, looking guilty—Don't be afraid, he's not scary at all, why don't we go up and pet him. The strange thing was, this seemed to work on the KGB guy as well as it did on you, because when he returned the books to you after rummaging through them for a few minutes (squeezing the covers and spines carefully to see whether anything was hidden there), he braved playing along in the role so casually foisted upon him by this pale, deathly frightened woman, handed the books back to you as if he really were a nice man, awkwardly, like someone who had never had anything to do with children, and said, "Here you go, *dyevochka* . . . you got some nice books there." The books were all shuffled into a different order, and you confidently pulled the blue dreamy boy to the top once again; however, something was no longer quite right—something sweet and pleasing, the books' promise, had been extruded, removed, and you did not feel like taking them out on the balcony anymore. You held them in your arms, and this became your most precise, your only unequivocally clear memory of that September day: you are standing there, and your hands are occupied with your books.

It was perhaps at that very moment, when she rushed to take you into her arms, to embrace and shield you with her whole body, that a realization flashed through your mother's mind, an obscure, alarming truth: she would not be able to shield the both of you. She had no room for two. Thus you, by virtue of your fully realized, irrevocable presence in this world, edged your sister out of it. Because how else to explain that it was you your sister kept calling out for, for several years afterward, with that distant hum of a name you could never make out, and it was only to you she manifested in the vision of a light-haired head, turned so the sun lit up its soft curls? You were sitting with your feet up on the couch reading a fairy tale in which the traveling salt traders made a flute from a guelder rose branch, stopped at the house at the edge of the village, and when the farmer's daughter raised the flute to her lips, the flute began to speak: Gently, gently, my sister, play, do not stab my heart today; it was you, sister, who drove us apart, plunged a knife into my heart . . . You don't have to plunge a knife into someone's heart to end them—simply having already been born is enough.

You found out that you had a sister much, much later, when you were twelve or thirteen—your mom told you, and your parents had a fight about it because your father thought that children shouldn't be told about such things: like with all men, he could only be convinced of a child's existence at the moment he could hold the baby in his arms and lower her into a warm bath, so it's possible that your mother was unconsciously looking for an ally in you, a girl about to become a woman; however, she did not know about the visions of the little curly-haired head that no longer returned to visit you, about the onslaught of indistinct, moaned names that would make you mutter them under your breath for days at a time—but there were things you did not know either. You had no idea what it was like for her, being in her third month of pregnancy, to lose fifteen pounds in seven days so that all her dresses hung on her like on a closet hanger, and to be called from work for interrogations every day: to have to get up from your desk in the sudden cotton-batting silence with all eyes fixed on you, and have the driver in a military uniform waiting for you in a car downstairs—and to walk around for an entire month with your eyes wide open as if stuck between your eyelids, dry, but hot, like after crying. Every fear has its volume and weight—Natalia's filled her already-diminished body to the brim, pushing out through her eyes and, probably, the final straw (the clang, and the raising of a giant lid) came not even that night when she sat weeping in the kitchen the way that one sobs two, perhaps three times in one's life (Bastards! Animals! Damn them!), already know-ing that her husband, Anton, was right, that she, what had become of her, could not possibly bear a healthy child—the final straw came later when, having washed her face with ice-cold water and feeling the cold slowly taking possession of her, still living, the marble cold of a tomb-stone moist with beads of dew, she drew upon the full force of her icy body and spoke to the terrified hot little lump of life that desperately burrowed into the deepest recesses inside her, Forgive me. Forgive me, baby, my sweet little girl or boy, my darling—your mother dare not suckle you on her fear.

And there was another thing you didn't know—that a few years later, in the middle of that brief time when your parents *were not* expect-ing to be arrested any day, your sister would appear to your mother. Natalia could never quite make out her face—it was obscured by a pale, shimmering smudge, as if seen through tears; the whole dream came to her in black and white, a vision seen at night or in luminescent lighting: out of the darkness a tiny moonlight-pale girl wordlessly reached out for her, as if drowning, with long, pale arms, and outstretched fingers, weepy and quivering, draped over an expanding spiderweb of threadlike tendons. The arms reached with a pleading tremble for a human touch—*Mommy,* that gesture mutely begged, *Mommy.* And here's where Natalia was plunged into that crumbling abyss of terror after which comes nothing—her own desperate scream woke her, and remained clanging around her entire unhinged body as she sat at the edge of her bed curled into a ball, teeth chattering as her body temperature fell (only the face of a clock on the dresser glowed in the darkness: it was 3:00 a.m.) and rather than the release from the nightmare she felt the crush of the full weight of the crystal-clear awareness that this terror *was not her own*—and that she would now have to live with this knowledge evermore. That terror came from without—it swept in from out there, out of the mute luminescence of the night, where it held in the amniotic fluids her rejected child, her little girl cast out into the moonlit cold— only now was it revealed to her that it was a girl, because the abortion was late term and difficult, permission barely granted on the grounds of "mental-health indicators," and in reply to her blubbering question as to whether it was a girl or a boy Natalia heard, "Who the hell can tell now," and it was at that point that she dug in and, with teeth clenched and tears dammed, demanded that they show her that which was or would have been her second child. Because, no matter how crushed she was, the idea that this child, this tiny crumb of existence as fragile as a breath of air, this bud of already sovereign flesh that had managed to change all the clocks in her body, so adeptly setting up and furnishing its first earthly abode, could disappear without a trace, unrecognized, unnoted by anyone, unrevealed in any way, would be as intolerable as a pair of white-hot metal forceps applied to her brain—that there should be no sign of it, no remembered feature, not a mite, no eye color or shape of the skull, nor even sex, nothing whatsoever, naught, as though she, Natalia, had only been pregnant with fear and not with a human child. What she saw—what floated in the cynical gleam of a zinc basin—looked like slices of raw liver in black clumps of oily blood, and that indeed was the sum of your sister's earthly existence, this "who the hell can tell now": the curette had cut lengthwise and crosswise, like the mythical self-wielding ax—everything that had been rooting in the moist steamy ground was uprooted, cleared, grubbed, stripped, scraped down, down to the yellow clay, to the white bone, to the permafrost, to the petrified layer of lye at the bottom of the pit, to the rattle of cattle cars on buckled rails across the snow-swept tundra. Twenty years before, it was one such cattle car that carried Anton, delirious with fever, and among the prisoners there was a woman, whose name he fixed in his memory for all times and bequeathed to Darka—a deposit into the bank of indivisible time—the woman who collected shearling coats, or even furs—there were aristocrats in that car, old Galician professors, high clergy, a former envoy to the Imperial Parliament in Vienna, with his whole family, whom everyone still addressed as "Your Excellency"— their heavy furs still held the ethereal dust of prewar European hotels, women's perfume, flakes of opera house gilding, tasseled velvet drapery, while the shearlings smelled bitter and hard as such coats should, with the acrid stench of old sweat and ineradicable dirt under fingernails, the waft of cattle pens and millet gruel with milk, the animal-lair breath of a peasant hut, and the grim, churchy smell of beeswax candles. That woman shouted all of those things away from their owners, pushing them to crowd under shared covers, and heaped the goods over the eighteen-year-old boy burning up with fever, and laid herself on top so he wouldn't be able to struggle free. For three days she held down, with her own body, this mountain of lifesaving warmth that sucked death out of the boy and into itself; for three days in a packed cattle car some- where on the immeasurable distance between Lviv and Chita, this woman labored to give Anton another life from the collective suffocat- ing, furry, woolen, felted mass of their ruined lives, as if from a common

11

womb. On the third day Anton's fever broke, and in a few days more they arrived to where they were being taken, and Anton never saw that woman again. For Natalia—gutted, violated, and crucified on that gynecological chair—it became abundantly clear that the crazed ax had never stopped chasing Anton—along the rail tracks, for twenty years, chopping and slicing away the mounds of protective warmth thrown together by various women, nests to nurture new little lives—isn't that what the KGB lieutenant colonel meant when he told him during an interrogation (in Russian, of course), long after Anton was rehabilitated, allowed to earn his degree, allowed to teach, "You were in the camps, and now you don't want to work with us—you'll have cause to regret it"? *Regret it*, whimper like a dog with a broken spine, beg forgiveness of your children for bringing them into this world—that's what they wanted from us, vermin, bastards, monsters, not on your life, I will raise her, my Darka, my girl, the only one left to me now, I will not let her slip away the way I let this one, letting you spread my knees and turn her into these pieces of raw liver in clots of black blood, my baby, will you ever forgive me? . . . This—or something like this—was your mother's experience at the time, so it is no wonder that when she finally did see your sister on that luminescent night and felt, if only for an instant, her first and last terror she carried with her out of this world, she immediately knew it to be the answer to her mute pleading. So it must have been, because after that Ivánna never showed herself again—neither to your mother, nor to you. Another twenty years passed, half of them consumed by Anton's slow dying, and only then, once the heavy lid closed down behind him, and only a biting winter wind was left in the empty cemetery to tussle the black gilded bows of the wreaths and the chrysanthemum blooms stuck in the slimy mud kneaded by countless feet, did Natalia have another dream: in that dream Anton was walking away from her; she saw only his back and there was night all around, but out of that night stepped a little girl in a white dress who took his hand—she did it so confidently, and so parental was her husband's instant response, that Natalia, for whom the entire scene unfolded in silence, felt utterly at peace, and thought as they disappeared in the distance: Well that's good, he's home. It was strange, though, that this time she did not recognize the girl: all her attention was focused on her husband, and the next morning, when she told the dream to Darka, she did not understand her daughter when she said, looking aside, "It was her." "Who?" Natalia felt as if she had tripped on something in the middle of a fast run: for the first time in what felt like a single clotted infinity, this dream promised her *peace*, and she responded to her daughter's abrupt surgical intrusion into it with the same cold internal spasm she experienced at every unexpected ring of the doorbell, or a hand-delivered telegram, born of the apprehension, no, certainty, that once again, something was going to be taken away from her. But you, her sweet Darka, now a grown woman, hands falling free along the lines of your strong and beautiful young body—neither a cigarette nor a cup of coffee occupied them—said with barely felt cruelty, or rather, with a tantalizing urge to grab your mother by the shoulders and shake her as someone who refuses to wake up, "That was the child who was never born—and so now they've finally met." Natalia then realized that it was true, that's exactly how things were, and in the flash of gratitude to this, her living child, her very own, only now discovered ally who was able to make sense of everything so quickly—another insight flashed and left her mind: that the ax had finally passed them and left, cleaving off one half of the tree, and the lost half now brought itself together, in that riveting of the girl and the man's hands, out there, on the other side, which meant the half that remained here—Darka and her—were out of danger. That was the meaning of the long-forgotten if ever-known peace the dream delivered her into.

And Natalia began to cry.

You held her then, because your hands were free—freed by your father's death. It took two lives to ransom yours. Two whole lives.

But you—you slipped through, Darka.

GIRLS

TRANSLATED BY ASKOLD MELNYCZUK

Darka saw her on the bus, the sweaty, June-soaked bus, brimming with people and their smells: sweet, almost putrid—female, heavy, equestrian, yet oddly palatable, and even stimulating, sexual—distinctly male. Suddenly all the smells switched off, leaving only the girl's profile on the sunny side of the bus, angular as a Braque: abrupt, soaring cheekbones, a fine pug nose, full lips, and a sharp, childlike fist of a chin—a capricious, fragile geometry that occasionally seeps from an artist's pen, piercing the heart, as at the touch of a brand-new Christmas ornament when you were a child (I remember it: a blinding white ballerina, tutu frozen in an upward sweep, an inconceivable liquid legato of arms and legs, so delicate and small-fingered that touching it with your brutish five-year-old's stumps seemed blasphemous), such faces are catapulted into the world in order to reawaken us to life's fragility. She had the disproportionately long (instead of Braque, Modigliani) neck of a wary fawn ("Fee-fi-o-fawn," chanted the other girls, but Darka couldn't bring herself to say it: the fawn was simply Effie and none other, because these slopes and angles, lines pushed to the breaking point, suggested something else entirely), it was the same kind of neck Darka remembered emerging from the open collar (stiff, angular, extending over the shoulders in that style from the seventies) of the school uniform, flashing cleavage. Ah, Effie the fawn! In the chemistry classroom her spot was near the window, where the light fell on her face and neck that same way, trailing down into the shadow under the second button, which deepened as she bent over, giving the sun her downy left cheek. Only, Darka realized now that this could not be her childhood friend, that the real Effie, like herself, would be well over thirty, and yet amazingly enough, it was her, newly returned in her incomparable not-quite-twenty-year-old, eternally teenage prime: every woman's beauty has (as every figure has its ideal size, where one pound more or less makes all the difference) its own age of perfection, one in which everything opens to the fullest, and which can change in a minute like the bloom on a desert flower or may, in happier circumstances, depending on the care and watering, last for years (so, optimistically, reasoned Darka, whose spending on watering—meaning on moisturizing, creams, and lotions—has recently begun to exceed her outlay for clothing)—Effie was intended by her gracious creator to be junior size, and who knows into what life turned her eventually? Effie: *ephebus*, the word exactly.

Effie-who-is-not-Effie, on the sunny side of the bus, senses she's being watched and turns her head (the butterfly brush of lashes, her glance sharp as an elbow: Look, look, said Effie, rolling up her sleeve, See how sharp, want to feel it? And here too—she pushes down her collar, stretches her neck as a spooked beast, props forward her collarbones, Cubist honed: held breath, the gaze dead, strange, a little frightened, whether with its own daring trustfulness or because of your unpredictability: she loves me, she loves me not (or, as she played it: hold me, thrill me, kiss me, kill me)—of course it's not her, and neither is this woman as young as she looked in profile—Darka turns her eyes away, and looks politely out the window where at this moment the monument to Vatutin rises out of the dappled green of Mariinsky Park—dull, bald, and smug, a sculptural epitaph to Khrushchev's era: a peer, Darka sneers (the monument went up the year she was born)—and at that instant she decides she will, damn it, go to the school reunion (a stiff envelope with a gold seal, an invitation, removed yesterday from the mailbox, and uncertainly set aside—there will be time to think about it), though the prospect wearies her: what could be interesting about this pathetic act of individual self-assertion vis-à-vis one's own adolescence, what's compelling about the grey and the bald blissfully morphing into boys again, and the artificial, elaborately decked-out women who sneak glances at your wrinkles, hoping they have fewer themselves? But she'll go—whatever happened to Fawn-Effie-Faron? Suddenly, she needs to know.

***

Darka once read an article by an American gender-studies luminary that claimed axiomatically that boys tended to be competitive, and girls cooperative. Only a boy could have blathered such nonsense so glibly. The struggle for power, not for its dividends in the form of grades (suggestive of subsequent financial security), not for success with the opposite sex (which had not defined itself as being opposed to anything yet), and not even for the applause meter spiking at the Christmas pageant (which principally feeds the vanity of one's parents, and only later flexes the muscles of your own), but for power in its nearly unalloyed pristine form, like the sweet narcotic of pure, dry white spirit, and all the more intoxicating—the exclusive and uncontested right to lead the class either from the schoolroom to the playing field, or after school to what they called a cats' concert, to be staged below the window of the fat girl from the front row you don't like, the one who chews her sandwich wrapped in wax paper during the break and then leaves hideous grease stains on textbooks—to lead the class no matter where, no matter whether for good or ill, because the difference between good and evil doesn't exist, just as it never exists in the presence of absolute power—this struggle, setting aside primitive tribes for the moment, is found precisely among girls from ages eight to twelve. Later, thank god, they develop other, more civilian concerns.

By fourth grade, when Effie appeared in their class, Darka already had the rap sheet of either a budding criminal or a future political leader (the boundary between them being vague, and heavily dependent on nurture rather than nature): at least two girls from her class had to change schools, one of them in the middle of the year, the black-haired Rivka Braverman with bluish-white starched bows in her glistening braids, whose father's chauffeur drove her to school in her father's government-issued glistening black Volga, and after school drove her to music lessons.

Rivka had a plump, confident ass and a disdainful mouth melding into folds of flesh. She smelled of homemade vanilla cookies, vacations at a spa in the Caucasus, third-generation antiques confiscated during the Bolshevik revolution, and a five-room apartment of the sort reserved for only the most privileged of Soviet families, in a building erected by prisoners of war for the elite. Such a start in life does little to encourage an instinct for self-preservation, so it was Darka, whom Rivka carelessly attempted to treat with all her studied arrogance toward those who had never darkened the threshold of such a five-room apartment in a building erected by prisoners of war, who taught Rivka her first lesson in survival in a society sufficiently transformed so that neither her grandfather the prosecuting attorney nor her father the chief manager were able to secure for her what was most valuable: a more bankable nationality to declare in that fifth blank on her passport. After Darka sicced on her a mob of classmates that included the red-haired Misha Khazin and Marinka Weissberg, who chased her all the way from school to the entrance of that apartment building built by prisoners of war, in one breath chanting, "Kike, kike, running down the pike"— and Rivka really did run like the Wandering Jew of all Treblinkas, her plump bouncing ass suddenly, pathetically deflated—and the next day in class the group murmured to themselves so that the teacher facing the blackboard heard only a monotonous buzz as though the room had been filled with bumblebees—*Zhid, zhid, zhid,* the *zh*'s especially

18

greasy, thick, repulsive, until the teacher would snap—"Let the damn bee out!"—and the buzz would stop for a bit, and then would start again, so that finally Rivka leaped up and shouted, "Again! There they go again!" and ran out weeping—after this, no matter how Braverman Senior threatened the school, no matter how many parents were called in for meetings, it was no longer possible for Rivka to stay in this class with the propeller bows of her braids held high, or in any other manner.

Darka herself was shocked and frightened by Rivka's unexpected collapse. Her hysterical crying had aborted their game of king of the hill, and for a few days Darka herself lay in bed with an inexplicable fever. Her principal sorrow lay in the fact that Rivka, arrogant and hateful, with her muscling into the class presidency, with her hideous pouting mouth (a clear legacy from her grandfather, an agent of the cheka, the brutal secret police, a fact Darka could not have known at the time, but intuited unerringly) with which she talked her way into the coveted position of nurse's volunteer assistant wherein she would examine her classmates' hands and send the ink-spattered back to the washroom for a scrubbing, with her methodical nerdiness and unblemished faith in her own perfection, who had once dared to point out reluctantly that Darka *too* was an A student ("It's you who's an A student *too*," Darka blurted back), with her glistening sleeve protectors, and that second pair of shoes she carried in a special pink bag, real pumps, delicate and also pink, like a little princess's, with heels—"You don't have any like this and you never will. My daddy bought them for me in Copenhagen"— that Rivka was abruptly revealed to be *a child*, just like Darka, and because of her, because of Darka, that child was screaming with grief. Darka's parents also grew worried as she began groaning in her sleep. She'd gladly have made peace with Rivka, would have apologized, made up, cheered her up, had she only known how. Her experience of peacemaking involved only her mother and father, who, no matter what happened, always found themselves in the pastoral position: "Go and sin no more," they'd say after a time, and it was possible to skip out with a leap, lighthearted, with quickly drying-as-in-a-sun-shower tears. Here, however, something had broken irreparably—in Rivka, in the world, in her very own self, and through the broken hole, as in a fence, there crawled a thick, hot, brown darkness, and when Darka's fever finally fell and she returned to school, she found that Rivka was no longer in her class.

We can count among the long-term consequences of these events the mixed feelings of guilt and shame that from then on dogged Darka in her every encounter with a Jewish person, and that would only fade upon closer, personal acquaintance. The direct, immediate consequence was that Darka shrank, grew subdued, and dove deep into books (that began the period of intoxication by reading) right up to the end of the school year.

Then, the following year, a new girl appeared.

Darka remembered the first time she met everyone who'd played any real part in her life, even though the memory may be hidden at the bottom of her mind's drawer—a snapshot of another-other-stranger, cut out of the chaotic backdrop that became the rest of the world, singled out by god-knows-what intuition, like a promise. Laid out with the rest of the sequence, the snapshots charted a series of various and unexpected poses, from the lightning charge of first direct eye contact, the voltaic arc of it short-circuiting (blue eyes, grey eyes, green eyes, each with the same enchanting glassy gaze of antique crystal, men's eyes, but who knows what hers looked like in that instant?), to those taken as though with a hidden camera, when the object has not yet noticed you and not begun to suspect that he or she will soon be someone in your life, profiles, three-quarter shots, even shots from the back of the head: napes can be outrageously singular. Yet, no matter how long she rummaged through her memory, she could never find that first shot of Effie. Effie had not come from the outside; she'd unfolded from within Darka like one of her own organs. Like the dormant gene of an inherited disease.

What Darka remembered were Effie's nylon pantyhose—most of the girls in the class still wore white and brown cotton ones, wrinkled, droopy kneed, and for some reason eternally sagging because they were made too long in the seat, oh, this damned command economy—did socialism set as one of its goals the breeding of short-legged and suspiciously tubby little girls?—with the crotch always drooping from under one's skirt so that everyone, above all the wearer, expected that any moment they would slip all the way down, and so our childhood passed, in the Land of the Slipping Tights. First graders simply hiked up their skirts and purposefully yanked them up, and that very same fat girl from the first row (her name was Alla) did it once in fourth grade when she was called up to the blackboard, the most natural gesture, the same as rolling up your sleeves or smoothing your hair, but in fourth grade they mocked her mercilessly, the boys practically fell out of their chairs, pointing their fingers, and the treacherous girls too yukked it up, and maybe because of that Darka was so impressed with Fawn's legs, those long, vulnerable, lanky legs of a newborn fawn, but covered smoothly, as if with a tan, with a fine transparent wrap. In the sun-drenched classroom they looked golden. It was as though Fawn had no childhood, nothing to outgrow, all the barely visible, minute feminine skills of proper self-presentation, which take one's entire adolescence to master (and some need a good chunk of their adulthood too), all that plucking of eyebrows, trying on various haircuts (the shag, the flip, the Sassoon bangs—a chirping language already incomprehensible to boys), nail polish with glitter and flowers, until settling in tenth grade on, thank god, a reasonable color. Fawn seemed to have been endowed with everything at birth, a fully drawn, precise, and delicate gold-legged figure: Braque? Modigliani? No, Picasso, *Girl on the Ball.*

Effie, Effie, my love.

Darka remembers more about the legs—the unbearable internal burn that you eventually learn to recognize as jealousy when the English teacher (and really as though copied from life, from the grotesquely bland, flat-chested, formless, ageless English women of de Maupassant whom Darka was already devouring surreptitiously) makes Effie stand in the corner: teachers—that is, female teachers (there was only one man, who taught phys ed)—somehow teachers did not love her, but why? And Effie stands there in her short-skirt uniform, in front of the whole class, lightly rocking on her golden fawn's legs, and Marinka Weissberg whispers to Darka: "Doesn't Fawn have nice legs?" Darka cringes, this isn't a subject for discussion, but Marinka keeps on, "Long too. Mine are twelve centimeters shorter. We measured. You know how you measure, here, from the hip"—the blow is so shocking that Darka inadvertently opens her mouth to catch a breath, and then under her breast the burn spreads with a slow fire: just yesterday she and Effie sat late at the lake in the park, first feeding the Effie-necked swans, and when the swans went to sleep, the girls watched the sun set on the burning, splintered, intense dark-purple streak of water, wide eyed as though frightened. Both gazed with Effie's wide-open eyes: "So much beauty," she said, her thin—so thin they looked shadowed with blue—eyelids twitching like the wings of a butterfly: "So much beauty in the world, how to grasp it all? You know, Dar, sometimes I can't sleep all night, I keep thinking, my head goes round and round, how to hold it, this world's so huge? And you know"—the lids dropped, along with Darka's heart, the skin above Effie's top lip, full as if ready for a kiss, beaded with sparkles of sweat—the effect of an extraordinary and invisible struggle inside her—"You know Dar, I think either something very beautiful or very terrible will happen to me," her knuckles squeezing the bench turning white. "Something, some way in which I'll finally be able to capture everything, hold everything, contain everything, you understand?" Darka trembled within, not from the cold, because her cheeks and mouth were hot, but from the feeling that in her cupped palms fluttered a butterfly, because everyone knows that if you blow all the pollen off the butterfly's wings, it will certainly die. Never again in her life would she so desperately want to protect someone, before no one

else did she feel such numbing awe as then, with Effie, all later relationships were mere shards, reflections of this sensation, like those splinters
of purple fire on the water (a bit like loving a man, when you pull apart,
exhausted, but then after a few minutes hungrily reach for him again
because you don't know what else to do with this flesh, impenetrable
as a wall, aside from taking it one more time, because there's no way to
come together so as to never part again—but that's coarser, more primitive. For that matter, as you grow your self-conscious flesh, everything
becomes simpler and more linear, or maybe, Darka wonders now, being
an older sister is an inborn instinct, like being a mother, and it was her
only-child's sisterlessness that had been an absence swelling inside her
for years and at the right moment poured onto Effie, Effie who in fact
needed something different)—deafened and blinded, Darka bent low
over her notebook, trying not to look at Fawn standing in the corner
though she smiled wanly in her direction as if she knew what she and
Marinka Weissberg were whispering: that Effie yesterday entrusted to
her the most precious, most fragile part of her inner self meant to Darka
a kind of vow to eternal and absolute fidelity, so, aside from the shock
that the beloved turns out not to be transparent, that she leads a separate
life and can have secrets from you (measuring legs with silly Marinka,
giggling, hiking hems to press their hips against each other—She never
did such things with me, not even a hint of it)—in addition to that
shock, there was the grief of injured love that demands everything at
once, unsatisfied with bits and pieces, and therefore is destined to doubt
that which it has actually received: Is it possible she lied to me yesterday?
How is it possible to be so, so hypocritical! Darka remembered she'd
used just that word: during recess, she passed by Effie in proud silence;
it took her stupefied senses an entire class to recover from the shock,
while at the next recess Effie herself approached her: "What's up? You
mad at me?"

"I have to talk to you," said Darka in a tight voice she didn't recognize herself, a lump in her throat. After school they again sat in the

park at the lake, wrapped like fairy-tale heroes in a cloud, an air of Shakespearian thunderstorm, a tempest—betrayal, breakup, the parting—Effie, flashing eyes full of wobbly tears, passionately assured Darka that the thing with Marinka had happened long ago, which was supposed to mean, before Darka, that it was all silly and meaningless and didn't matter, and Darka brightened, the sky cleared, as though pulled out from under an avalanche, yet for a while she still pretended to be offended, partly from an innate sense of form and partly out of an unconscious bartering with Effie for new concessions, new guarantees of undivided and exclusive affection, a scenario that Darka later on inevitably repeated with men except that with them it was much easier, while Effie was about as supple as Picasso's acrobat, dodging to avoid Darka's onslaught, from despairing repentance to a sudden collapse into a complete and trancelike absence and self-absorption, to half-hysterical recitals of poems meant to explain everything (that year they buried each other in poetry), until, exhausted by the endless back-and-forth, Darka heard her own voice cry: "Forgive me!" and then she was sinking to Effie's nylon-warmed golden knees, embracing them and greedily breathing in, through tears, their surprising smell of bread, the odor of home reached after long travels: in the bedroom under your parents' door the light pours, Let me fluff up your pillow, the tickle of her soft and living, like a kitten's hair on your cheek, two girls cuddling under the covers, pressed into each other, whispering, sudden outbursts of laughter, Stop, you're deafening me—the same as you, but different, that's what a sister is, that's what I'm embracing, tightly, so tightly that it can't be tighter, never to let it go—two wildly intertwined girls on a bench in the park at night, her budding breasts under her school uniform thrust into yours, her lashes tickling your neck, like in that myth where the cloud of the gods rendered the lovers invisible to mere mortals—nobody walked down the path, nobody rustled the fallen leaves, there was nobody to be surprised when Effie began kissing the trail of tears under Darka's eyes and then pressed her lips to hers and gasped, stunned for an instant, Effie's heart thumped inside Darka's chest and both froze, not sure what to do next, and then Darka felt between her lips something quick, wet, salty, and very large, it floated in her mouth like a naked hot fish blacking out the rest of the world and she did not immediately understand that it was Effie's tongue but once she did, she was seized by another, incomprehensible sort of sobbing, which she gulped down together with Effie's tongue, squeezing her skinny body even tighter: her shoulder blades sharp as wings, the keyboard of the vertebrae under the coarse uniform suddenly brought to memory her first realization of what it meant that something was alive. She had just turned two years old, and stood speechless above a basket full of tiny fluffy white rabbits, unable to step aside or turn away, until one of the adults said from above, "Would you like one?"—up until that instant she struggled to come to terms with the idea that such an astonishing miracle breathed and moved, and then with the equally astonishing news of what one could do with such a miracle: one could *have* it. At that most honest of ages, possession meant just one thing: it meant that, out of an excess of feeling, one should put the thing in one's mouth and, ideally, swallow it, as one did the petals of the prettiest flowers from the courtyard garden, which you plucked and chewed, your drool turning bitter and green when you spit, and over years that original meaning of the word doesn't change, only gets clouded over. It takes a lifetime to understand that long ago the grown-ups lied to you, that in fact nothing living, neither a flower, nor a rabbit, nor a person, nor a country, can, in fact, be had: they can only be destroyed, which is the one way to confirm they have been possessed.

❖

"And here too," said Effie—but this was another time, at home, before a large tarnished mirror in a dark-brown frame—she first unbuttoned her dress, exposing a double bra strap on her Cubist shoulder of protruding horizontal bones; she'd long ago begun wearing a bra, Darka had seen, when they changed before gym class, Effie's matching snow-white underwear unavailable in any store but there, amid the smell of old, rough mats stacked up in the corner and the reek of old sweat, in the middle of it, it was just underwear, but here, when Effie, not turning her hypnotized, dark eyes—pupils dilated—away, slipped off her bra, a tender, pearl-pink nipple popped out of its cup like an outthrust tongue and at the same time Effie's fingers, stumbling over buttons as though asking permission, cautiously unbuttoned Darka's sweater and she saw, alongside Effie's, her own nipple only darker, redder, like a cherry pit, here all the blood at once rushed to Darka's head and everything grew blurred. Effie leaned lightly over her breast, and Darka felt her wet gathering mouth, and goose bumps, and her own rapid breathing, and everything began flowing, or was it Darka herself who was slipping into the unknown, something heady and hot, something forbidden and tempting, compared with which all of her will to power, being first in her class, academic triumphs, captainship of the volleyball team, all this was small and insignificant as she went down and emerged new, dark, dangerous, and big as the world—oh Effie, Effie, two girls with their shirts undone in the depths of the mirror where Effie touched her kissed breast to her own and said: "Here too," pointing to the other one, and that was how it began.

And so it whirled, sweeping all away.

All their school recesses spent shoulder to shoulder at the window-sill, wandering through the park after class, drunken talking, talking, talking, insatiable as two mutes who'd suddenly discovered the gift of speech or infants who'd just learned words, but they really were just learning to speak, learning to translate themselves into words different from what the adults required of them, about the meaning of life, the future of mankind, will there be war, about their own childhoods, it's amazing how much you recall at that age—when I was little—and then you don't remember a thing until you're old, when, they say, the sluices finally open again, you can't even remember what those things were that you spent hours gushing at each other, so the day felt too short, except a few splinters, of poems for instance, Brodsky's "So long had life together been" (Effie), Kalynets's "Lady with eyes larger than asters" (Darka), but that was prompted by the grown-ups, it was the fucking legacy of the '60s that still dripped from family to family after the tap had been decisively shut off, while all of one's own content that filled the cup to overflowing had drained away somewhere, leaving only silt after the passing of a stream—the memory of a bench, of a windowsill in a school corridor, a memory of Effie's concentrated face—did she know how to listen with shiny eyes and half-open mouth! and all that in the shadowy, autumnal light of sad, nostalgic longing for the long-gone unreachable heights. That whole visible daily aspect of their friendship (sixth grade: just as the kids enter the chaotic process of gluing and ungluing in twos and threes, like molecules, friendships forming and dissolving several times a year so that none of the teachers ever paid these two much attention)—it all continued, this material world, yet invisibly tightening and shrinking like dresses that now pinched in the armpits under the abrupt combustion wind of that new, suffocating, heady element of their friendship that unfolded without witnesses and demanded more and more, at least from Darka, because all their trembling embraces, all their hot kisses and more frequent, growing caresses exploded not on their own, not from a purely physical compulsion, as would later occur with boys, but each time and inevitably as the resolution of yet another emotional upheaval, a little drama, the improvisation of which they were wonderfully adept at: in the fit of peacemaking after a new argument that took them to the edge of breakup (which were as frequent between them as thunderstorms in July), in an ecstasy of reconciliation to the sound of the Doors, to which Effie would respond by collapsing onto the carpet and pounding her forehead into it, shouting, I can't, I can't, I can't, and Darka would gather that dear warm downy head (smelling like the fur of a kitten), her whole body trembling at the unfathomable mystery of feeling things, at how far more subtle and spiritually richer Effie was than she (that was how Darka put it in the essay titled "My Friend": "My friend has a richly subtle and spiritually rich nature" and was stuck for a long time on the repetition: one of the two had to be crossed out, yet neither was willing to leave), really, it's a miracle, Darka now thinks, they managed to study that year, where had they found the time for it, or, to be more precise, where had Effie found the time, since she never managed things as well as Darka, yet succeeded in passing all her classes, even earning As, and not only in music and gym (a good student, which automatically meant a good girl, or as the vice principal said during the PTA meeting about her, a girl from a well-to-do family, because that was what she was, with divorced parents who spoiled her competitively: stereo, French underwear at twelve)—where did she find it, the time and energy?

Because they also read, insatiably, with all their might, living through the work as though it were their own inner life—their own times fit them like a glove: these were the years of the book boom—years of the hunt for limited-edition books from Moscow, bound in fragrant fresh leatherette the color of dark amber, or bottle green, or marine blue, all spines gilded like the epaulets on an officer's uniform (and looking for all that like the boxes containing expensive cognac next to which these books were meant to cohabit on Yugoslavian furniture, signaling lives of cultured leisure and the ever-expanding well-being of the Soviet people), and Darka, whose family could afford, at best, cheap mimeographed copies, and not always of the safest works, borrowed from Effie high-ranking uniform volumes of Akhmatova and Mandelstam, as well as *The Master and Margarita*, which Effie read first, before loaning it, rehearsing for her most of the first chapter almost verbatim up to and including the part where the head is cut off by the tram, but Darka never managed to memorize the final chapter: she was called to her first interrogation right as she was finishing the book, and that is how her childhood ended.

YOUR AD COULD GO HERE

Much later, as a grown-up, Darka finally risked asking her mother just what horrible thing had been discovered at that point (oh, if only it hadn't been!) and which had stormed through the entire school for over a month? To an adult, the story seemed utterly banal: the girl "from the well-to-do family," not yet fourteen, secretly, without anybody knowing (not even me!), hung around with sexually mature seventeen-year-old boys, went with them Sundays to the deserted Trukhaniv Island, and later the mother of one of these boys (you can imagine this mother, someone should have drowned the bitch!), raised a fuss across the whole school (idiot!) because her dear little boy had the foreskin on his penis torn, or rather, bitten through (so what's the big deal? It would heal before his wedding!). Darka's mother was only able to tell her about the torn foreskin because for her, apparently, the story had been an unforgettable lesson in anatomy. Okay, I agree, said Darka insincerely, hoping to coax more information from her, the story's not pleasant, certainly not for the girl's parents, but when you think about it, there are many worse ways to lose your virginity, which don't always lead to broken lives, and a girl with such a turbulent debut might, in twenty years, why not, surface as an affable matron with a decent academic career, while the poor mangled boy may, to the delight of his mother, yet become a PhD, an oceanographer, a selenographer, or some other -ographer, why not?

(What Darka herself remembered was her first glimpse, through a crack in the principal's office door, of Effie's mother—young and dazzlingly beautiful, sheathed in leather, draped in pendulous Gypsy jewelry, in sheaves of turtledove, grey veils of smoke that swirled like burning incense around an unknown goddess—apart from the brief shock at the fact that someone had the nerve to smoke in the principal's office, she remembered it as the first time she became aware of a different species of human that somewhere, no, *here*, beyond the glass wall, though you can't get *there*, thrives—a richer-than-rich, glamorous movie idol with an unfathomably intense life who has been given the

29

world for her pleasure forever.) Darka's mother, however, also remembered the arrival of a detective, something Darka barely noticed (maybe because the children were questioned in their parents' presence and parents were, to kids at that age, still more important than any strangers, so Darka retained the vague impression that it was her own parents interrogating her). A detective? That means it wasn't simply a matter of horseplay in fresh air. What else was up? The chewing gum and American jeans (the height of luxury) that were given to or traded by one of the kids near the, oh god, Intourist Hotel (where all foreigners stayed), merited that terrible word—the most terrifying word there was—"dealing" in quite likely smuggled goods, because trading with foreigners was, after all, a crime. Were they setting them up for a later date, to keep the kids from racing into the future with extravagant appetites, teaching them instead to aim lower, and sin in secret?

You must have seen Skalkovska has (Effie immediately became, and remained, Skalkovska) that pin with the American flag? Did she tell you where she got it?

Chills, my god, what a nightmare, plus the reek of a political informer—was it the mother of the victimized, skinned, half-circumcised boy who'd used this as a way to break up the group once and for all? What could Effie, her Effie, have to do with this? And above all how could she have maintained her life on such strictly parallel tracks, as invisible as pantyhose without a wrinkle, without ever giving herself away to Darka?

(There was, however, one moment that Darka, with the sudden jealous clarity of all lovers, did register, one splinter she caught: Ihor M., from tenth grade, in the hallway, among the red-scarfed peons whom the upperclassmen shoved aside blindly like ants, suddenly stops: Fawn, he says, with an unusually intimate, creepy, utterly adult tone, and a strange smile on his lips, and Effie steps toward him like a ballerina, heel to toe—and while they exchange a few hushed words, Darka sees nothing but her bent leg, toes lightly pressed to the ground, and her heart breaking out of the pain of uncertainty, suspiciously asks Effie after she returns, "How do you know him?"

"We're neighbors," says Effie, puckering her plump lips into a chicken's ass—it was the kind of grimace she put on when called on in class, driving the female faculty utterly mad. This was the single glimpse, quick as a scratch, of Effie's distant and incomprehensible, beautiful and frightening—and how could it be otherwise—secret: because she was all mystery, that's what she was, and neither Darka nor those hideous boys whose brains leaked out in their sperm, not that there was much there to begin with, could have dreamed of holding her for more than a moment, a moment brief as the flutter of a butterfly's wings.

At the time, of course, Darka knew nothing about any foreskin, and for that matter neither did anybody else, except for the parents, among whom the news might even have caused a surge of sexual activity: the atmosphere was electrified. All Darka knew was that Effie had been dishonored, irretrievably thrust into some dark nightmare, into a quagmire, opened suddenly where the ground was supposed to be hard and well lit, and Darka's parents loudly complained about "the little prostitute" and even went in a delegation from the PTA to the school principal to demand that Effie be immediately removed from school and the rest of the children, implicitly tender and pure, be therefore forever segregated from her immoral influence. (What Bolsheviks they in fact were, what monsters, Darka discovers, with cold surprise, twenty-five years after, that entire generation en masse, the loyal and the dissidents, the thinkers, the free thinkers, and the thoughtless, my god!) And she also knew that Effie had *betrayed* her, this time not childishly, but in fact.

Forever.

(Shameful, and frighteningly obscene, and at the same time so unsettlingly grown-up, the vision made Darka's head spin: with boys, with the thing that dangles between their legs that just two years ago they'd spied on in gym class, elbowing each other: "You can see everything on B!" And exactly what was it they saw? With big boys who "already know everything," and therefore must have done to Fawn who-knows-what and she let them, the grown-up strangers, and they look at her as Ihor M. did—none of this associated in Darka's mind in any way with their own sapphic games, and the only thing that wounded her was this: How could she have done that with strangers? How could she let strangers take off her panties? Never mind what followed—that blurred in Darka's imagination. But the worst thought was: Effie, what about me? What about me? A mixture of feeling ignored, disrespected for her gender, her age, and of course for her sex: no matter what, Effie *had been chosen*, this was obvious, chosen by those boys for a different sort of life, while you, Darka, metamorphosed in a stroke into one of those comic, clumsy, hunched honors students escorted everywhere by parents, even to the movies, as if by guards: she didn't let you in all the way, didn't let you touch something essential in her, which means that everything about your friendship was a lie because at the bottom of the most luminous, ecstatic explosions of your oneness, which seemed so clear, there was always this gigantic dark cave full of sealed shameful treasures, oh, what an idiot you were!—and nightly weeping into the pillow, deeply buried so her parents wouldn't hear.

And therefore, when at the class meeting, as the leader of the Pioneer Council (the *comrade leader*—the drumbeat as before an execution, the red flag carried in, plush red with yellow fringes) and as a *former friend* of Skalkovska's—sure, there was no getting around the need to distance herself, as she was told by everyone, the vice dean, the class tutor, and all the king's men, otherwise Effie's fall might drag her down so low she could hardly imagine—when she had to announce the Personal Case of Comrade Skalkovska and take the floor (and again at first the strange resonance of a voice squeezed by your own throat so you can't swallow, it echoes inside your head, you're listening to the sound of your own head) she denounced Effie in a way no one would ever have foreseen, she least of all.

. This must have looked like the unbridled, escalating attack of a mean little dog, nipping, drawing blood, and again, to the meat: Remember! Remember what you said about all the classmates, that they're all narrow-minded nonentities! (Naturally these good-for-nothings closed ranks, and Effie wound up completely isolated.) You put yourself above the class! Above the group! You decided you were better than the others, that you were allowed more than the others were, and look where this has led you—your comrades (that's right: first you create a group identity, then you speak in its name) are now ashamed of you! And so on, an oration worthy of an A+ with two exclamation marks after it, but alas there's no such grade.

And it was not an excess of administrative zeal (as it might have appeared to an uninformed outsider), and even less was it a desire to save her own skin (as it might have been appropriate to say had they not been children) but rather an ardent, overwhelming drive to *possess* Effie, even if for the last time, to have her back, begging forgiveness, repenting her betrayal. (And because Darka did not have *her own power* over her, she pursued instead the one offered her by the adult world, that of the Comrade Leader of the Pioneer Council—and the drums beat, oh, how they beat, they sent a chill up your skin, this shaman's drum, the prehistoric tambourine; that's right, all turning points in life should be staged as solemnly as tribal initiations, and what is one's first act of collaboration if not a kind of initiation?) Consequently, Darka's words should have been read to contain a secret message, revealed in ultraviolet light: Remember! Remember how you said I was your only soul mate, the only one you could talk to; remember how I said, when we listened to the Doors, that it sounded like doors were really opening, and you knew what I meant, you said, Yes, those cast-iron doors! Heavy as those at Saint Vladimir's Cathedral. And I really saw them as that, and I screamed with joy that you did, too, you did—we stood before the doors together, we breathed as one, Effie, why did you slam them in my face?

But Effie-Skalkovska stayed silent. And did not intend to remember a thing, nor to repent, nor to beg forgiveness. She didn't even look at Darka—she looked out the window, at the playing field lined with poplars, occasionally biting her lower lip, she cried—and it was clear it was something very personal, something a galaxy away from Darka, her fiery speeches, and this endless meeting. The doors, which Darka hadn't been asked to enter and tried to break down, remained shut.

What if, Darka speculates now, she was pregnant? That, thank god, she would never know. Because you can't exactly roll up at the class reunion to, basically, a stranger, with a glass of wine in your hand, and ask, as casual as if you were talking about the weather: Hey, did you by any chance have an abortion in sixth grade?

Now, from the vantage point of this dull bare plateau that is called experience, Darka could consider something else: namely that Effie with her innate vulnerability, her innate fragility—she was like a package, its contents cushioned in layers of paper, stamped *Fragile* on all sides in runny ink and sent on its way, yet without an address—this perfidious, secret, gracious, spoiled, truly vicious and irresistibly seductive, inwardly aflame Effie-Fawn, simply had to find, at an early age, her own way of protecting herself, especially from the all-conquering Darka, defending herself with what was most obviously hers, her body. Putting it between herself and the world like a cardboard shield: Take it, take it, feel it, you want it?

(I certainly didn't leave her any other options—why should others have?)

❖

For one, two, or three years after that—in seventh, eighth, yes, and ninth grade, too, they passed each other like planets on distant orbits, greeting each other with a nod, though for a long time Darka avoided Effie's eyes and was careful not to get stuck alone with her: the awareness of her betrayal, which couldn't be undone, poisoned her, from the bottom of her soul, where it lay like immoveable rock raising up muddy miasmas so that in the upper grades Darka even had fits of nausea, especially in the mornings, very much like morning sickness, problems with her gallbladder; she got scoped in the hospital, and was advised to swallow a spoonful of sunflower oil before breakfast—and then she noticed, with embarrassed relief, that when they were in groups, Effie would answer her remarks calmly, almost warmly. She did not pretend Darka didn't exist, so Darka decided finally to risk speaking with her one on one, politely and purposefully—what's the big deal, really, let's get over it—asking Skalkovska when she'd be on class duty, and Skalkovska politely answered it would be Thursday, and so it went, sideways, as between strangers. By that time they really were strangers to each other, having outgrown their childhood episodes along with the cotton tights and splayed children's shoes, snub nosed, which got tossed into closets or attics, where they gradually aired out the pigeon-toed warmth that once filled them, and all the falls, scratches, and bruises they witnessed, the jump rope, hopscotch, the sand carried into the house (while mother scolded), and sticky as lacquer (to be pulled off with fingers) traces of jam, and after some years, when you found them again, amid the dust and the cobwebs, you dragged them into the light to see they had become old rags. No, they weren't girls anymore, they were ladies and young women, sighing, well, well.

(This is a lie because in fact nothing passes—no matter how deeply you bury it, what happened keeps growing darkly under the skin of years like an indelible bruise.)

Somehow, the dust settled. Perhaps an influential parent from the Bad Company managed to turn down the heat, or maybe the school wanted to protect its own reputation—the school had a fine one—and who needs it all, the endless meetings, commissions, inspections, good Lord, enough, and so it all died down. Dried up. For a while Skalkovska suffered her isolation but that, too, slowly dissolved. Only the teachers, or more precisely the female ones, continued to rage (rumor had it only the gym teacher—a man—tried to defend her at that first teachers' council, but it sounded silly, what kind of defense could he mount?), treating her badly, really badly, which she definitely did not deserve, but she remained even keeled, straight backed, expressionless, a good student but not a star, and was once even sent to the regional academic tournaments for her English, or something. And yet a teasing, seductive odor wafted off her like that slightly cloying yet barely noticeable (except up close, lifted by the body's warmth) and thus all the more lascivious (so they thought) scent of what must have been her mother's perfume, it tickled their noses, entered their bloodstreams, darkened their faces: "Skalkovska, leave the room!" (Shaking her head like a pony with its mane, biting her lower lip, whether getting ready to cry or to laugh, she concentrated as though she were leaving forever on packing her books and notebooks into her bag, then her long narrow back with a keyboard of buttons running down it and short skirt would walk down the aisle between the desks to the door, never turning around: Darka could never keep from staring at her back, as though she were expecting something, but her back was buttoned tight as the door that she had just closed quietly behind her, which teachers were eager to take as a provocation, repeating her punishment, again and again: "Leave the room, Skalkovska, that'll teach her.")

And in ninth grade, before the end of her last term, she finally did leave for good. And after her, the gym teacher, an Olympic medalist in swimming, a forty-year-old with thick grey hair (why do athletes so rarely go bald?), with acidy sweat and hair sticking out of his nostrils, was also let go. It turned out that he and Effie had been carrying on an affair all spring. Someone had seen them.

Heaped in a corner of the girls' gym room, the old mats, rough to the touch as though steeped a long time in brine, and a dry, sunk-in smell, familiar as the odor of old abandoned stables, the smell of children's sweat, or not only children's, but also that other, violent and acrid?

❖

All the time, somebody is living your life for you, one of its possible, never-to-be-realized versions. All those feelings that really do bind us to others, from love to envy, grow out of this half-secret longing for other lives—intuited, recognized as doubtless ours, lives we will nevertheless never possess. And somebody defends us, something shields us, lives them out for us. And we sleep without nightmares.

❖

"Of course," said Darka's mother, "it's all the fault of the parents: one look at Effie's mother tells the whole story." She said this while cutting her nails with a sharp whipping sound: she was using tailor's scissors, because they didn't have a proper manicure pair. Her triumphant voice was a monument to her own motherhood, which was utterly beyond reproach. And something apart from this, which even then raised Darka's hackles, though she kept it to herself: faceless and impersonal, with all the pressure of the ten atmospheres at the bottom of the ocean, the truly terrible eternal righteousness of the *tribe* against the individual who broke its ranks.

Darka's mother also had her most intense life experience when she was thirteen. She'd stood at the top of a hill with her sled, red and gasping, waiting for her turn to go down—and suddenly she saw how the snow-covered slope flowed down from under her feet in the lilac-colored shadows of the trees: in the sun the snow glimmered with billions of sparks, and each one was a planet. The planets burned, shimmered, and as the poet whom she had not yet studied at school said, spun into alignment.

The girl stared while the light grew brighter until she could almost hear the ice tinkling. She didn't know the ancients called that sound the music of the spheres. That this was the voice of the infinite. She knew

only that she had to look away, otherwise something terrible and irrevocable would happen, she'd go mad!—a bolt of black lightning flashed
a boundary marker in her mind: Get back, get back!

And she turned away.

Everything that followed in her life was fine with her: marriage,
poverty, children, sickness, a job she didn't like, as well as the little joys,
like a new apartment or a leather coat. It's true, the leather was only
pigskin, but had been well tanned.

It could have been worse. Much worse.

❖

After all, thinks Darka, going through the outfits in her closet: her club
jacket will reveal the burn from the iron on her forearm, the yellow
dress begs a tan, and I'm pale as a cheese, and so on (it's fine to laugh
at yourself, but a reunion is yet another test, this time of your life-in-
progress, which hasn't exactly fallen into place perfectly but that's all the
more reason to hold your head high, dress to the nines, flawless makeup,
silliness, but there it is, and what for, what's the point?)—after all, you
can't have infinity, can you? Yet that apparently was what Effie wanted—
but this second idea, following the first, plays over the surface of her
thoughts, never sinking in: Darka sees herself in the mirror holding up
a long silk dress on a hanger, and her expression is unexpectedly stupid,
entirely childlike—what an obvious discovery, you can't have infinity.
And all our striving to gather up more—money, men, impressions,
diplomas, dresses, cars—is nothing but our pitifully meager effort to
reach infinity by adding one thing to another and then another. There
has to be a better way, but what is it?

❖

At the entrance to the restaurant they were figuring out who wouldn't come, for whom not to wait: Misha Khazin emigrated to America, long ago, back in the early eighties, Kraichyn's in Paris at a conference, Artemchuk is somewhere abroad as well with a sick child—thyroid problems (Chernobyl)—and Soltys, well, they'll commemorate him separately, and it would be good to someday make a trip to the cemetery, absolutely (at this moment everyone is confident that someday they'll certainly go)—at Berkovtsi, in that unfenced area where row on row of short pillars topped with red stars stand at attention, announcing that they all did their noble international duty in Afghanistan, though they say it's permitted now to put up crosses. That overwhelming feeling at the very first moment—of a group of strangers, unusually quiet (everyone overwhelmed by the same feeling perhaps), greying, balding (men), and decked out (women)—and then at the next moment, as though the film projector begins to rewind, there begin to emerge from them the figures of children they were twenty years ago until the two frames, the past and the present, finally click together and then from their lips come the sincerest of cries: You haven't changed! You too! You haven't changed a bit! (Who but our classmates will give us back those selves that no longer exist—not for anyone, hell, not for anyone? Of course, if you don't count your parents, but then, that's why they are your parents.) So who else are we waiting for?

Holding out her bent finger: Khazin, Kraichyn, Artemchuk (the Soltys forefinger remains half-bent and uncertain: where should it go?). Hey, look, Sashko Begerya's here, too, though he didn't graduate with us—he went to the technical school after eighth grade—at last Darka gets up the nerve, as though she'd just remembered:

"And Skalkovska?"

You know, what's her name. That's how it comes out. And yet she thinks that for a second everyone falls silent. Your sin is a sin, my dear Darka, and there's no statute of limitations on it.

But no, that's not why. Almost immediately Darka realizes that none of them really remembers the incident from all those years ago. Nobody remembers Darka's speech at the meeting, and even if they do recall something, nobody gives it the weight it's gathered for her over the years (one may say over her whole life, because she never did anything like it again, maybe cruelty too requires a single vaccination, though vaccinations sometimes also prove deadly). Dear Effie, my beloved golden-legged girl, my lost sister, with an addict's blazing pupils in which tears burn like candles at the impossibility of taking the whole world into yourself, or all the men in it, what are they saying about you?

Because they are talking, they are lively, the ice of estrangement melted by the insatiable human craving for sensational stories: You're kidding! No! Really?—the way they'd suck onto a plane crash with two hundred dead, preferably with a list of passengers along with their ages (taking special note of the couple with a baby who were going to show him off to his grandparents), onto all the mighty who have fallen and now allow us to pity them: presidents caught with their pants down before the entire planet, bankrupt oil magnates, pop stars busted for drugs, and the one who yesterday was crowned the king of the Jews and who today appeared humbler than the humblest of us, thereby revealing how he'd cheated us and so we with all due rage shout, "Crucify him," asking for revenge for yesterday's humiliation.

They are talking, or rather it's a little plump brunette with a dark mossy mustache talking, who turns out to be Marinka Weissberg, while the others around her chime in with their, What? Really? And then?

Last summer, Marinka says, by accident, on the street, "I didn't recognize her." She says that you, Effie, now weigh about 190 pounds, huge, a barrel, because they gave you insulin when you needed lithium—"But lithium also adds weight," one of the boys, now a chemical engineer, says authoritatively, while another, a doctor, though not a psychiatrist, in the same professional tone, interrupts him (oh men, how hard you work to earn your self-respect from us!), taking an interest in the diagnosis: "If it's lithium, then it's manic depression, and that's the end of the story, you spend your life on medication." "Oh my," coo the girls, a gust of self-satisfaction (or does Darka imagine it) wafts through them, the whisper of wind in the treetops, then gone—but does Marinka know the diagnosis? Did she tell her why? She told her she'd had a miscarriage after which her husband left her; they'd just come back from vacation, from where, from Switzerland (another round of leaf rustling, this time sharper edged, and Darka sees a few suppressed sarcastic smiles), where she swam in a lake where there was a sign, **WATER POLLUTED**, and must have caught something there that caused the miscarriage. The pseudopsychiatrist, also Vovka Lasota (former nickname: Bucks, who knows why, but nicknames no longer apply), now claims the stage (one of two: either he's a decent doctor, or this is his only way of asserting himself because there are no salaries being paid and his wife at home nags endlessly) and declares, casually and patronizingly (for which Darka quietly begins to loathe him), that mental illness doesn't necessarily depend on specific causes, *they*, meaning *not us*, those other ones, separated from us with a tall wrought-iron fence, are always seeking a cause, often making it up, and they're good at it. (But you, Darka sends him angry pulses, of all people should know that that fence is no boundary, that tomorrow you too might land on the wrong side of it in a washed-out dark-blue robe like a marine uniform and even more washed-out pants with your aluminum bowl for food and a dazed, drug-clouded gaze, don't you?) And if it's really serious manic depression, the guy blathers on (with a touch of skepticism about the diagnosis, as though to say, I'm not sure of course, I haven't seen the patient myself), if that's the case, then it's not psychosomatic, it's organic, like schizophrenia or petit mal epilepsy (in a minute he'll rehearse everything he's learned at the institute, what a good boy, wait, he isn't married, where's his wedding ring, how is it possible such a catch is still available?), in such cases, the etiology isn't clear, the disease surfaces only later, usually after thirty (once more the female rustling, bees, on and on, Just imagine, you're just going on with your life . . .). "You go on and on and never even taste it," Darka says aloud, trying to derail the conversation, and the conversation turns, your school-age authority hasn't faded, and defrosts immediately into its fresh power, along with your public persona from back then, but the tracks turn unexpectedly: "You know," says one of the girls, "it's a nightmare, of course, it's awful, but she, Skalkovska, was always, well, weird, wasn't she?" Everybody nods in agreement, gathering together defensively, hastily erecting between themselves and Skalkovska that wrought-iron fence with the sharpened pickets at the top, hammering them in one by one, as though it might really protect them from something: someone with servile readiness remembers the time she danced a rumba on the chemistry table, "Girl on a Ball," of course, she took ballroom dance lessons, and at that moment everyone was having all kinds of fun, until the assistant principal walked in, but there was something odd in that dancing, and the speaker, the farsighted sage she is, noticed it.

"Then you should have said something then, why did you keep it to yourself all this time?" Darka grins through her teeth. "You might have saved her life."

They fall silent and embarrassed. They are in general not bad people. We are all of us not bad people. And yet why is it that, no matter what we turn to, it all goes so rotten? Marinka comes to the rescue: it turns out she hadn't gotten to the end of the story because she then invited Skalkovska over, it was nearby, they'd just moved uptown, finally leaving her parents, and it worked out very fine, they now have a two-bedroom apartment on Mykilsko-Botanical Street with windows facing the botanical garden; the subject is a live one and everyone has something to say, especially the girls, who immediately take a warrior's interest in the details of the trade-up: what kind of apartment did they leave, from what neighborhood, how much more was it, Marinka is puffed out with the pride of responsibility, she promises a few interested parties her top-notch real estate agent's phone number, Tell him Marinka and Vadik sent you. Vadik, then, must be the husband, and it was this fine upstanding Jewish husband, can you imagine, that Effie attempted to seduce when Marinka, a good-hearted soul, went out to get a snack, leaving them tête-a-tête. "He told me later, I literally didn't know where to hide."

Literally. Nymphomania, Vovka Lasota delivers the new diagnosis—and why nymphomania, Darka wants to object, why not the hysteria of an abandoned woman, and quite possibly the habit of being an easy one to get, with that instantly recognizable defenseless fragility of hers, which not even two hundred pounds can hide, and which for many, and above all for men, is balm for all their wounds at once, so that our upstanding husband may not be the innocent lamb that he convinced Marinka he was, or what if Marinka convinced herself, because what other choice would she have had? And what's left for Darka but to force out what she intends to be a caustic remark but which instead comes out mumbled and pathetic: "Isn't it nice for medics, you have a diagnosis for everything, and here, have some pills."

In response Vovka Lasota winces and asks her not to refer to him as a medic since he is neither a male nurse nor an orderly but a doctor, and the head of his department, and as a matter of fact he specialized in gynecology and would be happy to share his phone number. "Thanks," laughs Darka, and it comes out in a bass, otherwise her voice would have betrayed her. "Thank god, I've no such need."

Meanwhile the crowd has begun moving to the tables, which glimmer from afar with coquettish kitschy bouquets of white napkins blooming from the glasses, Why the hell did I come here, and what am I to do here, god, what emptiness—get drunk, maybe?

✛

Vovka Lasota sees Darka home. In the taxi she notices that his Chekhovian beard smells of cologne, Givenchy she thinks. He kisses her under her dress strap, mutters something about his divorce, Darka says, "Be so kind as to shut up," and wants to add, Or I'll scream, it's the last thing she needs at this moment, another male confession, but she decides to leave such a complex sentence for better days, focusing herself instead on getting her key into the lock, which she manages on the third try. The worst thing is that she remembers everything, even more clearly than before: instead of drowning in the drink, it rises to the surface and swirls through her mind, and it sucks. Lasota meanwhile has turned into a hot bumblebee and buzzes in her ear how he'd wanted to approach her since they were in eighth grade but was afraid, attacks her from all sides with his heavy breathing and the pressure of a strange body under the bulging, already superfluous clothes, so okay, actually it's not okay, and it won't save her from anything, and she can't even focus, but she'll try, she'll try, why not—the beautiful dress drops unceremoniously to the floor, and when he enters her abruptly, with a groan, and the familiar warmth inside her awakens the body's previously stilled memory, which grows instantly louder than everything else, she surrenders herself gladly, out of genuine gratitude to Lasota for this brief respite, which he naturally takes as a sign of his own male irresistibility and so encouraged, he does it well, yes, quite well, and Hey look, it's getting really good, oh, oh god, oh, and then she lies like a stone with her face buried in his shoulder, and he asks her above her head, in a voice so deep with emotion she is ashamed of her utter lack of any reciprocity:

"Did you know I loved you?"

It looks like he also needed revenge. Isn't it convenient? Men indeed. How one dimensional they all are, how linear, like a simple arithmetic ($x:y=z$; $z+a=b$). Slipping into sleep, as consciousness loosens its bulldog grip, she remembers how Lasota, who himself was not the worst of students, once asked timidly for her help with math—the only time she might have discerned his wish to be alone with her, and with this pleasant thought, or rather, using it to squash, like a beetle under a saucer, a different thought, the dark and formless one, for which she has no more energy, Darka finally falls asleep.

She awakens instantly as if shoved and pops out of bed, where, shamelessly, as though he belonged there, lies a loud, breathing, snorting man, along with all the bed smells of a stranger. What was it, a fit of nausea? Sour mouth, room dark, in the window a lone streetlamp burns, what time is it? She's prodded by some internal physiological fear, but her foot gets caught in a cold pool of silk, her crumpled dress on the ground, her best one, she picks it up, shakes it out, tosses it in the direction of a chair (it rustles, landing), god it's cold, she's trembling, her teeth chatter, goose bumps on her forearms, large and wide spaced like scattered grains; of course, she fell asleep naked, but that's not why she's cold, could it be the alcohol, it's bad—she wraps herself in her disgusting husband's robe (when will that idiot finally get his things?), and stumbles, blind and uncertain, toward the kitchen, where the digital clock says 3:30 a.m., holy shit, and she lowers herself down to the edge of the seat carefully as though she were made of glass, trying to breathe evenly one two three inbreath one two three outbreath, a meditation session, almost fucking yoga, ah, okay, now she can put on the kettle, a few familiar stabilizing gestures, and the blue flame flickers peacefully below, very touching. No, it wasn't her teeth that were chattering, it was something rising from within, a clatter of the castanets—this line of poetry, which repeats itself mechanically as if the needle were stuck on a spinning record: "So long had life together been"—Brodsky, stupid verse, stupid as green firewood and crackling just the same, and yet it stuck—and suddenly, hands leaning on the stove, Darka starts to cry, the sob coming not from her throat but from her belly, like a groan, and she again has to hold her breath one two three so that she does not shatter: Why, why, what is all this for, this fucking life, my God? And it's no longer clear whose life she's weeping for, only that she needs somehow to endure, to survive this terrible unfairness, somehow digest this burden of injustice, this eternal human scream to heaven: My God, why me? and her grief, alive and burning, is for everything we did not become and never will.

Blotting her eyes with her fingers, she reaches for the cigarettes on the table, strikes a match, and standing there in the kitchen with a cigarette in hand, she seems to herself larger than the darkness. Okay, let's sum up, and what have we got? A certain reputation in her field, a modicum of financial security, provided such a thing is at all possible under our circumstances, and two published books, one of them based on her thesis, plus a university textbook, plus two divorces, and honorary membership in three Western academies, which is worth exactly shit but will do for an obituary. *E la nave va.* The show must go on.

Why the hell, of the two of us, did I have to be the survivor?

And here this disgust with herself, this nausea, the toxicity of the self—the eighth grade, the scope, a spoonful of sunflower oil, yes, then, just like now—in a lightning flash reverses itself, and Darka is at last rattled to the core, she is turned inside out like a sock, her stomach in her throat, she barely makes it to the bathroom and there, leaning against the cold tiles above the toilet, with more and more tremors, doubled over from a silent cry, half falling in a cold sweat, no longer a human figure but human-size intestines pumping backward, she throws up last night's dinner, and herself at the dinner, and the night with Vovka Lasota, spasm after spasm, a brown sharp-sour stinky mass of life's undigested garbage spilling over the top, how does it all fit inside us, the decomposing corpse of her last marriage, all the scandals and humiliating settling of scores, all the pent-up hatred for the world and herself, a hot burning spray of hard bits through her mouth and nose, she can barely take a breath between fits of heaving, her knees buckle, but this is right, it feels right, this is how it should be done, to the bottom, to the scraped-out dregs, to childhood, to those first jealousies and first betrayals, to become sterile, pure, and immoveable, like the white tiles that hurt the eyes in the blazing light, because nothing either very beautiful or very terrible, nothing like this ever happens to us, you poor child, you still have to work really hard to get either one of the two—and here again Effie made it, everything came out as she had predicted—while normal life just rushed through the rest of us with this jiggly, thick brown stream, just look how it glistens in the toilet, even the walls are splattered brown, and the flushed water roars like Niagara, and you feel this otherworldly cold because your whole life has been cast out of you, and you are standing in your bathroom like a Jew in a gas chamber, leaning against the tiles exhausted, covered in tears and your own shit, your fingertips blue, empty, empty as after an abortion, and those you loved have been flushed out of you down, down the sewer pipes.

✦

Later she takes a long, thorough bath, and brushes her teeth three times because the odor seems permanent, and when she steps out of the bath, it's starting to turn grey outside. Vovka Lasota lies in her bed with his head wrapped in the sheets like a Bedouin corpse ready for burial, and just like the dead Bedouin, he has nowhere to go (sure, divorce isn't easy on anyone, especially on men, who soon seem like abandoned dogs who'll lick anyone, seeking a master). At Darka's appearance the corpse shows some signs of life: he pulls his head out of the sheets and smiles, somewhat like a victorious man after a successful night, and somewhat like that boy who approached Darka during recess and, looking past her, ears red, asked her to help him after school with this math homework. Which, in fact, she never did.

And only now does Darka realize that she doesn't have it in her to tell him to get out. At least, not right away. She can't turn on anyone the terrible megaton blast of the unmediated, naked—nothing could be more naked—and merciless because indifferent to the human essence of life, the blast that goes clear through you and wipes out anything from your adolescence, your childhood, any scrap of warmth you've managed to collect around yourself over the course of your life, leaving you face to face with things as they are. And no human can be left there like that, alone, with things as they are. Nobody deserves that.

This she owes to Effie. At least this.

"Get up," Darka says to Vovka Lasota, in the most casual voice on earth. "Let's get some breakfast."

THE TALE OF THE GUELDER ROSE FLUTE

TRANSLATED BY HALYNA HRYN AND
NINA MURRAY

She was born with a crescent moon on the crown of her head. That's what her mother told her later, that's what her mother remembered of that first moment, the first cry of the child raised from her body all the way to the roof beam by someone's strong arms as she looked up at her from below, unable to blink away her tears—on the round, smoothly protruding forehead that was a touch too high for a girl there glowed, a little off center, a finely chiseled crimson sickle, like a waning moon. Except that mother stubbornly repeated that it was a new moon, until she came to believe it herself, for everyone knows that a new crescent is for good fortune, while an old crescent—well, that's why it's called old, it brings on ill dreams, best not to let your thoughts stray there, all the more because with time the mark grew hidden by hair, a thick crop that stole away from the unseemly broad dome of the girl's forehead, better suited for a studious oblate, and no one, even had they wished to, could now discern which way those crescent tips pointed. Only when her mother washed the girl's hair could she still feel under her fingers a springy curve, where the hair grew particularly generous, black as tar and stiff as wire, and as unruly and curly as if it belonged not on the girl's head, but, Lord forgive, on her sinful flesh, on parts where the child was still blessedly smooth, and at times the mother's fingers would hesitate on that curve for a moment—with the needle-prick of the memory of the old midwife sneaking in a sign of the cross over herself and spitting over her shoulder at the sight of that crescent, because she thought it a brand of the heathen, or, not to speak it under the holy icons, a mark of the serpent's tooth, which all comes out the same: everyone knows whom the heathens worship!—it took a good while for the midwife to mellow, long enough for the baby to prove herself, knock on wood, quiet and docile as the bedeviled never can be, not to mention the changelings that the she-devils slip into mothers' cribs as soon as the midwife turns away (and the old woman must have turned away once or twice, and knew her sin!)—those scream without cease as though scalded. The mark, therefore, required a different explanation—like all *true* signs, those visited upon us by powers beyond our comprehension, whether in broad daylight or in our dreams, it spoke in its own language, potent and dark, forbidden to a common soul, and when like this presents itself to you unbidden, your choices are few: either haste to glean some wisdom from the local seer (only borrowed wisdom won't take you too far, and the overly curious oft got themselves into a heap of trouble by following this path, and then didn't know how to rid themselves of it), or have the sense to pray to the good Lord and wait for the force that had reached out to you to manifest itself of its own accord. And so it was that the mother waited, nurturing a secret notion that her firstborn was destined to become a princess or queen, because obviously she wasn't meant for a common peasant—a fate like that wouldn't merit marking the girl with a moon like that—while a certainty was taking hold within her, slow and inscrutable, that her child was chosen for a truly extraordinary fortune, one that common people's children dare not even dream of—only hear, spellbound, in tales passed down from grandmother to girl from time immemorial.

On winter nights, when the wind in the chimney howled and sobbed, as though pleading to pray for all travelers caught without cover in the open, and the swollen wedges of grainy snow brushed down from the roof past the windowpanes one after the other like someone's heavy steps, and everyone in the house would start and turn toward the noise, craning to hear if something had knocked at the door, the mother, nestling her daughter's head in her lap, told all the tales known to her, one by one, steady and clear, as she combed the girl's fair locks, gentle as silk, one hundred times in one direction, another hundred in the other—of the golden-haired maiden that the prince spied by the river where she bathed, and then asked to take in marriage, of Milady Hanna who came to the king's banquet hall three times—first by a four-in-hand, and then by a six, and then by an eight of steeds all black as serpents, who burst from the willow tree in her yard, and all the gentlefolk and the nobles marveled at whether she was a duchess, a princess, or a bright star that lit up the palace—and as she told these stories, she combed her daughter's hair so smoothly, braided it into tiny braids so tightly, that the girl's head began to glow in the firelight like a freshly glazed pitcher, but no matter how many times she licked her fingers to slick back the unruly forelock, it always sprang back with a defiant twist that would neither be cut (it grew even thicker!), nor braided in—and why should it be? Let everyone see, mused the mother not without pride, perhaps this will be the very sign that will make her known to the one she is meant for. And the child learned to hold her head high when going out (like Milady Hanna!), and the village folk, as always, saw everything because they have such good eyes to see, except that they did not see the most important thing, that which only your good Lord knows of you and which, in the end, like it or not, you take to your grave, and that is why, do what you will, you'll be judged crooked while still alive—because no one knows what truly impelled you to act, and what folks do not understand they deem evil, and this in fact is the original sin that has hobbled us all since our forefather Adam. Thus when neighbors asked the moon-marked girl, "And whose are you, that you put on such airs?" it was not because they wished to hear her simplehearted "My mama

Maria's"—also an odd and inappropriate answer, if truth be told, befitting the girl if Maria had been a widow, or unwed, or at least a Cossack's
wife whose children hadn't seen their living father in who knows how
many years, but not when she was a proper goodwife to a common
tiller, who was a father, and not an uncle to that strange girl-child that
she wouldn't even mention him, except only when a particularly coy
and inquisitive housewife would keep pressing her, hardly hiding her
pleasure in mulling over a poisonous implication, "And where's your
daddy?"—to which the child would retort, "At home," and flash her
dark-cherry eyes from under her brow in such a manner that her inter-
locutor instantly lost her desire to give the child the proper lecture she
really ought to have had—after all, that was the purpose of beginning
the conversation, to school the child (since nobody seems to have taught
her properly at home!) that it is improper, unseemly to act so grand: you
have to cut them down to size while you can, when they are still little,
lest it be too late, for who sows a habit reaps a heart, and who sows a
heart reaps a fate, but let it be as it may, Lord knows, all of us common
souls have our own children and our own troubles, so live the best you
know how, only do not say afterward you were not warned . . .

Of course, had there been someone on hand to tell all those good-
wives what kind of burning ache had been carving away at Maria's
heart for years and years, turning it into a festering, hungry void that
even sleep could not tame, they wouldn't hesitate to sympathize, even
sincerely, and similarly might have been a little kinder to the child—
but there was no such person. Maria herself carried her still-pretty lips
tightly pursed, which, with time, made them grow thinner, and her
house and her garden were always in good order beyond reproach, so
who in the world would ever conceive the notion that Maria wed her
Vasyl out of anger—from pure spite, and nothing else, just stunned
her father like a thunderbolt, while the matchmakers were still shaking the first snow off in the entryway—winter that year came early,
exactly on the Feast of Intercession, and the men's newly cleated boots

stepped on the floor loudly, gaily, and frighteningly in the chorus of boisterous voices, and at the sound of this special and oh-so-memorable bustle Maria felt everything inside her seize up in a single scalding knot, never again to be loosened, because rather than burst out in tears, Maria spoke, from the depths of the deep injustice visited upon her by her father, sharp like a crack of the whip, "Will you not let this one have me either?" This was the first time she had spoken to him since they received those other, earlier matchmakers, so eagerly awaited and dreamed about, listened for while another living sound boomed in her ears—the loud, gay, and frightening pounding of her own heart, and he replied to their opening of "Our prey—we followed its trail from the road to your yard, from the yard to your stoop, and here it roosts," after sitting silently for a while, that these folks are not from around here and have come from afar, so perhaps they'll have a drink—and that's when she did howl, clear like a beast, somebody's hands (later she realized these were her own) clamped over her mouth, and the world around her and inside her came crashing down, like the rafters of a house going down in flames, and this was the only thing that could, and did, survive that blaze—her scorched and defiant, Will you not let this one have me either?—her challenge thrown down in blind pain: if it can't be him, her one and only ("You stupid girl, you'd have cried your eyes out with that rabble-rouser, you'll thank me one day when you come to your senses!"—while all she heard ringing in her ears was a song, drowning out all this supposed good counsel, for she had no words left of her own: "I'll go by the meadow, not the riverside, and I'll meet with the soul mate ne'er to be mine" and they did meet, once only, after that match-making night, secretly, and the next day he vanished from the village, headed off for parts unknown, leaving behind him a chill that would stay forever . . . "Farewell, my soul mate, ne'er to be mine, we loved each other to the end of time"—you are stupid, girl, oh, how stupid you are . . .)—If you won't let me have him, then here, take my life—she dropped like a bowl, If it breaks, to hell with it, and if it keeps whole, it's all the same to me. The old man shrugged his shoulders, not making much sense, like all men, of women's warring, which is governed by discrete, complicated, and unfathomable ways of risking one's life, so it is best to let the challenge fly past: "You want to wed this one, go ahead." "And so I will," Maria shot back: there was no turning back for her, only the blind, desperate chase to make known to her father the grave injustice he had caused her—That'll show you! was all that spun around in her head, an echo of the vow she had just uttered and could not take back, and that is how Vasyl came to be a hostage in a duel of which he, poor heart, had no inkling, and their firstborn, Milady Hanna (that is what we shall call her henceforth, no matter what they christened her), the wonder of wonders with a crescent moon on her forehead, came to grow up as her mother's daughter, whose else could she be, loose bulls may roam, but the calf is ours, is it not, and the father matters only when the mother lets him, and mother was raising not only a daughter for herself, but a carefully tended, second-generation desire to be avenged, like a family treasure secretly accumulated and grown far beyond the limits of common imagination, as though everything that fate had denied her, Maria, was taken as a credit toward the second life, her daughter's, and was to be returned, like in an honorable transaction, with generous interest. Maria's father died shortly after her first child was born, but he sometimes came to her in her sleep—always angry and red faced like a vampire, and each time she rushed to remind him of something, to prove something to him, *to show him*, to finish the conversation between them that never did take place, but each time something got in her way—the old man disappeared, and she was left to sleep with the feeling she held a precious ring between her lips and was afraid to part them lest she swallow or lose it.

And so it came to be that the second daughter—for it seems Maria was destined to bring forth girls alone, as if an angel stood vigil over her marital bed to make sure the couple issued no boy by way of whom Maria's father could return to haunt her for the rest of her days—the

second girl, the little Olenka, was not in any way marked by any heavenly bodies, and besides was frail, beset by maladies, and a crybaby.
A meager child, Maria would sometimes think with regret that was
partly maternal and partly, may the Lord forgive her, from her wounded
pride, especially if she were to compare Olenka to the older girl, who
had the makings of a beauty already in the cradle, and turned into one
very quickly—the second daughter was her father's girl, as good as cast
over to Vasyl as a consolation prize. He doted on her beyond measure,
like he would have over a son—he even took her with him into the
fields, and made her dolls with chewed-up bread as though he wished
to feed all his vigor into her through his spit, making up for what she
was denied at birth. And were Maria to, for example, rap the little one's
knuckles for reaching her hand for food out of turn, he admonished
her on the spot, with authority that did, indeed, make her shy for a
second: "Leave the child be, she needs to grow!" Whenever Olenka was
sick, she would raise a sorrowful meowing by night, not in a demanding
manner babies have when something needles them, but a slow, grown-
up, inconsolable wail, steady as autumn sleet, which drove Maria to
distraction as though it revealed an inconsolable truth about her life
that she would have never, ever admitted to herself—Will there be no
end to this plague?—then Vasyl would get up, silently take the little
one into his arms, and, likely a bit embarrassed by such an unmanly
task, take her outside, where he cradled her, rocking gently, until everyone in the house fell asleep again. One time the elder girl woke to his
voice by the window: sitting with Olenka on the porch, her father was
singing, in a quiet but pure tenor, a voice unfamiliarly young, flowing
like wellspring water, as if indeed a wandering stranger paused by the
window to confess his grief to the trees and stars because he had no
one else to confess it to: *Loved I a maiden for nigh a year, until my foes
made me pay too dear.* The house was close with warm, greasy breath,
and pitch-black darkness, only once in a while did the pale thin blade
of the moonlight glisten through the shutters, and Maria moaned into

the pillows in her sleep, and that lonely voice by the window confessed its grief—like a soul seeking redemption. The girl lay shock-still in her bed as if she had overheard something shameful about her father, which prompted in her a swell of vivid, teary-hot sorrow, but at the same time awakened in her a different, crueler insult—the voice was *not* singing to her, that voice, that seemed to no longer be her father's, so unreachable in its high masculine loneliness, had no idea she even existed in this world, and had she not been too young to understand what she was feeling, she would have whispered to herself a sacred wish: to be the girl in the song—I want it to be *me* that someone loves that way when I grow up! . . . Instead—especially inasmuch as growing up was a very long way off indeed—the next morning for some completely frivolous reason she gave Olenka a good beating: the little one cried ferociously, smearing snot all over her face; Mother, irritated by this spectacle, gave Little Hanna—Hannusia—a robust if not very sincere spanking, and Hannusia walked around for the rest of the day in frowns with her bum burning: everything had turned out nothing like what she wanted, but what she wanted, she didn't exactly know.

The two of them, in fact, did not much relish each other, and the more they grew, the more the secret tension embodied in them came to the fore. Barely had she begun to walk when Olenka discovered how easy it was to drive her sister to distraction, and she embraced the habit of doing so the way other children, for example, take up playing with matches: strike it, throw it down, strike it, throw it down. Whenever there were no adults in sight, she would get under her sister's feet, intent on causing trouble—small, to her size: trip up her spindle, perhaps, as she was learning to spin, or tug at a ball of yarn so that it unraveled all over the floor, or else simply, for pure sport (and this was her favorite), settle in at her feet, and looking slyly upward to know when the game began to grate, make loud noises by vibrating her lower lip with her fingers like a jaw harp: "Brrn-brrn-brrn-brrn!" And again, "Brrn-brrn . . ." "Will you stop before I drum on your ribs!"—"Brrn-brrn-brrn-brrn!"—"Leave me alone, you leech!"—"Brrn-brrn-brrn-brrn!"—"You're a pest!" and with this last desperate cry, the older girl would finally throw herself at the younger, who only made as if to try to escape—and how could she, she hadn't learned to run yet!—and would begin pummeling her in earnest, without a thought for her strength, with all her rage, which thus only grew in intensity, rising and burbling like dough in a kneading bowl, threatening to spill, and always, at the decisive moment, fogging her sight with a dark, unleashed wave, Take this, and this, and this!—she'd knock the little head against the floor, feel the tiny, soft body spasm from either the blows or from the thrusts of weeping that rose inside it, and would go on until suddenly, as if with a wave of a magic wand, her rage would recede and she'd see herself from the outside—eyes hollow and empty, standing over a sobbing little girl on the floor: What am I, mad? "Will you promise not to do it again?" Hannusia would ask uncertainly, hoping to end it in a more or less dignified manner, but the voice from the floor would trumpet—and where did it fit in that morsel of a girl?—through coughs and sobs, "Nooo!"—and the next day it would begin all over again. Neither their mother's spanking nor her constantly speckled knees from having to kneel on millet in the corner, nor even their father's belt, the only thing that actually vexed her—and not so much the pain as the humiliation of it: Olenka, the snake, would be given an apple, whereas she was thrown over the knee with determined huffing and puffing, with her skirt thrown over her head and so, not having a way to explain to her father what a great injustice he was about to visit upon her, she would resort to ungodly screaming and carry on until she almost choked, and only then would she catch, not without some satisfaction, through the salty mist in her eye, the familiar hollow, confused look on her father's face, as though he, too, was asking himself, as he brought the belt down upon her, What am I, mad? Nothing, nothing was as deeply grinding for Hanna as that exhausting daily combat with that little viper, fox's snot, little tick ("Quit teasing the baby!" Father would yell), who, despite being a baby, found a way to win against her, the older and smarter one, every time ("Why can't you be the wiser one!" Mother would scold), and drive her straight into the dark and blinding wave of un-self-possession, thus provoking each time herself to be beaten, and Hannusia beaten as a consequence. Later, in moments of clarity, Hannusia would realize with the insight that desperation some-times gives our thoughts that the only thing Olenka truly wanted was to see Hannusia's rage come to the surface—only that and nothing more, as if that rage were a goose Olenka was given to mind (a huge, fierce, hissing goose, with a long snakelike neck and an ugly black maw, edged, if you squinted and looked closely, with fine sharp teeth like a pike's), and so Olenka minded it good and well, grazed it on rich green grass, and the goose roamed and ate to her heart's content. And grew fatter.

Sometimes their father acted oddly, as though he felt guilty and wanted to atone for his guilt: once, for example, he brought Hannusia silk ribbons from the fair, red and blue ones, like for a real maiden, and Olenka only got some nuts and raisins—eat them, and there goes your fun. Hannusia, feeling happily alien to herself—no longer Hannusia, but a real Milady Hanna—gingerly held the delicate bundle as though it were a living thing, and felt another warm and ticklish invisible bundle stir inside her. That day the family didn't go to bed until late, the house smelled of freshly baked pies, cherry liqueur, and drunken cherries poured out of the jug, and seemed to shudder with the settling dust of the day's commotion and the as-yet-uncooled excitement of the adults, and she, as was her custom from the time she was little, took her happi-ness, too large to be fit indoors, outside—to the moonlight. The moon was already high, and glowed steadily with its thin burning-silver light dented with the bluish shadows of the gorges, and as was its custom looked silently into her face in a way that promised someday it would speak—the girl felt her breath knocked out of her, like the cork from the long-kept jar: a strange force emanated from the earth like a steady breeze, and another entered her body and surged upward, raising her hair, and it seemed she was just about to rise into the air and float away, as she did in her dreams, over the orchards flooded with moonlight. In the next moment, a shapeless shadow separated itself from the barn and moved toward her: Father, she realized, and let out her breath at the same time, which felt like thumping down to the ground, only golden shivers ran up and down her body. "What are you doing standing here?" asked Vasyl. "Daddy," she burst out, giving him a start as if he had tripped over something. "Daddy, what's that dark spot up there on the moon?"—"Ah," said Vasyl, "that is the brother who raised his other brother on a pitchfork, two brothers they were, Cain and Abel, and the good Lord put them up there so that people could see them and not forget about their sin, and you go to bed." Hannusia looked at the dark streaks on the silvery face of the moon more closely—and indeed made out two small shapes that seemed to be standing somewhere far out in a field, one slightly above the other, and both oddly splayed out and between them a thin diagonal strip, like a ditch or a groove—exactly even with the top shape's chest . . . "Why did he raise him up on a pitchfork?" she asked again, although she really wanted to ask something different; namely, Why would the good Lord keep them up there forever, on the moon, and especially the one on the pitchfork—doesn't that hurt? Why are they not treated differently—that was the question that vexed her, deep inside: If they are both put up there for punishment, then why were they both punished equally? "Go to bed," Vasyl replied, hoarsely and sternly, like she was an adult, and she understood, more by instinct than with child's reason, that he had nothing more to say to her.

It was about that time that she began to grow more beautiful, all of a sudden and keenly (too soon, the womenfolk rustled among themselves, twisting their lips in judgment—unless a decent woman should turn up among them and slap her hands against her skirts: Tut on you, old hags, cawing like rooks before the snow, are you jealous of other people's children because your own are a bother?)—as if an unseen painter-carver worked his magic on her day by day: her eyebrows grew darker and glistened like velvet, the child's plumpness melted off her face like snow in spring, and her features acquired the angles of a royal profile fit for minting on a silver coin; her posture changed, her gait became more fluid, as though what the girl carried were not merely her budding breasts that had just began to rise beneath her blouse, but a basket of precious painted Easter eggs to be sold at the market, and the tar-black curl sprouting from the crescent-moon birthmark that burst audaciously from under her red ribbon ("The Jewish lock!"—Olenka teased her) looked like the final stroke of the master's brush—a signature under the painting. Young lads began to click their tongues as she walked by—Who's going to be getting you when you grow up?—and in Maria's heart, along with pride, nestled and grew a certain disquiet, as if she had planted a homely flower and come to find a tree of unknown provenance heaving itself out from under the earth, and who knows what kind of fruit one could expect it to bear. She could guess the child was dreaming queer dreams at night, because Hannusia would wake up with a mysterious, unconscious smile that stayed on her face unhidden until noon, and wherever she went with that smile, all heads would turn in her direction, like sunflowers following the sun, all eyes longed to rest on her face, as though each urgently wanted to find out, then and there, what this mighty strange thing was that the girl held inside her. And so it went, until an old woman pilgrim on her way to Kyiv stopped to stay the night—although god only knows where she really was headed, alone like a stone, and why she chose to knock on their door, which had nothing to distinguish it from the others on the street, but she entered as assuredly as if they had been awaiting her. Tacit, almost a little scary, all in black, she looked up from the bench at Hannusia, who had just brought in a pail of water and made to fire up the stove, and asked out of the blue: "Will you come with me to the convent, girl?"—"Goodmother, she's much too young for a pilgrimage," Maria replied, suddenly timid, unnerved for some reason by this old woman with deeply sunken eyes that seemed outlined by charcoal, as if their own deep-well blackness wasn't enough. "That was not my meaning," the old woman spoke, resonant, like a heavy church bell, and Maria's head spun, she thought the old woman suddenly grew taller, her head reaching way up to the icons perched under the ceiling—"Your daughter, goodwife, is better off at the convent. It is not you who's fated to find joy in her!" Maria drew her shoulders together, in an effort to chase away the sudden cold under her ribs, and spoke peaceably: "Ain't that the truth, we raise daughters for others' homes," and then added, perhaps involuntarily trying to avert an ill prophecy poised like a cleaver over her older daughter, "And I've got two of them!" The old pilgrim fell silent, as though giving Maria time to comprehend the folly of her declaration and turn red, and Maria did indeed turn red like an obedient schoolgirl, angry at herself the whole time, and then the old woman said suddenly, gently, like an angel descended upon the house: "The younger one is no cause of grief to you, goodwife, she'll be looked after even without you, but to this one the Lord has granted a great might, which can lead to great temptation, not in body, but in spirit, so send her to the convent, that is my good counsel." "I don't want to enter a convent, goodmother," spoke up Hannusia from where she stood by the stove, and once again the room spun before Maria's eyes: in the reddish glow of the oven, where the fire now burned gaily, her daughter's eyes also seemed to burn like two hot coals, her face emitted a deep cherry-red heat, the ribbon had slipped on her head, and the curly dark lock snaked down her temple like a black rivulet of baked blood: magnificent she was—you wanted to kneel before her—but otherworldly, too, as though it was not her child, as though that great might the old woman named a moment ago now made itself manifest and transformed the girl in its own image. "I'm not a goodmother, I'm a holy mother," the guest quietly corrected her: a strange, kind sadness came into her voice, the sorrow of old souls who had seen much in their lives and knew full well the futility of human vanities. "If you don't want to, then don't go, nobody's forcing you, dear, it's just how are you going to protect yourself when anyone who wishes to comes and drinks from your well and you won't even know it?" "Pray kindly, what is your word against, Holy Mother?" Maria leaned forward, shaking off that momentary, as if spellbound, numbness, ready to shield her child with her own flesh, if need be, from whatever threatened her, but the old woman only shook her head: "What I had to tell you, goodwife, I did, and there's nothing more I can do, it's not in my power, except for this last small thing, in thanks for your bread and salt." She turned to Hannusia and asked, "Fetch me some water, child, if you would be so kind, but watch you don't spill any." Hannusia, a good girl, obediently scooped a beaker full from the pail and brought it toward her, with visible trepidation and, it seems, even gasped slightly as their hands touched—and the following instant all three women cried out in one voice: the pilgrim woman's body, not just her hands, quivered, and she dropped the beaker—it clanged, rolled away, hit the table leg with a dull thud, and a flash of garnet, shimmery in the firelight, spread on the table. Maria, for whom things swayed and lost shape for the third time, could have sworn that what spilled was not water but wine, and on the rag that Hannusia was just wringing out—she had spun around swift as a squirrel to clean up (a heedful girl, the old lady praised her, apologizing for her awkwardness)—she clearly saw dark stains the color of royal crimson. Hannusia, on the other hand, felt them to be sticky and hot to the touch, so she hurriedly tossed the rag into the stove and closed the lid, but when she woke up in the morning (the pilgrim woman was gone: she left long before light), she saw the bedding under her stained the same red. Well, you're a woman now, said her mother, somewhat embarrassed and thus adding to her daughter's simultaneous pride and modesty—the guests have come to you now—reasoning, in her mind with some relief, that the old woman's visit had been a good thing after all and that she probably wasn't a pilgrim at all. Since that day, Hannusia no longer woke up after a night's sleep with that mysterious smile everyone would stare at—the one that seemed to suffuse her with the light of some secret knowledge in which she knew no better than to rejoice—and perhaps should have feared—that smile vanished, washed away. The girl became more ordinary—more like common people's children, lesser to the eye, and people also turned more kindly toward her.

And now Maria found herself intercepted at the footbridge, or by the well, by mothers of growing sons with their intentionally vague talk: the first time it happened, it was all she could do not to burst out laughing in that Maskymykha woman's ugly face, but, being a good woman, she kept proper, teeth all but clenched, outraged to the core by the fact that any old yokel dared compare their spawn to her Hannusia: A good girl she is, to be sure, but not for your kind, you rubes! The notion that Hannusia could eventually wed one of the simple neighbors' lads stabbed her with such a blast of anguish over her own wasted years that she nigh lost the will to live. When Vasyl, after quietly clearing his throat to get her attention, began telling her how he was approached (he, too!) by not just anyone singing Hannusia's praises, but Markian himself, the owner of the large homestead that sat apart from the village, and that homestead, good Lord, it's pretty as a picture, isn't it?—she didn't answer only because at that moment she was overwhelmed to the verge of tears by a sudden, sharp disgust at him, her husband, at his gentle throat clearing, which always seemed furtive, at the sound of him scratching the mottled rough growth on his chin, which was threaded now with silver (how had she not noticed before?), at his faded bushy eyebrows with a few particularly tough hairs like stubs of feathers on a poorly plucked chicken, at the weave of red veins on his nostrils, which made his nose look like last year's shriveled apple—and once again, as when she was young, right after the wedding, she gagged on the pungent smell of his sweat, which at the time struck her as the smell of rotten onions but then seemed to fade away with the passing of years: she got used to it, and her soul howled like a wolf inside her—Lord, woe is me, what have I done that you punish me so? She turned away, touched her dry eyes with her fingers, waited until it passed and her voice no longer revealed anything, and then said, as good as she'd cleaved a furrow: "You make the match you want for your daughter, and leave mine in peace." Thus it was first spoken between them, what later, once the girls had grown up, entered the talk about the two of them evermore, neither to be washed over nor scrubbed off: they were Father's daughter and Mother's daughter. And there you have it, a woman's life—before you know it, there's a daughter ready to be wed, and you're an old woman, no matter that your brows are still jet black—and lo! What about my own life, what is this ice-hole that swallowed it in the daily grind of house-field-garden-chickens-geese-pigs-cows, infant maladies, sore back at sundown, and you don't remember when you last looked up at the sky? Shush, old woman, keep quiet, lest you sin . . .

Up ahead of her, however, up ahead Maria could see a straight path running through the hills on a sunbeam, making her dizzy with the tickling inside her head, just like that night with the mysterious wayfaring woman, and along that path went her Hannusia, and the whole world marveled at her beauty and her stately bearing, but who's that clinging to her?—ah, can't you see, it is her mother—of course, Maria nods graciously, herself clad in gold and silver, floating ahead like a peacock—then the vision would fade into a glittering rainbow fog, and Maria would again go at her work as keen as if it were a dance, as if accompanied by invisible musicians at her pleasure, and only the knowledge that it was just around the corner—she only had to persevere a wee bit longer, bide her time a little more, good things come to those who wait—this incredible, unheard-of fortune for her child, and only this knowledge made it possible for Maria to endure year after year, so it should be no surprise that every intrusion from the outside, every human interference into that which alone fed her eternally hungry soul, vexed her as much as Vasyl's touch at night, when he wanted her and she wanted to sleep, and sleep, and nothing more, so she'd kick at him like an unbroken mare. The unease that would steal up on her did not come from people, or from the way that they treated Hannusia, but rather from the intuition that behind that rainbow fog in which her daughter's future remained hidden thus far, something was beginning to stir, something was being kneaded and shaped in order to soon be irrevocably brought to the table: eat till you burst—something very different from what she could dream up in her head, different if only because it was real, no longer imagined, and thus inevitable. The pilgrim woman was the first warning sign, and not too long after Maria was given the second: the three of them went to the annual fair to sell wheat, leaving Olenka at home, and at the fair, in the midst of the crowd, Hannusia suddenly stood stock-still, unable to take her eyes off the salt traders' caravan dealing in swift trade in dried roach fish and bream—"God help you, what is it?" Maria tugged at her shoulders, alarmed by her chalk-white face. "Mother," Hannusia asked in a hoarse, almost bass voice, "why is that lady sitting on that wagon?"—"What lady, where?"—"Over there, can't you see her"—"There's no lady there, come to your senses!" Where Hannusia pointed, a not-yet-old, well-built salt trader ran a brisk trade, flashing at his buyers a white-toothed smile bright against his tanned face, and himself looking like a sturdy Gypsy bear in his open shirt, and judging by the merriment around him, he had the wit to go with his haggling, and Maria's heart skipped a beat: It's him!—the one she dreamed of marrying, only fifteen years older!—but an instant later she knew she was mistaken and took a deep breath, wiping the sweat off her forehead: "What lady, what is the child on about?"—"She's sitting right over there, Mother, right beside that man, all in white, and her fillet is white, and her surcoat, must be a yeoman's wife, if not a sheriff's"—"Bless you child, are you possessed? Cross yourself and spit over your shoulder"—"Mother, I am telling you, she is right there, let's go over, you can ask her yourself who she is." Wrought by unease, Maria did ask someone, just for the sake of asking, which village the salt traders were from and found out it was far away, and that's where the matter ended and would have been forgotten altogether, if not for the fact that some time later they had word that the village where the salt traders returned from Crimea was beset by the plague: their own community hummed with worry, the most fearful began tarring their gates, and old people counseled that if the pestilence were to move in their direction, the village should, by ancient custom, have a plowing-round, whereby all the able-bodied women, as many as there are, come together at night and harness themselves to plow a furrow around the village that not a pestilence would dare cross as long as no man spies on the doing. Maria went about as if struck by a beam, for she had no doubt now that at the fair her Hannusia did indeed see none other than the plague itself on that wagon of fish, and if only she had listened to her child, perhaps it could have been averted—by not letting the caravan go on and burning their cargo, although, Maria justified herself in her heart, who there would have, based on the word of a mere girl, consented to send up in smoke a half year's income? They'd have been laughed out of town, and done no good. Maria would sigh heavily, rising before the cock's crow, when sleep is most fragile, for the soul is most tormented by its sins, and kneel and bow her head to the ground before the icons, begging the Lord to forgive her, but at the bottom of all her however fervent prayers lay one stifled plea she didn't dare give voice to, a hard black stone: Our Lord and Maker, spare my child if you have blessed her with *such* knowledge! There was much more demand than obedience in that plea, and so the walnut-hued faces on the icons, perhaps tanned up in the eternally ethereal altitudes where they resided, remained unmoved. The Holy Virgin pursed her delicate tight lips in reproach, and the flame of the votive beneath the icon flickered only from Maria's own breath. Be that as it may, the plague, praise the Lord, passed their village.

And the next time it happened, she was no longer by Hannusia's side—the girl's power ventured out into the world more and more, and the mother inexorably was left somewhere in the background. Maria was feeding her chickens in the yard, cluck-cluck-cluck, cluck-cluck-cluck, dearies, when suddenly a breathless flock of kids rushed in—Auntie, Auntie, they dug a well outside of Markian's homestead, Hannusia showed them where to dig! Until then the village didn't have a dowser of its own, they had to hire one from two villages over—a pockmark-faced fellow would come over, lean as a whippet, and wander around with his divining rod, taking no food, until all the children, Olenka among them, roamed around with sticks like him, and only when he finally indicated the spot, after they lowered him in a large barrel into the shaft so he could dig the last spadeful of dirt and release the water, would he take a drink and break his fast: a well is a serious matter, even those with the gift of drawing the water must mind themselves properly so as not to lose it, and here you have it!—casual, simple as a *good morning*, the girl turned to Markian's wife and said: "What do you need that pond for, when you've got a spring out there past the poplars, no more than a man and a half deep?" They went to dig, and sure enough, found the spring, and the water clear as a tear and cold as ice on the teeth, so good—you drink and feel like you've been born anew. "Hey, girl, would you work your magic on my plot too?" someone blurted out just to say something, obviously jealous of Markian's good fortune—the good Lord does look out for the rich! Hannusia, proud to be treated almost as an adult, did work her magic—walked over and said: Dig over here, and so another well appeared in the village, except "over here" fell not on the jealous man's land, but, as if to drive him mad, right over the boundary fence, in his neighbor's yard. Maria and Vasyl got money and gifts from all that, and Hannusia, in addition to the quiet pique of yet another person (because that unfortunate who led her to his neighbor's yard blamed her for all his dashed hopes, as was to be expected), earned glory that was known across the whole district: word they had a girl who could sense water underground spread like a straw fire, and it was now Hannusia rather than the old dowsers who was invited to more distant villages, and the family, not to jinx it, made a little money from it. Vasyl was even thinking about perhaps buying another horse, but Maria insisted they had to invest in a dowry for Hannusia, fit for a princess, so that nobody would later dare make a peep that he took her in naked and barefoot. Maria would gladly work herself to death for this—this was a purpose exalted enough to fill her life to the brim. Vasyl, who didn't say anything about this for a while, then set his own terms: the dowry was to be collected for both girls equally, and even that, he thought, was maybe not entirely fair, because the younger one might need it more, while the elder was more than enough herself. This was perhaps the first time that he signaled how highly he valued the older girl, the one that was not-his, and much less fawned upon by him, and it must have been this implicit praise that moved Maria to give in and acquiesce to his terms. Thus Hannusia was to earn money with her unexpected ability both for herself and for her sister. Olenka, in the meantime, spun yarn—of all domestic chores this was her favorite: mainly because you didn't have to get up and go anywhere, just keep your eyes on the yarn as it was twisted. A steady child, Vasyl would say of her, with restrained tenderness.

It's true that as an adolescent Olenka had not only grown taller, but also more attractive—bit by bit she came into her own beauty that was more her father's than her mother's: she had Vasyl's muted, subtle coloring (in contrast to the blinding brilliance of her sister), the same large pale eyes with a slow, somewhat surprised gaze—she certainly was a steady, persevering child, neither especially quick, nor efficient in a way that made things spin and hum in her hands to the delight of all around (as people repeatedly said about Hannusia), and how could she have been otherwise, growing up in her sister's unrelenting shadow—no one could have guessed, but she herself resolved once and for all not to waste her effort, thus bowing out of any competition with the elder sister long before she could lose it, and went on quietly spinning her dreams, like a thread on a spindle—like she too was waiting for her time to shine. Quarrels, not to speak of fistfights, flared up between the sisters only seldom now—one winter day, for example, Hannusia was all set to go skating and couldn't find her boots, she looked every-where: in the house, in the larder, she even climbed up to the attic—the boots were gone! vanished into thin air. Flushed red, on the verge of tears, Hannusia turned on her sister—"What did you do with my boots? Mother, do not defend her, I know she did it!"—the boots were discovered the following day standing neatly under the bench, side by side, spun similarly out of thin air. "I knew it was her," Hannusia exploded—Olenka curled her lips into a contemptuous smile, but hid her eyes nonetheless: As if I have nothing better to do than hide your boots!—such scars remained, festered from both sides simultaneously because Hannusia, having the more fiery nature, was determined each time to get the better of her sister, *so she'd know*—so that, for instance, she would *admit* before their father that she did hide those miserable boots, blast them (definitely not worth the storm they'd roused)—so that, in her words, there would be justice, and it could be no one but Vasyl who was expected to dispense it between the two of them. Olenka, on the other hand, precisely in the way that she intentionally, deliberately eluded any attempts at reaching an understanding, like it was now her turn to say to her sister, Leave me alone, and to say it with her entire demeanor, her taunting smile, her turned back impenetrable as a tall fence, hop all you want, you'll never climb over it—hit her mark without fail, wounding her sister where it hurt the most, and then it seemed the air itself inside the house, scratched into boils, churned to madness by mutual blows, would swell to the point of ejecting one of them—Hannusia—way, way outside, outdoors, anywhere, just to get out of sight, where she could take a deep breath and fill her lungs with fresh, living air.

And Olenka would remain to spin.

Not long afterward Hannusia observed something else: right after those domestic calamities she would lose her ability to find water—in fact, she seemed to lose all her sense in herself, as if she were replaced, for a time, by a heavy, faceless cloud of grievance; the cloud was an opaque yellowish color and something dripped from it—pus rather than rain. One time she obliged to head out in this precise circumstance, because they had already sent the horses for her, somewhere almost out by the wild woods, to the bluffs, where they urgently needed a new well after they found blood in the old one—folks called the priest, and he blessed it, and they cleaned it, but a week later they found a hired hand drowned in this freshly blessed well, so now they had to bring water from the river miles away. Halfway there, Hannusia jumped off the wagon and told the driver in no uncertain terms that she couldn't go on, excusing herself as unwell—what actually happened was that she saw the drowned man, whom she'd never laid eyes on while he was living, suddenly right before her: first his cold stiff feet sticking out of the well, and then the rest of him, stretching out to full stature with vicious satisfaction and glad to stretch his numb extremities—he was blue all over, netted in wet strands of his own hair, and he was about to turn his eyes, cloudy as the last bit of milk left at the bottom of a cup, and look straight at her. At that very moment, scalded to the bone by an otherworldly, icy chill—not the cool moist breath of earth that helped her feel the presence of water so clearly she could only marvel how others couldn't, but precisely ice cold—that came from something immovable, also seemingly underwater, but *life*less—she was simultaneously cut through by the penetrating knowledge that she would not find *living* water today for any treasure in the world: that he would be waiting for her, this terrifying self-murderer, and walk her around in circles for sport, and she could not free herself of him because he was drawn to her like a fly to carrion—to the pus of her soul she dripped and dripped without end, unseen by the living, but apparently visible to the dead, so she leaped from the wagon as if running for her life— straight into a roadside pit filled with dust, almost twisting her ankle. That girl's off her rocker, the driver must have thought, tugging on the reins: Whoa, the horses stopped, snorting angrily so that a strand of foam came flying at her—the horses, too, must have been thinking something very uncomplimentary about her.

That fall the first matchmakers came to the house, sudden as a thunderclap—Hannusia had just turned fifteen, no one expected them, and everyone lost their composure, Vasyl among them, not to mention Hannusia, who bolted out of the house into the anteroom and from there, hidden behind the door with her suddenly dry mouth wide open, listened to the grown-ups' customary talk of the hunters and the sable, disbelieving her ears: Could this really be about her? She had not a single thought for the young man she was being matched with, as if they'd come not to ask her hand in marriage to a flesh-and-blood person, but stopped by to testify to the arrival of a momentous and ominous change in the way the world saw her. Sure enough, lads whistled in her wake when she walked down the street, and she got used to that, accepting it as her due, but when those who were bolder (she always thought them more stupid, because she learned well from her mother that she was not meant for the village lads, and those who didn't understand that impressed her by their unheard-of obtuseness alone) would try to woo her with their crude attempts at flirting—say, rush her on a solstice night in a senseless tussle, the only purpose of which was to throw a girl on the ground and feel her up, or else ambush her and squeeze her in a throng of similarly captive girls that burst in all directions with happy screams—she would douse him with a glare full of such bone-chilling contempt that all the huffing, snorting, eager-eyed fervor went flying out of the prospective suitor like a witch out of a chimney—but now something new has arrived, something at once mysterious and dirty, like those greedy hands that wanted to feel her breasts, yet in a strange measure raising her up—to the height of a princess in a tower that the best knights try to reach by riding their most mettlesome chargers, something that was remotely akin to her father's lonely longing song that one night for the girl he loved and would never have, and, swept up in the frightful whirl of these two different and yet somehow intersecting currents of feeling, Hannusia took a good long while to come around, long after the matchmakers were refused and left—of course they were refused, how not, she was too young to be wed, let her have some fun first, we, good people, don't have fields of daughters to spare. But if you ask me—Olenka said very solemnly, with emphasis, amusing her father (who could never resist when she affected maturity, as she knew perfectly well)—if you ask me, she should have accepted, if good people are asking, why be so choosy? Hannusia had a good laugh herself—Have our matchmaker here, do we, she's barely got ribbons in her braids, but is ready to wed—having, at the same time, no doubt that Olenka was dead serious and she wished her older sister out of the house as soon as possible, so as to become herself first in line. It's just that Father, as always when it came to his baby, failed to notice this.

About the ribbons—of course, that was spoken in haste, because although Maria did not allow Olenka to go out yet, neither did she permit her to cuddle up to her father, as had been her custom since she was little, reprimanding them both with such force that Vasyl shied away and went outside to roll a cigarette: back when she was still small and sickly, Olenka learned to crawl up onto his lap in the evenings, putting her arms around his neck, and pressing her ear against his chest to ask, Father, what do you have thumping there?—Vasyl would become tender, carefully stroking his daughter's warm braids with his awkward, stiff, and calloused hand, so unaccustomed to delicate movements, and this touch would stir up from the depths of his memory, from its silt and mud, the memory of Maria as a newlywed: her braids had smelled the same, and the same tenderness welled inside of him—like a gentle wind that slowly fills the body from the inside, only this time very slowly, and Vasyl knew that it would never fill him to the brim again, he had grown far too numb, ossified for that. Olenka gave him back if not that youthful melodic lightness, then the memory of it, but this was the dearest thing that he had ever had—the child was his pet, no denying it, and even though he had been taught, heard it a hundred times, that you can pet a dog, but not a child, he could not resist her hugs—except for her, he got them from no one. Hannusia was different, very different from the moment she was born, more mysterious or something—if truth be known, he was a little afraid of Hannusia. As he was of Maria, indeed.

He wished very much to have more children—a whole houseful of children, full of hubbub and squeals, like a sieve overflowing with spring chicks—as a boy he always had an irresistible urge to stick his face and whole head into their warm mass—a house with ten such warm curly heads under the quilt on top of the large warm stove, ah my little chickees!—but what could he do when after the second girl they were as good as done: Maria miscarried one after another, lost them, and he'd be angry with her not least because at some level he felt himself at fault, as though each time he lacked exactly enough manly vigor to give the just-conceived child enough strength to reach this world, as though in some decisive moment, of which he had no idea, each time something within him sputtered and faltered—something elusive, something that could not be defined by simple, tangible things like spilling too soon or some such thing, but rather something he lacked to have the power to command a woman's womb completely and definitively, leaving room for nothing else, while he could sense that for his every issue something impenetrable and immovable inside her would rise up to meet it, like a dark mountain from which he would slide back down. Afterward Maria would lie in silence, her head turned away, so that even her breathing could not be heard: at first, when they were newlyweds, he thought it was because of her modesty, and this warmed him with even greater tenderness toward her, but now he thought no such thing: she lay there, and he lay beside her, and soon—more by that marital instinct that develops over the years than by her breathing—he would know that she was fast asleep. And that's how it was between them, and when it came to the future, Vasyl only very rarely allowed himself to dream that when the girls came of age—there wasn't long to wait—they would see

Hannusia well married, and take in Olenka's husband-to-be to take over the household, and he, Vasyl, would have grandchildren to look after, a whole garland of babies, light- and curly-haired little dandelion heads, like Olenka's when she was little.

Because Olenka was not little anymore, and he missed her—sometimes he even felt like he detected in her that impenetrable and immovable quality that he knew in Maria, except that their daughter was incomparably kinder and knew, with her astute female instinct, to hide this new quality, and got her bees with honey: Daddy, why won't Mother let me go out, all the other girls are going, what about Odarka next door, she's younger than me, she's not even fourteen until after the Feast of the Transfiguration—and in the end she got her way, and started going out almost at the same time as Hannusia—which was a good thing, Vasyl told himself, they'll be together, one will watch out for the other lest they get into the kind of trouble girls find, although, of course, he and Maria had to purchase a goodly selection of new clothes and haberdashery much sooner than they had planned, fine red leather boots with upturned toes, wraparound skirts brocaded with gold, full-length sheepskin coats trimmed with Persian lamb, and all kinds of other finery, almost a full trunk, if you must know—you can lose your mind with how much the womenfolk blow on their harness!—and since money was tight because they could not sell the heifer until the fall, the family had to spend a large chunk of Hannusia's earnings on this affair. Hannusia, bless her heart, didn't utter a word in protest, to Vasyl's great relief: he feared the girls would start warring again, and suffered great anxiety in anticipation thereof—she seemed to treat what she called "the water money" as if she'd found it, easy come, easy go, and maybe that's why that money stuck to her—not excessively but, praise the Lord, fairly tightly. It only aggravated her that the younger one had the nerve to behave as if they were equals: after all, she had the same fine red leather boots ("I want the same as Hannusia!") and began putting on airs as though there really wasn't any difference between them—Father's

girl and Mother's girl, and that's it—she even occasionally allowed herself to utter something patronizing, as in, You, sister, shouldn't put red
edging on this bustle, it comes out too much of the same thing—a
joke, what can you say! And it also bothered Hannusia a little how easily Olenka accepted her money, calmly, as though it was due her—You
could thank your sister, at least, Maria would admonish, and in reply
the younger girl would look at her mother with that languid, somewhat
surprised look that had the effect of ending the conversation: Well, your
father sure spoiled you, girl, didn't he, whoever marries you will have his
hands full! Olenka only shrugged her shoulders slowly, and the shadow
of a satisfied smile fleeted across her face—as though she was pleased
with the idea of that unknown unsuspecting someone having his hands
thusly occupied.

As time passed, Hannusia felt more and more acutely as if her
parental home were pushing her out of itself—and not only by virtue
of her father and sister's mutually agreed-upon waiting, to the point
that she sometimes couldn't help but feel like they secretly exchanged
conspiratorial glances behind her back, so she got into the habit of turning abruptly—from the oven, from the well, or whatever she happened
to be working on—to try to catch them, which she never succeeded in
doing, except that Olenka asked her mockingly: What are these spasms
you're having?—which definitively confirmed her suspicion, not even a
suspicion, but rather an instinct, like in a young wild animal that knows
nothing yet about the hunt but still braces itself, catching the scent of
hounds on the wind—although it wasn't only this that weighed upon
her, giving their home the feel of a dark cellar that she now entered
mainly only to sleep, and even then it felt like going to a dungeon—but
the sovereignty her sister exercised in it, which had grown beyond any
reason, with their father's tacit backing. Olenka behaved like the mis-
tress of the house and not at all like the second in line to be married,
and her ubiquitous, ineradicable, and incredibly self-assured presence
poisoned the air for Hannusia. As soon as she began going out, Olenka

acquired a clutch of girlfriends, and they walked together like a laughing and giggling resplendent cluster of ripe grapes, which was yet to be picked apart, one by one, by young men's greedy hands—Hannusia, on the other hand, was considered to be haughty and treated respectfully, but from a distance: her beauty alone set her apart in any group. Whenever, for example, they went caroling at Christmastime, and a garrulous host would utter a light-minded, Come on, girls, step up with your big sack, which of you has it, oh, I thought it would be this one, the prettiest!—Hannusia, cleaved from the group with that one word, immediately felt herself alone in a dark wood, surrounded by the instantly raised thorny brush of tacit dislike, as if her friends joined hands to make a circle in which there was no place for her—much the way she ended up at every celebration: the Maypole and Easter dances always circled around her, they chose her as the one to be crowned at Solstice, to carry, inevitably, the first-cut sheaf of the year, and the wreath at the end of harvest; in other words, she seemed to have been chosen to be put forward for show at every occasion, displayed for admiration and praise—the most striking among the girls, but because of it also not one of them: not for naught was she marked with a crescent moon on her forehead, she would think to herself when alone, when the alienation weighed heavily on her heart, and, coming home from the winter parties or street gatherings, she would walk up to the looking glass mortared into the wall to examine that crescent moon looking out from under her hair, and it would give her consolation with its unbreakable promise of some great and imminent reward.

She always loved to swim—she loved to feel the water caress her body, the tickle upon entering, its marvelous, soft touch that fondled her in most secret, most shameful ways, and now she found another pleasure, to which she could have devoted hours if she had her way—how lazy she would become then, she laughed in feigned horror!—she enjoyed looking at her nude body, marveling at it as a discrete thing apart from herself: everything was so delicate and perfect, from the arch

76

of her foot and up, along the chiseled line of her calf and thigh, made, it seemed, by a single stroke of a master carver, the dome of her stomach like the church chalice bearing the blessed sacraments: when she first made this discovery, she recoiled in fear from such a blasphemous thought, but then each time she lowered her eyes, she found the same sight—a shallow chalice that glowed with a gentle pearly luster, it was here, inside her, it *was* her, there was no escaping it, and this involuntary, seemingly independent of her sacrilege gave her a glimpse of such frightening, sweet beauty that shimmered like precious diamonds at the bottom of a ravine that it seemed if you peered in more closely, you would lose your senses. Now more than ever before did Hannusia feel herself worthy of song—not just someone's grand and sorrowful, larger than life itself, love sung a-voice, the way she had heard her father sing that night after her mother—she knew now it was her mother he sang for, but this would not be enough for her now, just think: were such beauty as hers to be given to one man alone, once and till the end of his days, that one man would have to die from happiness on the spot, having seen her just once as she was now, reflected in the slow river water, having touched just once the silk of her skin, cool and yet somehow warmed from the inside—not one of the young men known to her could even be conceived to measure up to such a gift—no, it wasn't a new longing expressed in old words that she yearned for, but a new song, composed for her alone, one that would suffuse each and every one who heard it with shivers under their skin, with this just now apprehended sense of a tangible and accessible sacredness—a feeling sinful, terrifying, and sweet, in whose deepest recesses her light would shimmer, forever desired—Hannusia, Milady Hanna.

"Verdant willow, open up, Hanna has come," she'd whisper as she descended the riverbank and untied her sashes before stepping into the water, while in her mind she'd call out, Fold open, steep bank, let me enter, yellow sand, make way, deep river—everything, everything around her had to give way as she came to it, unfurling, smiling in greeting, lauding her—the riverbank with its leaves, the river with its waves, the birds with their chirping, and that's exactly what would happen when she appeared, everything was set in motion down to the depths of the earth where, like bees in a hive at night, secret springs slowly hummed—in such moments she felt she could hear the entire earth all the way to the sea, and if she were to press her ear to the ground, she would hear the rider on the open steppe, and the salt cart on the beaten road, and, were she to pull her thought tighter, she could, for a lark, heave a rock away from a traveler's path, or on the contrary, block his passage—this, of course, she never did, but the very knowledge of this ability, as well as countless others—an entire universe of them!— hers to play with as she pleased, filled all of her happy being, down to her fingertips, with an avid, tumbling force, and from its cresting swell she would leap from the riverbank into the water with a sharp cry, unable to keep within herself such an overabundance of joy. The water nymphs teased her from the rushes, calling out, Switches, switches, I smell the straw scent of witches!—the water roiled around her body in white foam, as if around a fired iron, as she came to the surface—Lying spawn!—she shouted back to the nymphs as she threw her head back into the clouds that floated, reflected, in the river, and her voice carried far and wide over the water, because the little imps were lying, she did not smell of straw—of a peasant's hut—but of wormwood; she had taken up the custom of rubbing herself all over with it, and carried a bunch of it at her waist, that's what peeved the nymphs—they didn't dare show their faces to her, but contented themselves with whooping out from the rushes, and even their hoots were less angry than sad, as if they, too, gave her a greeting, acknowledged her invincibility.

Because straw scent or not, the smell of her own home was becoming hateful to Hannusia—she only felt truly herself when she was alone, by the river, in the woods or the fields, and people, whether kin or strangers, kept her out of sorts, as if one day a *different kind* of people was supposed to arrive from somewhere far in the great wide world for her, people more like the ones who inhabited her mother's tales, and it was for these people that she dressed into her fine clothes and fixed her hair every day—a princess in the tower, while those around her, the blind and small minded, thought her a haughty mother's daughter who disdained the very best lads in the village and traded them as fast as a Gypsy trades horses, waiting for Lord only knows whom, while the father's daughter agreed with them so much more, a fine and well-behaved child, that's right, and a hard worker, too—local gossip to make your ears wilt. Hannusia honestly did not feel she was being too choosy with the lads—she always refused the matchmakers, who, during the first autumn of her maidenhood seemed never to leave her doorway, one set walking in, the other walking out, With all due respect, I thank you for the honor, goodfolk, but I still haven't had my fill of my parents' good care—never once did she send anyone off with a pumpkin as a token of her refusal (to her mind, it was beneath her to mock a poor fellow so publicly, as if she really cared about him!). All of this seemed to her somehow not-real, not meant for her, although, in its own way, entertaining, the way one is entertained by a puppet show put on by the seminarians at the winter fair, or some such. Girl, you have your head full of air, the older women would say to her and shake their heads—but air it was not, quite the opposite, hard and solid, like a coin worked into a string of beads, a certainty of her predestination for another fate, which everyone around her, except for her mother, from whom she always felt silent support, cheerfully and unanimously were determined to shake, and to withstand this threat she thought more and more often of the old pilgrim woman and the night her childhood ended and maidenhood began, which was pressed into her memory as brightly as a gold-clad icon, until the day she finally plucked up her courage to go three villages over to ask a seer woman known across their whole country what was it that she must do to summon her true destiny, and not the one people kept foisting on her, as if she couldn't tell their tin from her true gold—however, precisely on that day, as if on purpose to upset her plan, Olenka got a toothache, her cheek swelled up so badly that she could barely open her eye, they feared she'd caught Saint Anthony's fire, so it was Olenka who was taken to the healer—right in their own village, but Hannusia could not leave home at such a time, someone had to keep up with the chores until Olenka recovered—and this is what happened every time, as if Olenka had returned to her casual torment, like when she was little and put herself underfoot just to hinder whatever Hannusia was doing: no sooner did Hannusia fix to go out into the world somewhere—maybe not to the seer woman, but let's say as a bridesmaid to the other village, where she'd been invited, and folks rumored all kind of men from the regiment were expected, up to and including the colonel himself!—when at the critical moment—how unlucky!—Olenka inevitably fell into one of her mishaps, usually not as serious as it was aggravating, but which managed, nonetheless, to put a dead end to all Hannusia's meticulously executed preparations, and always in a way she could not really protest—how could you, for instance, hold it against the poor Olenka when she twisted her thumb or cut her foot with a scythe so she couldn't even walk for three days! It seemed silly to think so, but Hannusia could not rid herself of a gnawing feeling, like a splinter under her skin, that her sister *would not let her go*—not away from her, Olenka, because nothing would've pleased her more than to see Hannusia married off—she watched all Hannusia's matchmakers like a hawk, you'd think her skin tensed with that focus—but, queer as it seemed, toward Hannusia's own destiny, as if jealously guarding an invisible boundary beyond which lay that which was Hannusia's alone, something special that Olenka, and all the other girls, were denied even to imagine, so whenever her sister was about to cross that boundary, Olenka dragged her back with the burden of all of her mundane maladies, back to the thickets of their domestic routine, as if Hannusia were a cow with a rope around her horns. The devil take it, Hannusia'd think, angry at her own feelings, and would go brew linden-bloom tea for her younger sister, who lay curled up under the

quilt and shook with coughs, loud as a dog's barks, having contrived
to catch a cold in the middle of the summer, precisely when Hannusia
was supposed to be sent off with other women not just anywhere, but
to Kyiv itself to take embroidery to sell at the monastery: Hannusia
embroidered handsomely. Well, they would just have to sell her work
for her.

In public, however, Olenka never complained, was always cheerful and even keeled, smiling sweetly at elders and even more sweetly at
the village lads: shyly, dropping her eyes and fidgeting with the handkerchief in her hands or with the edge of her lovely apron—clearly,
still very young. She would become especially shy around those who
had asked for Hannusia's hand and were refused: you'd think she felt,
by virtue of blood relation, at fault with them and desired to rectify,
ever so delicately, the injury caused them by her family, as though to
atone, according to old custom, for the dishonor. Soon enough this was
noticed—one of Hannusia's recent suitors, who began to frequent the
tavern after his unsuccessful courtship, where he would buy a drink for
anyone who would listen and tell them, loud enough for the house to
hear, what a foolish business it is to pine for a woman, after all they're a
dime a dozen, just whistle and they'll come running. On the next feast
day, also, apparently having had a drink or two, he grabbed Olenka by
the hand: What about you, will you marry me? Olenka blushed beet
red down to the bottom of her neck, broke loose, and ran away, hiding
in a throng of girls, while the young man cocked his hat and marched
down the street, singing with great feeling: "'Tis with your sister I'll
spend the eve, her talk is different than yours has been"—which, in
fact, was an insult, and not a minor one, said Hannusia, hugging the
flustered Olenka by the shoulders and drawing her close—Now there's
a dumb bully, pay him no mind, while the song mocked them from
afar, "Her talk is different, her words aren't stark, her skin's not fair, her
brows aren't dark," felt at once cut to the quick by the bastard's rude-
ness—You scoundrel, I was too kind when I gave you the boot—and,

deep in her soul and despite herself, somewhat flattered and vindicated, not so much in her vanity as in her need of justice: finally Olenka has been shown, unambiguously and by an outsider, her place in relation to her sister, *so she'd know*—and here Olenka, flashing her tear-filled eyes—never before had Hannusia seen her, such a quiet little mouse, so furious—breathed straight into her face so that Hannusia even felt her sister's spit drop onto her own lips, "Just you wait, we'll see who comes out on top!" "Good heavens!" Hannusia spit to the side in pique, but all the same for a long time afterward she could feel the drops of Olenka's spit like specks of fire.

She forgot about that misadventure fairly soon—a new worry beset her: a few times now Markian's son, Dmytro, made passes at her, regally and carelessly—an exceptionally handsome lad, that could not be denied, just look at him on a Sunday when he'd wear his red sash that blazed like fire, and a rich man's son, and an only child to boot, so it's not like he'd need to borrow money for his young man's caprices— "Will you come out tonight?"—he'd ask, looking her over with a leer, as if he had already undressed her and was now assessing her naked, like a Turk at the slave market—would he take her right there, or keep walking?—"If you come out, I'll hire musicians." Hannusia pressed her lips together, which instantly made her look like her mother: "Thank you for the kind offer, but I have enough money of my own"—the first time, perhaps, she'd ever brought up her earnings, and it left her with an unpleasant feeling, as though he had tricked her into showing all her virtues at once, including those she did not value particularly highly, because she took them for granted—truly like presenting yourself at the slave market, as in, What do you think me, friend, a pauper?— but she had no other recourse against the innate and seemingly all-encompassing sense of superiority he exuded with every stitch, down to the last careful fold in his sash. Dmytro, for one, actually would have girls run to his whistle, he himself was not in the habit of chasing, and Hannusia could not quite find the means—and was very angry at her own helplessness—just did not know how to burst the bubble of that rich boy's pride, he was round and smooth as if glazed, nowhere to scratch him, and only squinted his eye at her, like a happy cat in the sunlight, in anticipation, and the more she pursed her lips, the more dismissively she tossed her head, the more it entertained him—like a small child's antics. He did, however, hire the musicians as promised: Hannusia deliberately dragged her heels and came to the dance last, when the company should well have given up on her, and smiled to herself when, obviously bored a minute earlier, Dmytro blossomed with a new joy when she appeared: "Aren't you a proud one," he said quietly, stepping close and squeezing her by the shoulders, painfully, like he wanted to knead her into a ball, like dough removed from the wrap of her clothing. His breath, tickling her ear, was hot, fired up by dancing, and for an instant Hannusia felt a sweet weakness in her body—she moved toward him and pressed—almost struck—her chin against his shoulder, thus swallowing the surreptitious smile of her brief victory—"Let's go then," he said simply, signaling the other couples to make way, as if it was clear as god's day that she would be dancing only with him, as if that's the only thing she'd come for, as if he had already taken her into his hands for as long as he wanted, and she did not like that, so when he spun her around as they danced—sharply, so that she became dizzy, each turn a new test: he didn't dance with her, he danced *by means of* her, his every move telling the crowd, "Look what I've got!" when he grabbed her by the waist and pressed her close, not so much asking as commanding: "Come out to the meadow tonight, I'll be waiting for you"—she just laughed at him (this time turning her head so as not to get it in the teeth with his shoulder again): "There's no holding off for you, Dmytro, is there?" He was so stunned he stepped out of the dance circle—dragging her behind him: "Look at you, aren't you shrewd!"—and stood there, not lifting his hands off her, which was beginning to look quite inappropriate, like they were embracing in public, and Hannusia gently but persistently freed herself—"Careful you don't outshrew yourself," he said, suddenly unpleasantly, all but menacing, and looked at her again in that evaluating way of his, except this time it was different—undiluted, sharp, cold, and clouded, like a breath-fogged blade, and that cold echoed in Hannusia—I see now we're really talking!—with a sudden and clear satisfaction that she did knock him down a rung, but at the same time she felt the prick of the insult in the fact that, goodness gracious, it was only now that he'd finally *seen* her—he saw only a thing before: the best girl in the village, a new trophy worthy of decorating his father's hearth. At that, Hannusia felt a real chill—the sweat between her shoulder blades evaporated—breathing at her from the maw of the infinite desert that suddenly opened around her, endless like the night sky; at that moment she could have simply told Dmytro, whose thoughts she could read as easily as if they moved in front of her, like a school of small fish teeming at the bottom of crystal clear water—I won't marry you, don't waste your time—but he wouldn't have believed her, because any sensible soul would say she could not possibly marry anyone else. And so Hannusia held her tongue—and soon enough came to realize with a heavy heart that Dmytro's family, once they took something into their heads, were not ones to let it go: people began to drop meaningful hints at her from all sides, and found every occasion, as if they'd plotted around her, to mention Dmytro in her presence, some with a nod and a wink—Now there's a fine young man, and the fields he's got, and the cattle!—and others shooting straight—So, when shall we have fun at your wedding, Markian's sure to spare nothing for his only child! Oh, how lucky you are, sweetie, sighed the more openhearted and poor of the girls, while the richer ones said nothing, since more than one of them had her sights set on the lad, and Hannusia, from all of that, slowly began to feel like a wild beast, driven toward the pit by whistling and hooting hunters: she was precious game, of course, a prize, and all around her commanded, nay, demanded she be mightily proud of this, yet even the rarest beast is prized for one thing—its pelt.

At the same time, her mother (and no need to even mention her father: he walked around all puffed up as though the wedding were just around the corner, even began humming to himself) seemed to stop bolstering Hannusia, withdrew invisibly from her daughter, as if to say, Do what you think is best, child—whether she'd lost her nerve in the face of the fact that the girl, after all, had turned seventeen and couldn't stay a maiden forever, waiting for her prince, or whether she'd judged that a homestead was one's own kind of fiefdom, albeit small, the two of them never spoke about it—they never spoke about Dmytro at all, avoiding the issue as carefully as a sinkhole in a swamp, and Hannusia couldn't have known that Maria was weathered and frayed for a reason altogether different: she began to dream of her dead father again—this time, he appeared to her laid out on a bench in their old home, with a lit candle that was for some reason placed at his feet, and there was no one beside him except for her alone, and she fretted she wouldn't be able to properly read the Akathist Hymn over him because he had only sent her to school for one winter, and so every night, in her dream, she would shut the housedoor with the dead man inside and head out blindly to look for help. Exhausted by that dream—for she had been to church, given alms, and had the priest serve a special liturgy for the repose of her father's soul, and yet each night her trial returned—Maria turned to the village healer, who read prayers over her and poured off wax, but the wax showed the same thing—a coffin, a church—"You have an old sin in your house, Maria, and you don't know how to carry it out, and it's high time you did," was all the healer could tell her.

So did each of them wage her own war, Maria—with the dead, Hannusia—with the living: because to her reckoning, the collision with Dmytro looked less and less like courtship, and more like he was simply taking her by siege, not a visible one—you couldn't quite put your finger on it—but one she felt acutely, along with his growing determination, like an impenetrable wall going up where love should have been. "You should know, girl," he once said when he appeared from nowhere in her path and seemed to drink all of her up with his eyes, "I don't like it when I don't get my way"—and another time he jumped out of the bushes where he'd been waiting to ambush her with a racket like a bear, giving Hannusia a fright, and blocked her way as solidly as he blocked the light of day itself: "They say you know witchcraft? Maybe you are a witch—let's see if you have a tail!" And the next instant, before she had a chance to cry out, his thick hand clamped tightly over her mouth, both of them were rolling about on the ground already when another paw—how many does he have?—ripped at her skirt, raising it over her clenched knees, as she flailed like a fish pulled out of the water because this was no innocent boy-prank—a fierce merciless force was about to overwhelm her, a force that was utterly indifferent to her and knew only its own thrust, its own violence, moist and terrifying, truly a wild beast that had attacked her, pinned her to the ground so that she couldn't even move her hand, growled and tore at her with claws and teeth: A werewolf! flashed through Hannusia's mind, and before she herself realized what she was doing, she went limp, stopped resisting, and produced a choked, and thus oddly lusty, deep and raspy witch's voice, "Dmytro, you silly, you're going about it all wrong, it hurts." The beast, too, froze in surprise, snorted in confusion, something along the lines of That's more like it—sensing this instant of weakness clearly, as if her entire body were studded with sharp, all-seeing eyes, Hannusia twisted and sank her teeth deep into the flesh of this neck, right above that collarbone she had recently rammed her chin into at the dance—Dmytro howled like a werewolf, jumped up, pressing his fingers over the bite as a stream of red seeped through, "You fucking whore!"—but she'd already lit it down the path, kicking up a trail of dust, her lips burning with a queer, salty taste—like an iron latch she once licked as a child, except that latch was cold and this was warm and alive, and made her want to suck on it more, gulp it, slurp it, more, more: unlike water, this only parched the more you drank it.

Not long after that incident, folks fixed to dig a well at the other end of the village and Hannusia, of course, was called for—and there again that smell hit her nostrils, sudden, salty, and sharp like the iron latch, it made her mouth water—so thick and rich it was, coming off the earth like lather, overpowering the measured, even breath of fresh underground water: Right here, she gasped from deep in her chest as if from a well, and her voice, again, was not her own—she didn't point, she commanded, and from the way everyone became quiet after her cry, she got a strange feeling, as if reliving what happened in her encounter with Dmytro: once again her body tensed up in predatory anticipation and was no longer under her control, it knew what to do without her—"Dig here!"—and, a moment later: "Catch him!"—pointing to an unremarkable little man in the crowd, who went visibly grey, glanced furtively about, and made to run. This all happened very quickly and if not for her (or perhaps it was no longer hers?) charged thousand-eyeness that could see everything—the crowd, the light of the sky, the old willow tree with its forked branches, the suffocating greasy fountain of red bursting at her from below—that man would have gotten away, but they caught him and bound him; he trembled, dotted all over by quivering beads of sweat, and then wailed, high pitched, like a wounded dog, and went limp, hanging in the arms that held him like a sack, because the pickaxes, whose scraping was the only sound heard in that heaviest of silences, revealed a long shape, dusted with earth, and people jumped back covering their noses because of the stench, someone started to cough, another threw up, the men digging were the first to take off their hats and cross themselves: "It's Ivan! By god, it's Tekla's Ivan! And they said that he went off to look for wage work." Hannusia took one last look at the now violently sobbing little man, who no longer tried to break free, and it was as clear as if he'd spoken: this was his doing, and only then she inhaled the stench—sickly sweet, strong enough to scoop your guts out, it came not from the pit but from the murderer, and strangely, rather than be disgusted like the people around her, she greedily, lustily snorted it, her nostrils flaring, taking in the reek that was, somehow, a continuation of the earlier steamy foul smell of spilled blood, and her heart stopped beating for a moment, squeezed by a mighty sorrowful torment, a premonition of doom—she remembered the drowned man she saw after she'd quarreled with her sister, she remembered the white-robed lady she saw on the salt traders' wagon at the fair, and thought for the first time she should have listened to that pilgrim woman and gone with her to the convent, if only on a pilgrimage if not for good. But she calmed herself with the remainder of the strength within her, it was not too late to go on a pilgrimage even now, she'll get herself together and go, she really should: it was not right—to start digging up dead bodies instead of wells.

There was never time to be found, however, for a pilgrimage—the harvest began, and in the daily work, from dawn to dusk so help us god, all senses and aspirations became wooden and dull—and the misadventure with Dmytro also began to recede into the past: there was no time to keep it alive by thinking about it, and it is only that which we feed with our soul that has power over us, this Hannusia took to mind firmly that summer, never mind that no one had ever taught her. With Dmytro, however much everyone considered them a couple, she was joined only by a double-edged fear: the threat of the beast he had set free, and Hannusia's terror of herself, that evil power he had awakened inside her, a match to the beast, and likely stronger than him—of course it was, and Hannusia, despite everything, found in that advantage a wicked consolation—the way she did in her secret devotional contemplation of her own physical beauty. Preoccupied with her own trials, she failed to take note, at first, how unexpectedly and lushly Olenka blossomed that summer—the girl turned outright beautiful, radiating youth like light, reaching out, it seemed, with every vein and sinew—and with such new grace and elegance!—toward both sunshine and people, bearing in the curved corners of her budded lips a smile meant for someone unknown. "Sister, dear, are you, by chance, in love?" Hannusia asked her in jest and was even more surprised when Olenka, rather than brush her off as usual, burst into laughter and threw her arms around her neck, hugging and kissing her, burying her face in her chest, pressing against her as fervently as a child looking for a mother's nipple—Stop it, you crazy girl, you'll choke me to death, Hannusia laughed—while Olenka, unable to contain herself, pretended to be a puppy and yelped, hopping and trying to lick her sister's nose, infecting her with her unbridled playfulness, and in the whirlwind of that happy moment, Hannusia managed to catch another surprise at a thing thereuntil unnoticed: how much her sister, with whom she had grown into one entity as one does with an unrelenting burden—an extra weight, an invisible thumb pressed on the scales of her life—was, in and of herself, *lighter* than her, not in body but rather—more transparent, somehow luminous, whether because she was without secret thought or simply less grieved overall—like a clear pond: there may not be much for the eye to see, but swimming in it is pure pleasure on a fine day. She'll make a fine wife, Hannusia thought, seeing her sister as if from outside, through the eyes of that yet-unknown lad she was now sure was courting Olenka—with the Lord's good mercy, she'll grow into one of those capable, quiet women who somehow, willy-nilly, manage to turn anything to their advantage and keep all things in good order.

She had no idea how close she was to the truth. And the truth did not wait long—it struck like a thunderbolt from the blue that same autumn, when the sky was indeed clear as if just bathed, its western edge afire with blazing jewel colors that would put the humblest soul astir, the eye traveled unencumbered all the way to the horizon, and over the fields, which lay naked and spent like tired children, flitted only the thin spider silk of Indian summer, when matchmakers began their rounds, and the very first ones who knocked on their doors came on behalf—nobody else would have dared!—of Markian's son, Dmytro. In spite of the fact that Hannusia determined in advance to refuse him, she—What a strange thing a girl's heart is, she marveled—still expected something from that proposal, as if the point was not whether she would choose to cast her lot with him or reject him but instead that she would receive from Dmytro's envoys an answer about her own fate that would definitively resolve her confusion, so at first she did not grasp why Olenka presented herself in the great room, and all dressed up—when did she even have time to fix flowers in her hair and put on her beads?—and for what reason she hovered around the stove, eyes lowered. Hannusia was all set to speak, to step forward with her hand over her heart, bowing deeply, when something in the tangled speech of the head matchmaker began to edge its way into her mind—then came the baffled mumbling of her father that it really shouldn't be done this way, goodfolk, to jump over someone's head, and that, as they know, he has an older daughter first in line, and the younger one would do well to enjoy her carefree years, a maiden's time is short indeed—and they prattled on among themselves, negotiating, but Hannusia no longer heard it, falling deaf and blind, because all her blood rushed to her head: Dmytro was proposing to Olenka! He finally found a way to get her—why no, not simply to get her—to kill her: before her internal sight, walls began to fall one after another in a house of many rooms, each opening up a new vision, one more frightening than the next— if Olenka becomes engaged, she, Hannusia, is relegated, by one fell swoop, at her age of eighteen, to the old maids, the ones passed over, beggars and not choosers who can forget all about love, lucky if they can find a widower to take them!—well, young lady, so much for your regal airs, there go all your dreams like morning dew, lordy-lord, just think of the gossip, how keenly they will yap, the women and the available men: Serves her well! Perhaps for the first time she could clearly see, as the next wall tumbled, and everything inside her turned to ice, how many people she had vexed, like a blight in their eye: the suitors she dismissed, the mothers of other grown-up daughters, her girlfriends—and all of it without meaning to—and once you added everyone who bore a grudge against her, because she didn't get the well dug in *their* yard, well, she might as well go drown herself!—not just the village, the whole world will jeer at her, they'll band together and tar her gates! Oh Dmytro, you must have stayed up many a night before you figured out how to bring me to heel: well, you came out on top, didn't you, because it's your law that rules, and all I can do is bring out a pumpkin on a platter and that only if someone comes asking first—as her thoughts raced, afire, like a witch astride a broomstick through all that, Hannusia came up short against a new wall, with a hiss: Olenka! Olenka, you viper, sister dearest, fox's snot, you plotted with Dmytro behind my back to knock the ground from under my feet! And knock it she did, and all that yawed from there was cold emptiness where Hannusia could only tumble, headfirst, for she had no more purchase on solid ground—Olenka stood there, flushed and pretty, shyly picking at the chimney mortar with her finger, May something come pick at your heart!—their eyes met, and her sister's look confirmed every detail of Hannusia's suspicion, blazing, as it did, with the triumph of a person who has just attained the most important victory of her life.

Olenka was betrothed. Although this was not what was meant to happen, Vasyl didn't miss the opportunity to point out as they sealed the deal with a toast (it did not sit well with him that Olenka would be moving out to the homestead and Hannusia would remain home unmarried), but let us nonetheless thank the merciful Lord, as long as it's all for the good—most definitely, the matchmakers nodded solemnly, clothed, it seemed, in all the wisdom of the world at once—man plans and God laughs, tactfully letting Vasyl's not entirely gracious reproach slip past their ears and understanding perfectly well there was no one who could let the prospect of Markian's homestead slip out of his hands! Maria, in contrast, was as good as crucified, rushing up to the icons to cry, accosting her younger daughter—Does he at least love you? I'm not asking after you, you little fool, you'll run after any pair of pants, you tell me what's in his heart?—and finally, not getting a comprehensible answer (because what kind of an answer could there be), swallowed her pride and went over to Markian's to speak to Dmytro directly—while the whole village was abuzz with the news, like someone had rung the church bells, and Hannusia dared not show herself outside the house. "You're not doing right, Dmytro dear, disgracing my child this way"—"What disgrace, Mother?"—she was unpleasantly struck by that premature *Mother*, it felt like mockery, as he stood before her, eyes dancing, handsome and as immune to judgment as a rock before the sun, practically snorting with pleasure at all that happened, just like a stallion being brushed—"What disgrace, I did nothing to your Hannusia." Then Maria told him something she had never told anyone in her life: "It's my sin, my boy, but you will be the one to atone for it—I wed my Vasyl in spite because I didn't get my way, and I would not wish such a fate for either my child or for anyone else's, don't you now walk this road after me"—that seemed to make an impression, hearing something like this from an older woman, moreover a future mother-in-law, but Dmytro quickly regained his balance as he obviously wasn't used to losing it for long: Olenka loves me, he asserted with the kind of confidence that under other circumstances may have even engendered respect, and added, anticipating the question already on Maria's lips, in a sincere, boyish way: "She'll be happy with me, Mother." There Maria's resolve collapsed, as she realized, all at once and with her entire being, that indeed, that's how things would be, that her younger daughter was already happy, and would only get happier with time; ruling self-same over Markian's estate, surrounded by her children, she'll be like a fish in water and will spend her life as cozily as at God's bosom, not troubling herself for an instant with the thought that her whole happiness, like it or not, was granted her at her sister's cost, and she would never have had any such luck had Hannusia not crossed Dmytro—but there will be no sin upon her, only blessings, the pilgrim woman was right when she said, You have no need to worry about the younger one, she'll be taken care of—in some way she, Father's daughter, was as indifferent as Dmytro, the apple of his father's eye, and at least in this way these two lovebirds were well matched, and would need or know nothing more in their lovebird lives—so Maria threw up her hands, Lord, where is your justice? Why was that crescent moon on her forehead, and was her beloved child granted gifts beyond all human measure solely so that her younger one could find herself a good match? She returned home in a fog (Hey, Maria, were you visiting with your in-laws? the rabble oozed its poison from behind the fences), while the words of a song spun around in her head, like she had jumped into a whirlpool: the tallest tree dries out at the crown, to the fairest child the Lord denies good fortune—is this the way it's always been since the beginning of time? But why, Lord—don't you yourself know the measure of your own power?

All these thoughts produced in Maria a powerful headache, as if she had strained herself lifting a weight heavier than she could bear, so it was with some relief that she did not find Hannusia at home when she returned. Vasyl said that the girl went to see the priest, so the same thoughts must have bored into her mind, too, she was Mother's daughter, was she not, and Mother's grief to recognize herself in her child at every turn—except that, thank the Lord, Hannusia had a quicker mind, had been taught to read, went to school for four whole years, so she'd have an easier time of it in this heavy quarrel with God—and with that Maria, in her mind, relinquished to her daughter the full right to judge herself, her sister, and all other people—as though giving her, once and for all, her ultimate blessing.

However, Hannusia didn't know herself what she wanted—she was driven to visit the priest by the simple impossibility of remaining for one instant longer in the house she'd come to hate—she could climb the walls from hopelessness, tearing out her hair like a wad of hemp, but you can't leave your own skin, no matter how hard you try, can you?— the very notion that in everyone's eyes she was no more than a rag used to stuff a pillow for Olenka and Dmytro burned her insides with fire, hot, and real enough she could almost hear her own screams, because it was unfair, unfair!—but nobody cared what was fair and what was not, so her quest for justice left her right where she started—all alone, by her parents' hearth, doomed to her old fate—the dull, exhausting labor of waiting for her destiny, which clearly had fallen fast asleep somewhere: day after day, year after year until her hair turned grey, the only difference being that until now this labor didn't feel to be in vain and therefore didn't feel like work at all, whereas with Olenka's future wedding everything was to turn against her—of the two of them, it was none other than Olenka who seemed to be touched by God's grace, as though it was always meant to be this way, and Olenka knew it while she, Hannusia, had only been fooling herself with nonsense she picked up who-knows-where, and now, when the fiction has been revealed, she will never again know that pure untainted joy of exultation that she had relied upon as her chief and sovereign consolation—because something changed inside of her, which frightened her, she felt as if she aged ten years in the one evening of that matchmaking, if not by a whole lifetime—something evil was taking possession of her, so abruptly robbed of her invincible power, something ineradicable like an incessant hot itch pulsing through her veins: Where to run to, what to do with oneself? And all the smells she breathed around her were fetid, as if everything inside and outside the house had rotted to the core, and a sound tormented her constantly the way one gets a ringing in one's ears sometimes, except this one was lower, duller—a pulsating noise like an echo after striking an ancient kettledrum, or the reverberating peal of someone's deep laughter carrying over far distances: Who was laughing at her, what enemy was celebrating? In the priest's chambers, where everything was cozy and pleasant, like walking on silk, and it smelled like church—of wax, communion wafers, old books, and something else dry and nice, medicinal herbs mayhap, the sound receded: it hid, and she knew that it would be lying in wait for her outside again—it grew darker, she could see the moon through the window, a full moon, orange and hot like a handful of coals, only etched slightly with broad lines of shadows where one brother lifted the other on a pitchfork. Only then did Hannusia realize what she was really after when she rushed mindlessly like a madwoman to see the priest, carrying with her the requisite donation of wheat and honey as if indeed she meant to invite him to the betrothal—and she asked the holy Father, How can it be this way, Father, that there were two brothers, Cain and Abel, children of the same man and wife, they couldn't have been doomed for one to be the victim and the other a murderer? Of course not, replied the priest, man chooses for himself whether to follow the path of God or the path of the devil—To be sure, Father, it's just that the Holy Scripture says the Lord had respect unto Abel and to his offering, but unto Cain and to his offering he had not respect, and didn't Cain work to produce his fruit just as hard as Abel did, without rest from toil? Did he not feel an injury that God rejected his work but gave his love to Abel?—she also wanted to add, but hesitated, not knowing immediately how to put it properly into words, that Cain perhaps wanted not so much to take revenge on his brother as to correct the injustice visited upon him by God: it was not against his brother that he raised the pitchfork, but to make the Lord know that he had upset the balance in the world, as though Cain personally wanted to place his hand on the other scale to make them even—but the priest was aggrieved by her visibly, as it were, scolded her for speaking sacrilege, ordered her to recite ten Our Fathers and ten Hail Marys, and not until she was about to kiss his hand and take her leave did the frown recede from his face, and he said, almost at the doorstep, as if it occurred to him just there: The whole thing is that the Lord could see Cain the way he really was, and gave a test to his pride, humiliating him in the eyes of his brother, and Cain, rather than repent, set out to duke it out with God and committed such a mortal sin that it will not be forgiven him for all eternity. The moon with the two brothers had risen higher and shone silently at them from above, flooding the porch and the path to the gate with such bright light you could gather needles, as the song goes, or letter psalms, and Hannusia's heart suddenly squeezed so tight again, the way it had once before when she stood over the murdered man in the ground—with the same mighty and sorrowful torment as is known perhaps only by those condemned to death or irredeemable sinners: Holy Father, she pled desperately, but tell me, *why did God respect Abel's offering but did not respect Cain's?*— Well, there you go again, the priest shrugged, no longer angry, but more like grumbling at an unreasonable child—I'm giving you chicken, and you keep to your feathers!—and aimed a finger at her, as if finding he needed to add more to the bargain: And ten creeds!

Turning down the third street—it was as bright as day outside, only strangely empty save for the voices reaching her from the far end of the village together with bursts of laughter: the young were looking for the next game, and Olenka was probably with them, betrothed and splendid—Hannusia stopped stock-still: a bright light flashed from right under her feet, a shimmering shower of sparks, she even cried out in wonder: in the dust of the beaten road lay unraveled, as if unfurled for sale at a fair, a wide and resplendent young man's sash—its expensive silk glistened in the moonlight, myriad golden tassels sparkled like sequins on water, so soft your hand reached out of its own volition to stroke them. Who would have been careless enough to lose such a treasure in the middle of the street, there's half a length of the most expensive cloth in it, enough for a skirt! One couldn't imagine it would be anyone other than Dmytro, except that even Dmytro's sashes, even the most festive, were roosters to a peacock compared to this one! Carefully, holding her breath, Hannusia touched the delicate fabric (and burned, almost to tears, with the distant memory of how, as a young girl full of hope, she likewise stroked the store-bought ribbons in her lap, the ones her father brought back from the fair: Father, Father, am I not your daughter!)—and as she touched it, everything suddenly came alive inside her, as if someone's warm hand gently compelled her to awaken: the sash felt alive—cool and simultaneously warmed from inside, like her own skin after a bath—with a sharp gasp of pleasure Hannusia buried her face in it, and then quickly, looking around to make sure no one saw, hid it at her bosom, laughing—for the first time in many days!—from the tickle of coolness that spilled like water over her chest. At home she for some reason didn't tell anyone of her find, keeping it even from her mother—she quickly did the dishes, made her bed, and lay down, stealthily shoving the sash under her pillow—and that's the way she fell asleep on the bench that served as her bed, under the window, barely squeezing out one Our Father, not to mention the ten she was supposed to recite—she felt very tired, and her sleepy hand went numb under the pillow clutching in her fingers the heavy and at the same time soft tassels.

She awakened suddenly, and sat up: Lo, what is it? It was dark, silence hung in the air, a pregnant silence—when outside the window, right up next to it, a horse let out a short neigh, like a laugh—Hannusia realized that it was this sound that woke her: Open up, an unfamiliar voice said to her, compelling and tender, a golden shot of hot embers penetrating her to the bone—a man's voice, deep and resonant, but where was it coming from? Open up, Milady Hanna, give me back my sash, or if you don't give it back, then be my wife—Hannusia began to tremble with her whole body either from heat or from cold, as if she herself was about to spill in a tinkle of golden sequins, swaying tassels that tickled up and down her spine—this was *it*, this was precisely what was meant to happen to her, this was what she'd been waiting for since she was a little girl, and here, finally, it has come, her winning lot, her princely reward!—Who are you, show yourself, she asked, opening the shutters, although in the depths of her soul she already knew—whoever it was, he was her fate: in the yard stood a team of four horses, black as the moonless night, tossing manes on serpentine necks, and against their background stepped forward a tall, tall enough to block the moon, shape of a man, she felt a breath of fire from very close, under her heart, as if the whole world whispered softly at her in one voice: Let me in, Milady Hanna, be mine, rule with me, for you are worthy, and I'll show myself when you show yourself first—Hannusia hadn't even quite reached for the latch when the window flew open on its own, impatient—wide open, and at that moment a hot torrent lifted her up, burning and filling her entire body down to its most intimate crevices, blowing her nightshirt off to the ceiling, and before she had a chance to take fright or cover herself—for this was the first time she had shown herself to someone else the way she alone admired herself until now, worried who might come to possess such beauty—before she could draw another breath, she felt the same hot wind spin up inside her, out to meet, it seems, countless men's arms, hard as flint, that all seemed to knead her at once, but these were no crude paws, like Dmytro's—these, despite their painful clasp, were sentient, like the tip of each finger was a tiny tickling tongue, and she melted in those arms like wax, softening, becoming all eager receptiveness, ready to take into her body the whole wide world—and the world rushed into her, sudden, hard and honed, and so icy cold she screamed when it touched her insides, pierced as she felt by a bell tower roofed in blazing tin. Off that steeple, she whooshed, straight up with a hiss, into the black wasteland that resounded with the echo of her own scream, with a chance only to think, in some broken-off corner or her former self that that's what it's like to die—and then she was no more, only the stars sparkled and twirled around her getting all tangled with their fiery tails, and there was no more pain, only the mad, white-hot bliss, the rapture of parting with your soul again, and again—as if she had a myriad of them. Faces sped by her in the interstellar whirlwind, one of them stung her as it passed as familiar, but just as she was about to recognize it, that same deep voice inside her said, That's enough for now—and the wasteland she'd spun in shrank away from her, with the fading clang of a bell, and Milady Hanna opened her eyes in her own bed, although there was no more bedding itself, only a bolt-upright whirl of sheets and the slow downward swirling of feathers from the burst pillows, like a hundred warriors had just laid down their lives inside this bed, and beside her lay, stretched naked to his full enormous length and, it seemed, glowing in the dark with every feature of his being, a most perfect man whose sight alone was enough to slay a human mind on the spot, sending it into madness. Something unthinkable, incredible, and off-putting lay in the fact that a man visible by mere mortal eye could be so magnificent—something that she could only vaguely intuit earlier, when with sweet terror she found in the outlines of her own body a vessel of the Holy Host, only then she thought that at the bottom of the abyss where she barely dared to peek, and from which she so gingerly shied, lay open and sparkling with the living light the gates of the afterlife—and here it was, this splendor, truly blinding, like the sight of it peeled off your skin, but what emanated from it was cold, ancient, and eternal, that same sorrowful, boundless-like-the-sea, mortal torment of a man condemned to perish that had so many times already crept up to squeeze her heart and now stretched out before her, made manifest and undeniable—and fixing her emptied eyes on the red stains of her maidenhood on the torn-up bed, she realized she had become that night wife to the most wretched man in the world.

Then the rooster crowed—and in the flash of an eye her bed was empty, not even a waft of warmth from that large body left behind, and Hannusia dropped into sleep, deep as a well, and dreamless.

The entire next day she wandered around like a sleepwalker, feeling only a steady issue that dripped down her thighs, from her womb, so agitated at night—and at night he came again, this time without a knock or a word of warning, a man coming for what was his own: no sooner did she begin to fall asleep than she felt beside her in the dark the familiar strong body, and she gave in to it, mindless like butter under a knife. Again they made love until dawn, and neither of them had had enough, because this time something new awoke in Hannusia: a thirst, the stronger the more she quenched it—it was akin to that salty, like the iron latch, taste of blood from Dmytro's bitten throat—how long ago was that?—only back then it was only a taste on her lips, and this was in her entire being, and so insatiable it overwhelmed everything else: all the power she knew gathered and transformed into this well-ing black thirst, in whose greedy waters neither one of them could swim enough. My queen, he whispered, as he pulled out her soul again and again, my bride, for a thousand years have I not known one like you—exactly what she yearned to hear, the only words that could heal the wounds common people had dealt her, as they oh-so-stubbornly insisted on judging her by their own measure and when she didn't fit that measure dared, their infinite meagerness nonetheless, disdain her—his healing words not only returned her to herself, it was like they took the whole world, with all the people who had been, were, and will be in it, and threw it down at her feet, and in this resembled that unknown song composed in her tribute she dreamed of hearing. Say it again, she pleaded, or perhaps it was her thirst that pleaded for more, the ecstasy of the body was no longer enough for it, it rose higher, spread wider, like high water in springtime—and he spoke to her, in different ways, with words and without, night after night. In daytime stupor—because she endured her days now solely in anticipation of night, indifferent to almost everything, except a bit vexed by the continued issue between her legs, which, shame to say, was acutely arousing to dogs: as soon as she stepped outside her door, they raised a ruckus across the whole neighborhood, or followed her in a line, sniffing after her like she was a bitch in heat—in her semiconscious wakefulness, which seemed to her less and less real than what went on at nights, she never once stopped to wonder why nobody in the house heard anything—the racket they made was enough to wake the dead and yet nobody woke up, nobody noticed anything, only Olenka complained that she started having nightmares, and Maria fretted that Hannusia seemed to sicken all of a sudden—Look at the rings under your eyes, and your face so grey, god forbid you've fallen ill—and disbelieving her own eyes, watched with fear as Hannusia's hair curled wildly all over her head so that you could no longer see the discrete strand that marked her crescent-moon birthmark—You, daughter, should go out and have some fun with the girls, take your mind off things, Maria would venture, only to have her daughter lower her head like a dog, and show her teeth, as if she was about to bite. Only smells could sometimes bring her back to reality—mainly those, thick and red, that filled her mouth with iron-tinged spit—they woke her up inasmuch as they roused in her that insatiable, all-devouring thirst she knew at night: when folks butchered a hog two streets over; her mother killed the speckled hen that, Lord have mercy, suddenly began to crow like a rooster; Hannusia herself got her period; at the neighbors' across the street, the daughter-in-law gave birth—in this last case she was possessed by such mad arousal she had to flee out to the garden and roll around on the grass, just to keep from running into their house to suck on the birth bed, gulping and slurping up everything that was living, hot, and red. At night everything was different—the way it should be, this new power made sense: You've come, praise the Lord, she whispered not so much from joy as from relief when she felt him beside her—but he grew distant, frowning and displeased: Why do you praise God for my arrival and not me?—she herself was amazed at such obvious, and until now unremarked, folly: Of course!—but he went on: Is it not your sister who ought to praise him, is it not her that he favors much more than you, although she's worth as much as a handful of sand to a handful of gold against you?—she trembled as if in fever with the joy of hearing, for the first time, her own thought spoken out by someone else: And why is that so? she cried, in anticipation of the answer that she had thus far been unable to find—neither from the priest, nor from her mother, nor from anyone in the world, and in her blind pursuit of which she kept coming up short against an invisible wall—he now promised her liberation, and she reached for him with her entire soul, yearning as if transformed into a pair of open, eager lips dripping with impatient spit, ready to slurp up his answer, whatever it was—and the answer rang out like a struck gong, but rather than setting her free echoed in her with the unutterable sorrow of perdition: Do you not know that he only favors his paltry creatures, only those meek in spirit are beloved by him, and as for the best and stron-gest, the most select, who are like diamonds on an earthly crown—he pursues them and humiliates them, and brands them with a mark of damnation to set them apart from the meek, for he fears they will take away his kingdom?—So it must be, she replied with some effort across the desolation of sorrow, having applied his word at once to herself and to him: it was wicked to be the best! That's the way the song went, she remembered: The tallest tree dries out at the crown—Of course it is, who would know better than I, all the choicest souls belong to me, only I know their fair price, and only I can give them what they truly deserve—she smiled bitterly, irritated by this cheap fairground boast-ing, because she expected a more sincere consolation from him: Why is it always—me, me, aren't you pretty miserable yourself?—he sucked in his breath, sharply, and she felt a waft of sulfur and burning in the air—so smelled his chagrin: her sympathy, which she had not dared to utter until now, obviously irked him: You womenfolk are a hex! Fine, I know the way around you—and he snorted with fire, sent quivering, caressing little tongues of it up and down her body, fixing to have his way, but she asked him, coarse because her voice caught in the terror of remaining forever banished to that desolation of the perished: Take me with you into your kingdom, I want to rule by your side, is this not why you chose me for your wife, why you gave me your sash?—she kept that sash wrapped around her waist under her shirt, so she could always feel her lover's presence on her body—Don't worry, he promised lightly, happily—too lightly, it felt to her, he could have been a bit more solemn at such an occasion—Do what I tell you, and I'll grant all your wishes—and fell right to granting, zealously, like a priest at prayer, her wishes one after another, without respite—until the rooster crowed and she was overcome, as always, by a short, dead morning sleep.

But what he said fell on fertile ground in Hanna's heart: It is only the paltry he favors, it is only the meek who are beloved by him—the knowledge smoldered inside her, who was ash to everything else, like a lit wood chip, growing into a dull, acrid yellow flame of bitter insult: Why should this world belong to Olenka? Because it was about to belong entirely to her—the autumn was quiet and clear as a tear, they had celebrated the betrothal, and the wedding was set for the Feast of Intercession, and Olenka walked around the village inviting brides-maids—not so much walked as floated, eyes lowered modestly, as if to permit all around her to admire more fully her so suitably rewarded virtues, while she demonstrated her utter lack of involvement or intent, and even conveyed how difficult it was for her, so young and inno-cent, to bear so much public attention, as good as if she were saying to everyone, Help me, good people, if you would be so kind—and that kindness rained down on her from everywhere: a fine bride, said both young and old, and even those who should have been looking at her askance for snatching up the best lad in the village from right under the other girls' noses could not resist her, made their peace, forgave her, and prepared to release their zeal by partying to the hilt at the rich wedding—something had to be attended to almost in every house, even the poor girls turned over their trunks to make sure moths hadn't eaten through their one good dress of fine linen, kept for the great feast days, some sewed new clothes, others mended the old ones, and Hanna fed her wound that flamed hot and yellow inside her, nursed it the way a mother nurses a child that will avenge her, the way her own mother raised her on her own grievance, although not nearly as great—with thoughts of vengeance.

Sunday came—Olenka's last Sunday as a maiden, the bridesmaids were already invited for next Saturday night for the girls' last evening. Waking up that morning, Hannusia felt that a change had come over her: her feeling of injury had hardened and sharpened into a long shard that scorched inside her chest so hot she could not breathe freely until she cast it out. In the hutch, she found a sharpened knife—and let out a groan of relief, passing her fingertips over the steel blade as cool as the long-forgotten whiff of underground spring water—she couldn't help herself and licked it: the taste was vaguely familiar, but weak, all squeezed out—the life was missing from it like salt from a meal. Let us go berry picking, sister—she turned to Olenka—What berries? You must be joking, it's the middle of September—Why don't you go, girls, get a breath of fresh air, chimed in their mother, who perked up too: she had dreamed about her father again, and the dream was heavy and evil, different, and on top of that, the neighbor's boy, feebleminded from birth, had upset her when he called happily over the fence this morning like a young rooster: Auntie, Auntie, a serpent flew into your chimney last night, it looked like a big star with a tail, I saw it!—of course he's a kid, and missing some marbles to boot, babbling whatever comes into his head, but her heart grew troubled regardless, and since Sunday dreams, as everyone knows, are only true until noon, she was happy for the opportunity to get the girls out of the house until then—See how warm it's been, the strawberries might have come again, and if not, you'll get plenty of mushrooms—Olenka agreed, not very willingly, and took the smallest basket, just for appearances' sake—obviously not intending to crawl under every bush but rather to nap in the shade while Hannusia foraged—ever since she became engaged, she had developed a new sense of propriety and dignity more befitting a married woman than a girl.

Hannusia indeed set to work like a madwoman as soon as they stepped into the forest—she needed to keep moving because of the burning under her heart, the burning of the man's sash against her body, and the torment of her entire body, which burned like an open wound. There was not an inch of her body on which she did not feel the hot breath of nocturnal lips, and this left her few choices—either scream like a banshee and gnaw at her own hands, to fill that yawning maw inside her body at least with her own flesh, or else race farther and farther ahead like one possessed, pushing through the thickets ferociously, uprooting the shrubs, scratching her bare skin until it bled because each flash of pain that bled as a dark-red spot as juicy as a ripe berry—there were no other kinds of berries for her to see!—seemed to bring momentary relief, and the blinding sulfur-yellow fog lifted around her. There was a crackle in the brush from time to time, like someone was following her, someone determined not to lose her trail and that, of course, was Olenka, who else had dragged behind her her whole life and will continue to hang on her to the end of her days, even after she leaves for her own household—especially then! No way to get rid of her, to tear her, like this chicory, out of your thoughts, out of your heart, she will forever rot inside you, spreading the yellowish miasma of victorious injustice—"And this shall not pass!" she cried aloud, rushing out to the clearing where Olenka lay in the last mild sunshine of the year, covering her face with a burdock leaf, like a lady who needed to avoid a touch of tan—the knife lifted itself from the bottom of the basket and deftly settled into her hand, giving her something to hold on to, and the last thing nailed into her consciousness in the darkening, thickening fog was the look in Olenka's eyes as she propped herself up to face her sister—as indulgently condescending as always, as imperviously surprised, as if to say, What is it now?—it suddenly broke, splashing Hanna with horror as cold and bracing as well water on her hot body, and it was pure luxury, indeed as acute as in her nighttime ecstasies—to plunge the knife straight into the warmly breathing body, so dense, yet giving way oh so easily to the knife, a body that convulsed along its full length in a short spasm (and this moment of resistance, too, was pure luxury!), and then grew soft, and a wave of rich, hot red washed up into her nostrils, making her sweetly dizzy, a wave she could drink, she could swim in, big like the whole world at once, finally, opened its doors—and flooded Lady Hanna in order to sate her hunger. She wielded the bloody knife above her head, drunk, barely keeping on her feet from this rich—never was there richer!—wedding feast that came pouring down on her and cried up into the noose of the sky that spun, unraveled, above her, ripping with horror, no doubt, crowns of trees—off to him, who sat up there above, never allowing anyone to see his face, and the echo of her victorious laughter rolled through the forest like the rumble of an invisible army: *Now you know!*

. . . It was dusk already when Hannusia stumbled home—Maria was sick with worry, the neighbor's foolish boy had come running over again—to assure her that he apparently saw a white bitch by the forest with its mouth all bloody, And she was so scary, Auntie!—she slapped her skirts when her daughter finally appeared before her, all disheveled, her shirt torn, with leaves in her hair, without a drop of color in her face—Where's Olenka, the father spoke up first—And how am I to know, Hannusia quietly rustled her chapped lips that were as rough as bark—am I her keeper? They rushed for the village healer to clear off her fright, and word swept the village like a whirlwind: someone attacked the father's and mother's girls in the forest!—a man was sent from each house, they searched and called out until midnight, with torches, form- ing a chain among the trees, but found nothing: Olenka was gone as if the ground swallowed her. Around midnight a thunderstorm struck, ferocious even for July, let alone autumn—bolts of fire flashed across the sky, generous as if emptied from a sack, the sky crackled and split open, something groaned under the ground, and in the roar of the storm, in the violent beating of the rain, half the neighborhood heard Hannusia scream—Holy of Holies!—an inhuman, deathly scream of rapture beyond which all that is living ends, and there remains perhaps only a limitless wasteland flooded with the light of the moon—no one had ever heard such a voice, and no one would ever hear Hannusia's own voice as they had known it after that night: the girl lost her gift of speech and neither the healers, nor the seers, nor the priest with his holy water could point to the cause of it. And soon after, Maria saw that Hannusia was pregnant: it must have happened on that same terrible day.

In the spring, a salt traders' caravan passed through the village, and a few men asked to be put up for the night at Maria and Vasyl's, having heard from the people there'd be room for them in the house, seeing how it was just the old man, his old wife, and the gravid mad girl—who wouldn't, in such circumstance, be glad for some honest company and conversation, with well-traveled and seasoned folk, who could spend the whole night telling of the marvels they'd seen in the far reaches of the world and not tell half of them—"But never, good sir, a wonder such as we encountered right outside your village," blurted, quite out of turn, a young dark-haired man with barely a furrow of mustache, who would have done well to wait until the elders were done speaking. The elders, however, nodded all as one in agreement, "What's true is true, show the goodfolk your flute, lad"—"Near your village, good sir, as we drove along the forest, behind the sign at the crossroads, this lad spotted a guelder rosebush, and he carved himself a flute out of it, and that flute—just you think of it!—spoke up with a human voice. Bring it over here!" "God bless us," Maria uttered in fright, pausing over the eggs she'd been scrambling for dinner—"What wizardry is this, pray do not play it here, there's been enough grief on this house!"—the griddle just then hissed angrily, the fire shot up sharp tongues, and a waft of sulfur, dense and grey, rolled through the house, but the young musician already held the flute in his long delicate fingers. As soon as he pressed it to his lips, Olenka's voice, thin and childlike, sang out: "Gently, gently, young carter, play, do not startle my heart today; it is my sister who made me depart, plunged a knife into my heart"—"My child!"—both Father and Mother cried out, it seemed, at once, although in fact everyone was struck so dumb that you could have heard the bells in Kyiv calling for vespers: by the stove, leaning against the chimney like a young maiden about to be betrothed, stood Hannusia—wearing only a thin shirt, stretched taut by her belly, rifled and disheveled, with dark deeply sunken eyes that glowed and crackled like hot embers, she was smiling—for the first time after the long winter, but so eerily it sent shivers down everyone's spines: hers was no madwoman's smile, oh no, everyone there would have sworn in that moment this girl was in more than full possession of her faculties because not only did she know perfectly well what was happening, but could clearly see beyond it, things that were invisible to others and of such nature they silenced the flute at once, and made it drop out of the young man's hands—but Vasyl bent to pick it up, shaking all over like an old man, as indeed he had just aged in a single instant, and tears silently rolled down his cheeks, when Olenka began to cry again: "Gently, gently, my father, play, do not startle my heart today"—while Hannusia smiled more and more broadly, about to speak any second—"Gently, gently, my mother, play"—and finally laughed out loud, slapping her hands together: "It came true!" she cried in a low raspy voice, like a raven had flown into the house—"He made it true, he didn't lie!"—and she laughed openly, heartily, holding her round swollen belly with both hands as it danced as if a whole nest of babies rebelled in there. "Mother, Mother, here is my song, mine alone, such as no one had heard since the beginning of time, here is my glory in my prince, he pledged to grant my every desire, just do as I say, and he did grant them, he did, he is no liar!"—she sobbed and laughed in fits, unable to stop, unconcerned as she ought to have been that she could well prod labor to start before its due time, repeating, again and again, "He granted my wish, he didn't lie"—until one of the carters found his bearings, stepped up, and gave her a sound slap on the cheek. She quieted down right away, holding on to her cheek and staring fixedly before her, and then said, in the most lucid voice on earth, pointing her finger at the salt carters: "And they—they will tell *the whole untruth*, and so it will go out and spread through the world"—and with that, she lay down on the floor, holding her stomach, and never rose again.

They ought to send for a posse—because, be the murderess sane minded or not, a wrongdoing is a wrongdoing, and nobody could any longer claim a good reason to doubt what transpired between the sisters in the forest—so they sent for it, and when the men came to put her in shackles, with all the village folk crowding into the yard, breathing hard and jostling each other to get a good look—they found the house empty, only a long wild trail on the floor—like someone had swept a tarred brush across it. Mother's daughter had vanished—escaped, perhaps, or vanished, or she still wanders somewhere, lost, on desolate moonlit nights.

II

I, MILENA

TRANSLATED BY MARCO CARYNNYK AND
MARTA HORBAN, EDITED WITH ADDITIONAL
TRANSLATION BY NINA MURRAY

On the surface everything seemed fine. That is, everything was indeed
fine, or so Milena assured herself as she hurried home from the television studio those dark winter evenings (her face still stiff under the
stage makeup she hadn't taken off and the small tender smile at the
thought of her husband's "I couldn't wait for you to get here" that of
its own volition puffed up her lips into the little pipe of a kiss—*Ah,
Poppet*—breaking through the makeup, as if through those wafers of ice
on the asphalt you had to watch out for all the time in the dark, even if
they weren't there. Mincing cautiously over the invisible slippery spots,
she would approach the building and, before going into the courtyard,
would sometimes walk under the chestnuts that separated the building from the street and, head tossed back, seek out her windows with
her gaze and find out, by determining which of them was lit, what
Poppet (Sugar, Pumpkin) was doing just then, unaware of the joy of her
approach. Most often the light was on in the bedroom—a washed-out
spot of blue on the lower part of the curtains: Poppet was watching TV.
Growing a wedding vegetable, as he often joked: for some reason, he
would start to get an erection in front of the screen. And he would also
say that he was watching for his sweet Milena.

Everything was fine when Milena worked in the news department, where her job was to appear, twice a day, before the camera with the moist light of oh-what-a-joy-it-is-to-see-you-again in her eyes (because the viewers must be adored, as her director was always saying, and Milena knew how to do this, sometimes she could even do it with casual acquaintances, if she was not too tired) and read the script someone else prepared, but that she occasionally improved upon, if not with words, then at least with her voice: Milena was unsurpassed at this, brilliant, to be perfectly honest, and anyone who had heard her and remembers her would confirm it, so I am not making anything up. With a voice like Milena's you could topple governments and parliaments in the evening and smoothly restore them to their offices by morning, and all without any opposition from the electorate: her voice sparkled, glittered, and spilled to overflowing in every possible hue and shade, from a warm chocolaty low-pitched intimacy to the metallic hiss, with a snakelike sharp *S* (assuming that it is not just in fairy tales that snakes hiss like that and that it is true anyone who hears that sound must soon die). It even had a few shades that no one yet knew to be possible: for example, the ozone freshness of dewy lilac at the start of the morning news at half past seven, or an ironic cinnamon-flavored heat (Milena had a particularly rich scale of ironic tones), or the wholesome crunch of toasted bread that was reserved for government announcements, and if anyone considers everything I've been saying to be a metaphor, they should try for themselves to pronounce, after a day's training, "President Kuchma met with the prime minister today" so as to make it sound sincere and even emanate domestic warmth. Then they will surely grasp why Milena, a woman who was on the whole as helpless as a sparrow, was fundamentally feared by her colleagues and her bosses alike and why, even though she never took liberties and always tinged the news with the expected color (Milena had always been an A student, both at school and at university), the sweetly painful richness of her voice stubbornly pressed to the surface, radiating out onto her face in barely discernible,

coquettishly secretive little grimaces, which naturally made her especially attractive but which did not always agree with the script she was
reading, so that it could possibly appear to someone who'd just gotten
out of bed that she was about to sneak in a snort of laughter in a thoroughly inappropriate spot, or say something utterly stupid she would
never dream of doing. In short, Milena was feared and even considered
a good journalist, and so someone in some oak-paneled office had taken
it into his head to give her her own show. And that's where it all began.

Actually, suspicious symptoms had appeared earlier, too, in her
news-department days. Insofar as her news was broadcast on channel
thirty-something, Poppet (Sugar, Pumpkin), with his own two hands,
mounted a specially acquired antenna (forty-five dollars, without the
installation) outside their window, so that in the evenings he could
watch his sweet Milena, because the building's common antenna got
only the first three channels. Since then, the TV delivered lots of various
"pictures," as Milena's photojournalist husband (who identified himself,
more pretentiously, as a "photographic artist" on his business cards)
called them, and he was now in the habit of spending his evenings in
the bedroom with the door closed, as if he were in a darkroom—only
the light there was not red but, if you looked at it from the street, a
ghoulish blue—picking over the buttons on his remote and hopping
from channel to channel like a bank manager calling up subordinates
on the intercom, and when Milena would poke her head into the half
light of the bedroom to ask what to make for supper, he would grin at
her with his teeth colored by the glow of the TV screen. After this they
would often start making love—Milena would turn off the TV at the
critical moment. Then her husband would go to the bathroom, and
Milena would lie there faceup and listen in wonder as the fullness of
her life moved slowly past her, thick and caramel-like.

And so one time when she came in from the cold, and straight from
the hallway into the bedroom, before she had even caught sight of her
husband's illuminated teeth, Milena heard a man's baritone greeting her

from the TV screen with a booming Good evening, love—turned out, an atrociously dubbed Brazilian soap opera happened to be on, and she and her husband had a good laugh at the surprise. Not long after, something similar happened to Milena's mother when she came for a Sunday visit. The two women's aimless, spastic jostling around the kitchen with their pots in an absurdist arrhythmic dance and their equally aimless jumpy conversation, all loose ends and interrupted sentences, cut off, dropped, and never picked up again, would tire Milena's husband rather quickly, and he would escape to the bedroom, where he lay low in front of the TV until the visit was over. Well, this time, his kindhearted mother-in-law, who was looking for him in order to enlighten him (she'd just thought of it) as to the proper way of sharpening kitchen knives (by running them against a step in the stairwell), headed for the bedroom herself, and, just as soon as she had pushed open the door, the darkened room, illuminated by aquarium-like floating flashes of color from the TV screen, screamed at her in a hysterical falsetto: Get out of here! Get out, do you hear me! Milena's mother forgot about her knives on the spot (she remembered them later, on her way home, and called from the streetcar stop, just when her daughter and son-in-law had turned off the TV, because the vegetable, as its gardener had claimed, had grown quite big enough). And possibly the very next day, when Milena, worried because her period was late, pressed a button on the remote in the bedroom to take her mind off things, an unbearably brash little cartoon frog croaked out to her from the screen, Don't cry, little girl, let me sing you a so-o-ong instead, and a cheery little tune poured out, and an hour later Milena's flow started. It was then that she had her first inkling that something had gone terribly wrong: something, or someone, had taken possession of the TV set.

She didn't know yet who it was exactly, and later, too, she only thought she had found out, because, as I've said, this was all happening back in the news-department days, before Milena launched her own show, which did so extraordinarily well in the ratings so quickly.

If anyone has forgotten, let me remind you: Milena talked to jilted women. There were old ones among them and young ones, pretty and ugly, smart and not very (Milena did not allow the utterly stupid ones into the studio): a peroxide blonde interpreter—fat legs, a short skirt, a plastic doll's light-colored eyes—talked about how many men were fighting over her just then, while a PhD in chemistry, with a nose that could be called Akhmatovian if she'd known how to wear it, insisted aggressively that at that particular time she was completely happy, and only once did she tear up as she was taking a handkerchief out of her purse, fall silent, sniff, and stuff it back in again (Milena did not cut the shot, not least out of a vague hope of moving the chemist's ex-husband to pity, in the event he was watching the broadcast). Milena's first guests came from among her girlfriends' friends—their classmates, hairdressers, beauticians, moms whose kids went to the same day care, and other various and sundry women who indulged in mutual confidences, as women do, on random pretexts. Later, when the show was better known, the guests came en masse themselves, just for the asking, and Milena simply marveled—sincerely at first, and then mechanically, by habit, mostly in conversations—at the insatiable lust for publicity human suffering carries within itself, and aren't we all so afraid of death precisely because that is the one thing you can't share with anyone? She took pride in the fact that she was helping all those women to recut and resew (well, at least to rebaste) their own suffering into a style they could wear, sometimes even quite smartly: she learned this from one of her first shows, which had subsequently brought in a whole cartload of letters. An awfully nice little woman, dark haired with barely a dusting of grey, mother of two teenage boys and boyish looking herself, her hair almost in a crew cut and her shirt probably borrowed from her older son, a librarian—in other words, broke, but sharp as a tack—expounded, smoothing out something invisible in her lap the whole time, on how she would be raising her boys from then on so that they wouldn't turn out like their father, with deadpan delivery that made the camera operators convulse with laughter behind their cameras, because the boys' father came out a phenomenal asshole, if he couldn't appreciate a clever little woman like that. Granted, everything didn't always turn out so well, sometimes quite the opposite, and in ways you'd never even think of. Milena couldn't sleep for two nights and took Valocordin and valerian drops with water when she found out that an ambulance had to be called for one of her guests because the day after the broadcast the stupid woman had gone and opened all the gas valves in her apartment. Everyone went into a tizzy that time, and the director had even rushed off to consult someone about getting a certificate from a psychiatrist just in case, because you could tell the woman was neurotic right off the bat, and her upper lip twitched on the right side, the camera brings out things like that like a microscope, there's no denying them, so it was Milena's fault for choosing her as a guest, that much was clear, but thank god, the whole thing had worked itself out, the damn woman pulled through, and Why in the name of fuck, the producer spat out in puffs of cigarette smoke, would you get yourself on TV if you can't look in the mirror without your meds? Stupid women! Milena breathed a secret sigh of relief at this gracious verdict and not being blamed after all, then immediately felt ashamed of her relief, and felt ashamed all day until her shame melted away. Milena did have her scruples, no matter what anyone said, and who would know better than I? So there.

That's what Milena's show was like, and she put it on, I'll say it again, with scruples. What I mean is she remembered well what she'd been taught at the university: that a journalist must show not herself but her subject, and if they wished to revel, if they wanted to all that badly, it would also not be in her misery but in her subjects'. And she really did have a genuine interest in all those women and in peering over the fence into the abyss: to imagine what would happen if she ended up in their position herself, if her Poppet took off one day and left her for good—an unnaturally stupid thing for her to conceive of, let alone imagine, like picturing a day when your legs all of a sudden separated from the rest of you and marched off down the street and left you sitting on the sidewalk on your rear end—but still, what then, what would she be like then, how would she feel? To try something like that on for size was titillating, terrifying, it made her dizzy (like when you were a child and listened, cowering under your bedclothes, to stories about highway robbers, or like your violent erotic fantasies when you imagine being raped by a whole platoon). Milena's pupils would dilate hypnotically on the screen, which, physiologists assure us, is the key to attractiveness, and her luminous voice would deliver incantations that ranged from the soothing empathy of a sister of mercy (Tell us, please, tell our viewers and especially our female viewers) to the angry low-pitched solidarity of a fellow amazon (And you put up with this for how many years?), although sometimes she needed to resort to her seductive voice, intimately cajoling when a guest would suddenly close up and wouldn't say another word, no more secrets, and go ahead, Milena, figure out how to crack that nut. Why, sometimes Milena would even let out one of her keen, low-pitched giggles of encouragement, short and lusty, as if to say, Oh yes, my dear, I've been there myself, and then what? That was usually how the most delectable bedroom bits were gotten out of the guests, prompting the flood of letters and calls to the show to rise to life-threatening levels. Milena didn't really like herself when she resorted to tricks like that, but the unpleasant aftertaste was more than compensated for by the megavoltage spotlight of professional triumph—Look what I can do! with the beads of joyful sweat between her shoulder blades and the half-admiring, half-envious way her colleagues looked at her—Better not mess with you, baby!—and that swelling sense of her own power, the biggest high of it all, like the gymnast's from his absolute power over his own body. Whenever she watched the show with her husband at home, Milena, her gleaming eyes fixed on the screen, would unseeingly squeeze his hand, hard, at the most dramatic moments—There it is, right there, watch this!—and would giggle, anxious with arousal, at every felicitous word that dropped from the screen, and he'd chortle, too, pleased, and proud of her success. Their professional ambitions did not overlap, and he had never photographed Milena, except well before they were married, in their courting days, and even then more as a pretext, because the static Milena was a mere shadow of herself: her voice, her face, the glint of living quicksilver in her—that, and not the still portrait, was her element, and Poppet preferred to take pleasure in her live, although he did find her photos pleasing, and generally considered Milena a beauty, which was, of course, an exaggeration, even though there were others besides him who thought so, especially when Milena got her own show and nothing seemed to foreshadow any trouble.

Now they were planning to buy a satellite dish and install it on the balcony. This would come to about $300, but it was worth it, because, although Milena conscientiously watched almost all her colleagues' shows, the output on Ukrainian TV, of course, could not satisfy her, and the Russian product was hardly better, three-quarters of it lifted straight from American scripts, while Milena was a patriot and always said that Ukraine must find and follow its own path. In fact it would be worth buying a second television, because her husband preferred to look at visuals, and, obviously, there are more of those in movies, whose story lines he would recap to Milena in two or three quick sentences (who's who, who's with whom against whom) that summed up the story up to the point at which she'd come home and snuggled at his side. His eyes glued to the screen, he would pull the blanket over her, tuck her in, gather her up to himself, tickle her cheek with his lips, and mutter, "This one here, the blond guy, he was abducted by aliens, but now he's come back." "Why did he come back?" Milena would ask absentmindedly as she pressed against him, staring now in the same direction, and so, after a little more fidgeting, they would fall silent and, lying side by side, eyes on the screen, and the third person in the room and their home was that Panasonic, so that as time went on the idea of buying another TV began to seem awkward and a bit bizarre to Milena, because wouldn't it be just like splitting up their bed or apartment? "After all, smart people can always find a compromise, can't they, Sugar?" Milena would say, which meant Sugar would watch what she wanted to watch with her, and the rest of the time he would be free to amuse himself as he pleased, to which the smart Sugar would respond with a cheerful Yes, ma'am! like the good soldier he was and just as cheerfully and resonantly smooch his sweet smart Milena, and thus compromise would triumph. But late at night Milena herself didn't mind watching something entertaining and thus distancing herself from the many faces and many installments of women's misfortune with which she now lived out almost all of her waking hours.

Altogether, that misfortune was quite strange indeed: made up, dolled up, flirty—some of the women were so committed to appear pert and happy on camera they presented with a forced, fake familiarity that was downright embarrassing, so when that happened, Milena would call out a categorical *cut* to the camera operators and spend five or ten minutes talking the overly emotional lady down to a more or less normal state. And yet, and this is what is interesting, every one of them was genuinely suffering, sincerely and unaffectedly, and Milena had even thought at first that slighted women came to her show mainly in the secret hope of bringing back their ex or at least taking their revenge, because some women did ask Milena whether it was all right to address him directly, and then would deliver into the millions of postdinner apartments their moving "Sasha, if you can see me now, I want you to know that I've forgiven you for everything, and I hope you are happy" whereupon Milena herself would get a lump in her throat: at that moment she could actually physically feel the choral, gurgling sob of the female half of the nation spreading out in the reality beyond the broadcast frequency—crescendo, crescendo—and a dark wave of public anger rising and swelling at this Sasha, millions of lips whispering, *Asshole*, millions of noses sniffling, the entire country caught, for a fraction of a second, in the shared orgasm of empathy—and all of it her, Milena's, doing, because it was she, Milena, who edited out the rest of the speech when her guest herself had not managed to stop with this exquisite opening, and proceeded, zigging and zagging like a car on a slippery road, irresistibly drawn into the ditch: "Of course, you hurt me, and very badly, I still can't see how you could have been such a jerk, and after everything I've done for you," tossing out long-rehearsed words faster and faster, seething, rattling, all but foaming at the mouth with her bottled-up fury, predatory flames in her eyes, and the hair on her head ready to spring straight up like on a witch taking flight. Milena's power was in presenting those women the way she saw them herself (they were better than that, so much better!), and when hers was unanimously voted "show of the month" and she said, now herself being interviewed (and focused with her every nerve on not, god forbid, having it sound condescending!), that to her guest she was a friend, a counselor, and a gynecologist all at once, it was, clearly, the absolute truth and no one would contradict it, but still Milena had the vague feeling it was not the whole truth: something still remained unexpressed, an exceedingly important, perhaps essential ingredient, like yeast in dough, was still left out. And so, something similar was probably happening to them too: even as the women came driven into the studio by the single, all-devouring intention of calling out one more thing in their ex-better halves' wake, somewhere deep in every one of them stirred the dark amorphous shape of a much more incomprehensible urge: to fly toward the light of the screen itself, like moths that used to fly, on humid and still July nights, toward the blue luminescence of the old black-and-white Slavutych TV on the summer cottage's porch so that up close you could clearly hear the dry crackling of faulty electrical wires or tiny sizzling wings. Did they (the women, not the moths—although who can say with confidence what a moth is thinking?) perhaps dream that by crossing over into that space beyond the screen, they would get back the soul that a man had taken from them, and not just get it back, but get it back completely renewed, enormously enriched, bathed clean in the glow of fame and raised up to unreachable heights above the lives they had lived until now, melded forever with the fantastic colorful shimmering of all the pictures in the TV at once, so that the Santa Barbara, the Dallas, the Denver dynasty, and the snow-white villas on the shores of tropical seas would all become their own, something that had happened to them, since they had been there, on the other side of the screen, too, and their everyday existence would acquire a special, perhaps even divine significance? Milena knew only too well from her own experience this magic of the screen: the spellbinding effect of your own face—in that first instant so alien you don't recognize it—in the frame, multiplied by itself a hundredfold in all its barely perceptible movements, how it envelops you, chained to your viewer's spot, in a ticklish warmth, like a bubble bath, and you soften, rise, and expand, feeding on the energy that streams from the screen, become so much larger than your common self that for a moment you can believe in your own omnipotence. "An energy boost," Milena's husband would say. "Just go read about lepton fields." (He would ⬚lip articles from popular science magazines and put them in a special folder.) "Why do you think that back at the turn of the century the Inuit would break ethnographers' cameras and run away from them as if they were evil spirits?"

"A photo is different," Milena would fling back, her face still flushed, eyes gleaming, because she sensed that if this comparison were taken to its logical conclusion, she would end up among the ethnographers and her studio guests among the Inuit, which she would not like the least little bit, and her husband would silently and agreeably switch to a different channel, one with reruns (all the more so, since on Milena's they were already running the last commercial), and the TV would aim at them the typical squinty look of a Soviet-movie secret police officer, and say, with that kind of officer's paternal warmth, "I'm looking at you, and I can tell you are really good kids!"

Somehow they both got used to this—to the TV gradually becoming an active contributor to all their conversations, and even, not infrequently, a counselor and a referee, and they stopped bursting out laughing when, for example, during an argument in which Milena, irritated not as much by her husband's misplaced jealousy as by the fact that she was not allowed to relax even at home, raised her voice to state (flattered nonetheless) that she needed that Italian man her husband felt she was flirting with at the reception that evening like a fish needed a bicycle, she could barely drag herself to bed at the end of the day already, an elegant respectable gentleman came into view on TV (which they now had turned on almost all the time) to declare, "My dear man, these days most Italian men are homosexuals, so this isn't going to give you much mileage," after which the argument fizzled out and they started kissing (noticing that people on TV were doing the same, only already lying down). Most of the remarks that came from the TV showed it to be significantly more cynical than either one of them: it would chat casually, as if about something self-evident, about things that neither one of them would admit to another other than in a fit of self-reproach, and this was highly salutary, they both thought, because once you've heard something like that from the screen, you no longer had to be ashamed and pretend otherwise. Milena, for example, would never have noticed on her own, or even if she did, then not anytime soon, that her husband, even when he listened and nodded patiently, was beginning to tire of her constant complaining about the studio head, who wasn't exactly finding fault with Milena's work, because there was nothing for him to fault her with, but remained probably the only person who had never openly shown any kind of enthusiasm or at least approval of Milena, whereby he greatly undermined Milena's straight-A-student's confidence, hobbled her, you could say, until she began to suspect that this demonstrative, as she believed it was, disrespect indicated a behind-the-scenes intrigue against her, a backstabbing plot to take her show away from her, while Poppet, on the contrary, held to the belief that the studio head simply had the hots for her and had chosen this way of keeping her in constant suspense, and so they kept on this subject, working it over and over like a bone, and would perhaps have kept worrying it like that until Poppet lost his patience if one night the TV did not lose its patience instead. No sooner had Milena started in on another diatribe at the door—"He gave me a ride home, and what do you think, not a word about yesterday's broadcast, not a single word, I can't keep working like this!"—than she heard, "So unzip his pants and give him a blow job" from a cold and terrifically vulgar floozy on TV, delivered in two languages, French and Ukrainian, at once. Stunned almost to tears, Milena shut up on the subject of her studio head, and, to tell the truth, stopped caring as much about him. The TV seemed to intercept their thoughts even as they were thinking them, to compress and edit them, sometimes even before they themselves had a chance to finish them or discover their own motivations. "Shall we hit the sack?" Milena's husband would say as he put his arms around her and slid his hands down her back to her buttocks. Milena would resist half-heartedly, saying something like, "My script for tomorrow isn't ready yet." "E-ekh, my dear!" the TV would intrude casually, in the guise of a seasoned old broad from a Russian backwater. "How are you going to hold on to your husband if you don't give him any?"—What if she's right, Milena would think, alarmed (and offended a bit, by things being put so coarsely, and for Poppet's sake, too, is the man to be treated like some kind of rabbit, heaven help us, like that's the only thing that matters to him?), but then again, who knows with men, you can live with one forever and never know for sure, and so she finished that thought already on her back, legs bent at the knees, while he thrust into her hard and without any apparent rhythm, so she wasn't getting anywhere, until she opened her eyes at last and gasped: riveted to her with the lower, moving half of his body, her husband held his upper half up in order to see the TV screen over the bed frame, bursts of color running over his face like at a nightclub, his eyes fixed on the image there with an odd, glassy look, sweat sparkling purple on his upper lip. What, what is it? Milena wanted to exclaim, pressed down by the weight of his body, which suddenly seemed to have tripled, crushed by the devastating sense of this humiliation, like under a steamroller, all the more devastating because so unexpected—*Who was he with?* Whereupon he moaned, and came down, limp, burying his face in her, now undeniably in her. Stunned, with mixed feelings of having been herself robbed clean, but also pity and reproach for her husband, Milena drew her trembling hand along his back, as if trying by feel alone to put back in place the reality of her life, which just a moment before had vanished, disappeared into nowhere. "Who were you with?" she asked quietly, to avoid asking, What were they showing? because that would have been a direct complaint, almost a quarrel, whereas she wanted an explanation, a reconciliation, and an apology. But he didn't understand the question: He raised his joyfully damp mug in astonishment at her, glowing in full color, "What do you mean, who? With you, Milena, who else would I be with?"

Milena tried to forget this incident, squeeze it out of her memory, thinking that maybe she had really imagined it, like the studio head's intrigues—didn't she then flip over onto her stomach and watch, together with her husband, a fun police procedural, with lots of female corpses, and when he trundled off to the kitchen to get something to nibble on, as he always did after sex, and then came back and asked her something, she mumbled in response without listening, and twice even waved him off when he persisted, with, "I'm trying to watch this," so at the end of the day, she could not, were she to be called to court, have sworn with one hundred percent certainty what had taken place in bed and what had taken place on TV. To be honest, this sort of thing happened to them rather often, because the TV not only interfered in their lives but lived its own life, too, and an incomparably more vivid one at that, more festive, uniformly bright and saturated, on all its fifteen channels at once, while the two of them each had maybe three or four (work, parents, friends) and only one shared one, and all of these, of course, had much less action on them, and broadcast in poor quality, with breaks, dark abysses, floating streaks of unnecessary moods surfacing from who knows where, and ghosts. Unlike them, the TV always had everything under control and was in an invariably chipper mood: each of its stories, however terrifying and bloody, always got a logical resolution; it never quit anything midway in the cowardly hope that things would somehow take care of themselves, and never, ever, left behind any loose ends—relationships that were not completely cleared up, defeats unavenged, ambitions unrealized, corpses unburied, or any of the other baggage you take on in a lifetime. It managed to put absolutely everything in order, to place all the right emphasis, and to insert voice-overs and subtitles wherever necessary, everything just so, and so it is no wonder, then, that when Milena's husband had sold some wealthy magazine all the negatives he had shot in one lot and then the bastards had started retailing his photos with no thought of paying him royalties, and he, like a pouting little boy, was telling Milena, for the umpteenth time, how he once again saw a photo of his in this publication and on that billboard, he'd have to repeat his report almost as many times before Milena managed to tear her glazed-over eyes from the screen (on which a very nice American newspaperman just decided to sue his crooked boss), becoming aware, at last, that her husband and the TV were not on the same page, so to speak, and having to ask, "I'm sorry, dear, what?" The dialogue that continued between them would have sounded something like this:

Husband: I'm saying they swindled me, that's what!

Milena: So why don't you take them to court?

Husband: What court, are you kidding? On what grounds? They paid me a bonus on top of the contract—threw me a bone, and now are free to rake in as much as they want. (Milena steals a glance at the TV.) With the taxes we pay, if I were paid by contract alone, we'd have been looking in the trash for cans to recycle long ago!

TV (in English and Ukrainian): There are no hopeless situations, man. We'll get the union together, put this story into newspapers—we'll teach the bastards to respect the law!

Husband (confused): What union? What newspapers? What law?

Milena (shrugs her shoulders and turns back to the screen).

And that, once again, is why it's no wonder that neither one of them noticed—and by the time Milena noticed, it was too late—what Milena's mother was the first—and, it turned out, the last—to intuit, except that, as was her custom, she interpreted her intuition the way she wished, and what she, who could not wrap her mind around the fact that three in a home is, whoever they are, a complete set, wished for, naturally, was a grandbaby. And so, one morning following Milena's show's broadcast, she called and asked, with a girlish excitement in her voice, "Milena, dear, I was watching you the whole time yesterday—are you by any chance pregnant?"

"No," Milena said in surprise. "What made you think that?"

"Well, you looked like you put on a little weight. You were sitting there so nice and smooth all over, and your expression was sort of distant."

Alarmed, Milena weighed herself on the bathroom scale (a ritual she performed every morning) for the second time in one day and even wondered whether the scale was broken, because her weight was of course the same as the day before, and the day before that, and the year before, and the year before that, and if she really had put on some weight, wouldn't Poppet have been the first to tell her? Just in case, Milena decided to wait for Poppet (he was gone until noon in his printing lab, and she left for the studio at lunch, so they usually missed each other, until late at night), and in the meantime rushed to review the tape of the show—with an elegant financial economist, a highly winsome lady, with a peppery dark Spanish complexion, who talked about how since her divorce she was banging (she clung to this word insistently) exclusively men younger than herself and what a positive effect this was having on her overall well-being, only this time, Milena irritably fast-forwarded her all-conquering financial economist as soon as she appeared in the frame, hungrily hunting for herself alone, especially in close-up: could that idiot operator have screwed something up? (Milena knew that in three-quarter profile her face seemed wider and rounded in a homely way, and, naturally, she never forgot this in front of the camera.) But everything seemed to be the same. And yet it wasn't. Even if she was neither puffy nor, god forbid, smooth, the on-screen Milena was nevertheless in some ungraspable way *different*, as if made of thicker bone, and the parts of her that were emphasized by her casual pose—her arm on the back of the chair, her hip turned up from the way she had crossed her legs, and her skirt pulled taut over it—were all as one distinguished by a heavy, grotesque, Toulouse-Lautrec-like monumentality that the delicate Milena had never, ever had, and the overall effect was somehow overfamiliar and preening, maybe even sexy in its own way, but only to a taste that was very plebeian indeed. Things were even worse as far as her face was concerned because it conspiratorially changed expressions in unison with what the irrepressible economist hadn't even finished or even started to say. From a professional point of view this was absolutely amazing insofar as it sent the viewer's imagination flying in the desired direction (for which the off-screen Milena, worried and ashamed, could not, in good faith, resist congratulating her on-screen self), but at the same time, there were moments when the on-screen face showed a downright indecent amount of pleasure, spreading out in a sated half smile, the eyes ready at any second, it seemed, to get bleary (which only Milena's mother, obsessed with her own wish for a grandchild, could have taken for the distant "wandering" gaze of a pregnant woman), and the whole woman really seemed to expand, so full she was of herself, so pleased she was with the way the conversation was going, or, perish the thought, so fully she shared in the economist's carnal delight in the muscular torso of her young bodyguard-chauffeur-masseur. Something dark and impure was looming in all this, a thick sludge that poisoned the charge that Milena would usually get when she watched herself on-screen: this time, her voice rocked back and forth, swinging like hips, her laugh was aroused, coarse, everything tingling with naughtiness—what happened to her voice? Where did this vulgarity come from that saturated it, dammed up like a stale breath? "What a slut!" cried the off-screen Milena harshly, as if slapping her hand on the table, and felt suddenly sobered, as if doused with water, by the sound of her own recaptured voice, and to this very same sound the on-screen Milena slowly turned to her that insolent mug of hers, shamelessly beautiful, blazing drunkenly from the studio lights, with its kiss-swollen slit of crimson lips, and winked at her arrogantly, triumphantly, all but flashing a grin: Of course, and what did you think?

Breathing quickly and for some reason holding on to her pulse with one hand, the off-screen Milena pressed "Stop" and then "Rewind" with the other hand. This time the on-screen Milena, turning her full face toward her, stuck out her tongue at her, which looked, between those dark glistening lips of hers, downright repulsive—it was pale, as if naked, and twitched at the end. The off-screen one hit the pause button to catch the wretched woman with her tongue hanging out: let her sit like that for a while. But she missed: the frame went by, and the on-screen Milena, suddenly brought to a halt, froze gaping in surprise like a tarty doll feigning offended modesty. She even pouted her little lips for *tsk-tsk*, as if she were on the verge of saying: Bad Poppet, you've hurt your sweet Milena! "Mock me, will you?" hissed the off-screen Milena, stung to the quick and feeling herself cover with a slimy cold sweat, like scales. "You just wait a minute, I'll show you!" She drummed on the remote's buttons, almost to the rhythm of her own accelerated heartbeat, forcing the on-screen Milena first to revive and expire by turns, then to contort and grimace in rapid spasms of a possessed marionette, and finally to move in slow motion like a sleepwalker, barely able to raise her hand as if under the pressure of a hundred atmospheres, but none of it was of any use—the other Milena did not reveal herself in any other way and turned into a very ordinary screen representation, tormented for no good reason, so god knows how much time passed before the off-screen Milena, who was just about to quit her schizophrenic clicking (and thus concede to the bitch that she had dreamed it all in her bedroom in front of the screen), heard the telephone ring, which reached her from far away, as if through a mass of water, and picked up the receiver—herself now in slow motion, hand fighting the pressure of a hundred atmospheres.

"Hullo," said an unfamiliar man's voice, clearing his throat, pushing onto her from the depths of the receiver like a storm cloud. "Hullo, is Milena there?"

Now she felt cold inside too: this was like the nightmares about the bear she'd had as a child, from which she always woke with a scream: the bear was coming at her, giant and dark, and his shadow covered her.

"Speaking." She tried to defend herself with her voice, switching instinctively to a silvery secretarial timbre, and whoever was on the other end paused, as if to think (as if to make sure his aim was perfect), and answered with affected recalcitrance:

"Listen, baby, I've got an idea for you. I'm tired of looking at you just on TV. So, call that girlfriend of yours, from yesterday, and let's make a date, I'll pick you up. Don't get hung up about the money, I won't haggle."

"What? How dare you? Who are you?" rattled the off-screen Milena in outrage, as she watched, with even greater outrage, the on-screen one sit up and fidget in her chair, eyes gleaming, her whole body vibrating impatiently with excited giggling—so she yelled, now utterly desperate, at the spot between the on-screen Milena's eyes, like an idiot: "I'll call the police!"

A nasty, knowing laugh came out of the receiver.

"No, you won't, you stupid hen. Think on it, I'll call back. I know where you live. And talk to your girlfriend. Don't worry, you'll like it!"

"Go away!" the off-screen Milena shrieked, her voice a squeak now, but the receiver had been hung up anyway (whereupon she heard from who knows where the first few bars of Beethoven's *Für Elise* played at an incredibly cynical, mocking dance rhythm: pa-pa, pa-pa, pam, pa-ra-pa-pam! They bubbled up like words from a drunk man, then someone very seriously muttered "Sorry," and the dial tone dripped noisily like water from a leaky tap). The receiver lay down quietly on its rest, and the off-screen Milena, just as quietly, in a voice that was white with rage, said to the on-screen one, "I will kill you," obviously with no idea of what she was saying.

Because what could she do to the other one? Even in the unconscious fever of the first hours—when the single urge was to rush somewhere, explain, prove, say, Look closely, that's not me at all (make a statement on air! Even as absurd an idea as that had crossed her mind, believe it or not)—Milena stayed lucid enough to be coolly aware, somewhere deep down, that the other she, itching as she was to tear her off herself like mangy skin, was still far from alien to her, and not just in physical resemblance. In her own way, the other (second) woman was quite striking, much more confident than the first, original Milena, more relaxed (that's for sure!), and, on the whole, perfectly suited to her purpose—there was no fault to be found with her from the professional perspective. Nevertheless, pent up inside Milena was a painfully vague, all but grunting with the effort to be articulated, recollection that back when she was just launching her show, she had imaged a different screen self—a warmer, more radiant one, one that fit into the vision of women's heart-to-hearts that go on in the kitchen nearly until dawn on the once-grasped and never again released crystalline singing note of souls growing closer together: Sister, sister, your heartache grows weaker, you are not alone in this world, your children are sleeping in the next room, and life goes on, let us be wise, let us be patient, these minutes are precious as music, as love, because you love her in these moments so deeply your heart could stop, you reel at the scorching pinnacle of her suffering, and here is tenderness, and pain, and pride in our brave and silent women's endurance, and a beauty unspeakable that brings you to tears, which glows for a while in both women (until the crowd on the bus rubs it off). That's what Milena, who had known no small number of such evenings, strove to achieve for her guests and herself. In one of her first scripts, which someone later cut without a trace, she called it helping-the-Ukrainian-woman-find-herself-in-our-complicated-times. And look what had come of it.

On the way to the studio (she could not stay put to wait for her husband after all: she needed to be in motion, she needed action), Milena covered her head with her hands and moaned: she suffered stabs of a festering and, most importantly, undeserved feeling of defeat. She had done everything the way she was supposed to, she put herself out there and worked hard, so hard that Poppet had been reproaching her (although he had recently stopped), and now that odious creature was sitting in her studio, winking and hinting at something filthy, and no one seemed to have noticed the difference! True, over the show's run Milena herself had learned many new things, had grown professionally, as everyone said of her, and would no longer make fun, the way she used to, of her news-department colleagues, for really coming to life only when there were catastrophes, fires, or murders, the more atrocious the better—it doesn't take a genius to realize that if you want people to hear you in all this racket and not change the channel, you either have to hit them, hard, with something, or scratch a very private itch, and do it so masterfully, too, that they'll keep coming back for more, changing your technique, so to speak, and whoever says that's easy is a loser who couldn't cut it himself, but! There was, all the same, a *but.* As the thought of that obscene complacent mug on the screen (oh, to smash it in!) washed back over her, Milena was blinded, as by a stroke of lightning, by a long tremor of hatred, very much like that of love, that ran down the whole length of her body. "What do I do now?" she mumbled to herself, ever so quickly, unconsciously speeding up her steps and digging her fingers into her coat collar, as if it were her enemy's throat: Milena was scared.

"Caw, caw, ca-a-aw!" She suddenly heard the cries above her. Milena raised her head: way up high, about halfway to the raw and empty sky that with springtime was already farther away, swayed tree branches in an imitation of a Japanese ink painting and circled a flock of startled crows. What a beautifully composed shot, and so apropos, she thought, you wouldn't have to edit a thing—and from that moment on, everything around her began to roll smoothly, like on TV, as if she had stepped right into that world behind the screen where one did not need to make any decisions. Only to watch.

In the hallways at the studio no one paid any attention to her, colleagues sped past her, goggle eyed and unseeing, and not a living soul lingered for a smoke in the stairwell. Here Milena remembered, with an instant chill, that she had rushed out of the house without her makeup, not even a touch of lipstick, and felt intensely embarrassed, as if she'd shown up in her underwear alone, and at the same time glad that no one had noticed her, so she could still slip out, dash home, put on some makeup, and come back with a respectable face, so as to ignite, with her hello to the guard at the entrance turnstile, the happy hubbub of greetings and hustle and send up ahead of her, like a flame along the detonating cord, up to the elevators, along the hallways, zigzagging into offices and studios. For some strange reason, the simplest and most obvious solution did not even cross Milena's mind—namely, to drop by the makeup department and pant to the ladies, So sorry, ran myself ragged, could you please put some war paint back on?—and to chat with them for a bit, share a smoke, take a breather before going to work, especially since the girls liked her, followed her show religiously, and one, who was divorced herself, even told her she unplugged her phone so that no one would spoil it for her. However, nothing even close to that dawned in Milena's tangled-up mind, as she stalked, instead, down the hallways like a sleepwalker, a ghost, toward the service stairs—she felt this compulsion to escape down the service stairs and no other way—peeking into open doors as she walked, while keeping her own face in the shadows as if it'd been burned. The next instant, her director all but fell into her as he charged out of his office, twisted out of the way, mumbled, in Russian, for some reason, "Excuse me," and brushed past her in a waft of sulfurous smell: a match, Milena thought, watching a curl of grey smoke unfurl above him as he fled into the narrowing depth of the hallway. The poor sucker is going to burn right at work one day, occurred to her, out of place and without pity, for somehow she lacked not only pity but any feelings at all, as if the light bulbs meant to illuminate them had all been unscrewed, and she was watching just the frames, one after the other, or rather, moving, involuntarily, from frame to frame on a flickering film, unable to stop, compelled to keep moving, while feeling anything, she remembered lucidly, would require her to step out of the flow and pause—and so it was that as soon as an emotion came to life inside her, like a spark, a gleaming little bug, it was shaken off on the run, edited out, blown off like ash into the air. People sped this way and that like comets, in intersecting sparkling cascades of tails as they burned out—more luxuriant behind some, more sparse behind others, whereby a constantly elevated working temperature was maintained on the premises and over the years, the walls, faces, and floor of the studio acquired that fine, barely visible bluish-grey tint that studio guests took to be the residue of plain old cigarette smoke, while it was not plain or simple at all, albeit indeed a kind of smoke. What a wonderful job I have, Milena thought with pride or, more precisely, an embryo of pride—the emotion flared behind her like a firefly, brushing imperceptibly against her cheek, and sizzled on the floor, without developing into a thought. Milena held her gaze before her, like a camera: the corridor was running into her, breaking in unexpected turns, and flashing increasingly goggle-eyed faces to meet her, but the main effect came from the fact the camera was hidden, because no one saw Milena—had no time to see her, actually, because the film kept rolling faster, jerkily, so people were no longer walking, but trotting and galloping. Before Milena's very eyes—that is, in front of her camera—the studio head's secretary, a long-haired blonde, becoming short haired and then a brunette, as she went, dropped a fetus conceived, evidently, just a minute earlier, which, with a gurgling froggish croak that Milena found vaguely familiar, slipped into the ashen twilight of the hallway and instantly vanished as if it had tumbled into the fourth dimension. Was it the studio head's, wondered Milena, a quick scribble in her mind, a question mark in the margin of the script, purely for the sake of form, because she really wasn't in the least curious, so the question tumbled off after the wretched fetus that had already been forgotten, including by Milena herself, who, nonetheless, remembered that she needed to reach the service stairs, and could only wonder, if the word was still at all applicable, why it was taking her so long to find them. Again, the director, now with a beard, popped out of a doorway, using both hands to jostle ahead of him, like a cart in a supermarket, two rather heavy women, who were glued to each other, as if in the act of making love, which somehow conveyed to Milena that one of them was supposed to be her new jilted heroine, and the other quite the opposite, her rival home-wrecker, and again she put an approving exclamation mark in the invisible margin—this was a great idea to liven up the show, as long as the women didn't get into a catfight in the studio—although right behind them, wiping out any traces of them, stampeded a herd of men in identical grey suits with identical pins on their lapels, which Milena didn't see clearly, some of them running bent under the weight of long banners with text that blurred into a single swoosh, and the last one even carrying the red-and-blue flag of Soviet Ukraine—but then, right after them, came dashing victorious athletes, whose feet sent off resounding echoes with their purposeful stomp, melded together into a yellow-and-blue whole, led by one who seemed to Milena, by now dazed from the onslaught of faces, to be racing with a lit Olympic torch, so the overall effect was cheerful and life affirming. But here a shot of the grey sky and crows was suddenly wedged in again: caw, caw, ca-aw! The branches swayed up high. Where had the ceiling gone? A double exposure, she erred in editing, Milena grasped, forgetting about her unmade-up face, and grabbed the first prop that came to hand—a door handle that gave way at a light push and revealed none other than Milena's own familiar studio, with cameras set for taping, and two chairs, lit up from all sides, on the podium. One, for the guest, was still empty, while sitting in the other one, obscured by the lid of her compact for a last quality-control look at herself, was an awfully familiar woman dressed in crimson, knees pressed together roundly under her skirt like a shield, also in a very familiar manner. "Where have I seen her?" Milena fretted while she noticed at the same time that the backdrop in the studio—and with it, the branding of the show—had changed: like an ad for Revlon lipstick, an image of gigantic, moistly parted lips that promised either to surrender or to swallow you whole in one gulp, was hanging there now. And there was something else looming behind the chairs, in the unlit background, something like a low couch, as in a psychoanalyst's office, but that she didn't get a good look at, because just then the woman in the chair took the compact away from her face, and looking at Milena was her own face—that is, not hers, but the face of that other Milena, from the screen, only this time it was improbably, not even humanly, terrifyingly beautiful, as if from the era of silent film: the eyes flamed like precious jewels, the lips blazed, the witchy eyebrows met on the bridge of her nose in a swallowtail, and her skin, matte with makeup, disdainfully immobile in the glaring spotlight, exuded that heavenly peace that only the screen can feign, and the only thought that occurred to Milena, bewildered and still dumb in the doorway, was, I wonder what they've been feeding her to get her to look like that! while the other one regarded her with displeased surprise as if wondering who this intruder was and just about to clap her hands from her luminous height for someone to throw the pest out the door. But this is my studio, and this is my show! Milena almost cried out, humiliated to the

135

verge of tears, including by her own appearance, so out of place here, so plain she might as well be invisible, so inappropriate she couldn't dream of proving anything to anyone but ought to run away, crawl into a hole, and not inflict herself on anyone's sight, because one look at the two of them was enough to say with certainty which one deserved a place in the studio—and it was not the derelict in the doorway! But still—how did the bitch dare, and where was everyone looking, the director, the studio execs, the viewers—and since when had she installed herself here?

On this last thought Milena had to step aside to make way for a procession that advanced, like a wedding train, from the hallway: the director—now clean shaven again!—the camera operators, not one but two makeup girls, and other dark figures, all of them engaged in escorting, almost carrying, a young blonde woman, in a pageboy haircut and barely conscious with emotion, with delicately curved cheekbones and a precious little nose on which drops of sweat had broken through the makeup. The woman's eyes were still and glassy as if she were in a trance; they did not express anything themselves, only reflecting the light from outside, and Milena, the one who was standing at the door, of course, was stung by a vague recollection of having seen eyes like that before, in someone dear to her (close, warm), and of that moment being connected to something extremely unpleasant. The blonde woman stepped forward precariously, as if her knees were about to buckle, and she was on the verge of crashing down, arms outstretched before her, with cries of ecstasy, because she was also breathing quickly and her lips were moistly parted, exactly like the ones on the backdrop, but it wasn't the backdrop that she was staring at so unblinkingly, like a calf at the sacrificial flames, but—Milena herself went numb, as she followed her gaze—at that other one on the set, who was now poised like a panther about to leap, and was greeting her guest with a smile so greedy, so evil, and yet so lush playing on her lips: Come on now, come on, closer, closer, as if she were drawing her in, like a spider, step by step, along an invisible length of taut sticky silk, until Milena could hear it humming. Or maybe it was the hum of the cameras that came on just in time to capture the blonde woman, already hooked up to a microphone on the collar of her blouse, as she neared the podium and raised—honestly, raised!—her prayerful, incredulous hands up, *Ave, Cesarina!* to the rapacious witch in the crimson dress, which itself became at once vibrant and fluid, as if filled with blood, and as the other woman, with a purposeful twist of her torso, bent to support her (*Come to me, and I will soothe you*) literally to snatch her, suck onto her because the poor thing was reeling, was ready to fall to the ground at the feet of her deity from an overabundance of feeling, and, oh my god, did she really just almost kiss the witch's hand? "Music!" someone called out breathlessly, running past Milena in the dim light and nearly knocking her down onto the pile of plywood cubes, boards, and other rummage stacked up against the wall. "Don't forget the music in this episode!" "Fuck off," a nasal voice responded clearly out of the dark, sending shivers between Milena's shoulder blades: the sound of it made her realize that something horrible was about to happen on the set, something so far beyond even her imagination that she just had to switch channels immediately, and, her mind grinding, like millstones, over the same mindless question of What is going on, what is going on, what, in the name of all that is holy, is going on, Milena lunged through the door back into the hallway.

She is going to slaughter her, the next thought caught up with Milena on the run in the hallway—she is going to spread her out nicely on that chaise longue of hers and slaughter her, slice her into little pieces with a knife, and that sheep of a woman will expire with a smile on her lips, are they all crazy in there that they don't see this coming? She rewound the scene in her mind and hardly had any more doubt that things were really heading toward a ritual killing that had to be urgently stopped, and the script required her, Milena, to stop it, and that was why she couldn't find her way to the service stairs. Once set in motion, the plot was unfolding according to the television's iron logic of resolution—a discovery that could not fail but inspire Milena to act decisively, and even enthusiastically. She tried to return to the terrible studio, but this turned out not to be all that easy to do: once again the interminable hallway bored into her view, snapping off here and there dark flashes of sudden turns, people speeding back and forth, and suddenly she ran into the noisy throng of a whole troupe of leading Kyiv actors, all of them, for some reason, in wheelchairs. She was jostled and pushed with her nose up against a brass plaque that was cold to the touch (and covered, like a windowpane fogged with breath, with a sticky film of that TV ash), and on which Milena, who pushed herself back with revulsion, read, to her great delight, the title, "Studio Head." Of course, that's who must put an end to this outrage! She wriggled with renewed zeal until she could feel the doorknob, turned it, and burst in: the secretary wasn't in the reception area (must've jumped out for another abortion), the door to the office was cracked open, and the studio head was in—Milena saw him from behind, facing his desk, a very wide oak table, about the size of a Soviet Khrushchev-era apartment hallway, grandly authoritarian, at the very sight of which Milena, and more than likely not she alone, used to experience a sneaky arousal, marveling at the same time how power could be so sexy even when represented by a table. At the moment, however, it was not the table that had her attention, but the studio head, to whom something strange was happening: black netted wings, narrow like a grasshopper's or a dragonfly's, appeared to grow straight out from the stiff shoulders of his suit jacket, and they were moving, preparing to spread, which made the jacket tug back and forth between them, comically flapping its rumpled vents. The next moment the wings flapped decisively, letting out at the ends what looked like bird beaks, and became, right before bewildered Milena's eyes, a pair of outstretched woman's legs in fishnet stockings and black pumps with pointed heels. Milena must have made a muffled sound because the studio head made one, too, looked behind him, and froze at the sight of Milena with his unzipped pants, while Milena herself was presented with a view of what was behind him, a sight that caused her to think, for the first time in her life, agreeably, Now I'm definitely going nuts, and it's nothing to be afraid of, sort of interesting: the first thing she registered, a single smear, was the crumpled stain of familiar crimson, then a terrifying flash of something naked and hairy, in stripes, and finally, her own unrecognizable face— *she*, that bitch from the studio, was positioned on the studio head's table with her legs triumphantly thrown up in a V-for-victory worthy of a rally. She swung one in the air, as if conducting an inaudible orchestra, and watched Milena with no expression at all, as if she were an insect. "Excuse me," Milena muttered stupidly, and the studio head, holding up his trousers, moved his lips in mirrored obedience, echoing her, but then he was impatiently kicked by the swinging fishnetted leg with its heel, and Milena heard a sharp cry, like an order for the firing squad, she'd never heard *herself* make that sound: "What'd you stop for? Give me more! More!" The studio head grunted, twitched, coughed out his half-swallowed "Excuse me" over his shoulder in Milena's direction, and again two netted black wings squeezed and pinched him from the sides, and he obediently resumed his trot-like thrusting to the accompaniment of that savage, vulgar whoop of "More! More!" Herself shaking with a repulsive dry shiver from deep within her gut, Milena shuffled blindly out of the office and shut the door tight behind her: an utterly futile gesture that did nothing to muffle the whoops, they kept coming, roaring in her ears, and the ceiling collapsed into oblivion from it, and there, flying above the swaying tree branches, cawing, were the crows. There was really nothing more to do at the studio.

Just as soon as she thought that, Milena found herself on the service stairs: the humongous multistory digestive tract of the TV studio now spewed her out easily, without resistance. And maybe it was for the better, a sleepy thought stirred heavily in her mind (once on the stairs, Milena suddenly felt terribly tired), maybe that's how things should be, since that other Milena (look, she conceded to recognize her, to call her by her own name for the first time) had gone much further than she would have ever dared on her own, no she would not have (the thought was interrupted by an exhausted yawn, so intense it brought tears to her eyes), while the other Milena stopped at nothing, took up the dirty work. The first Milena felt a relaxing warmth embrace and rock her (Let someone else, caring and strong, do everything for me, and later she can . . .)—the TV Milena is now a true queen, and no longer the perpetual good girl, Like someone else, she reproached in the tender grumbling tone her husband used, and dissolved into a smile, blinking her way out of her insuperable, deathly fatigue: to sleep, to sleep, pressed up against Poppet, his broad barely furred chest, one sleepy hand feeling its ticklish growth and the other cradling his warmly swollen tail, Poppet would put his arm around her, Mm-m, sunshine, my golden Sugar, calm her with the touch of his lips, a last bedtime kiss. I love you, Milena would say to him from the far shore of sleep, and all the others, well, to hell with them and all their games. And their TV shows. And all crazy women.

And with that, Milena dragged herself home.

The apartment was dark, only a low, bluish-grey light seeped from the bedroom through the new stained glass door. Milena, startled momentarily by the new door (when had her honey had time?), and by the whole ungraspable, disturbing feeling of unfamiliarity that one's own home evokes after a long absence (how long had she been gone?), reached for the knob where it had always been, startled again, with the very skin of her hand, when she found it on the other side, groped about, and finally went in.

And saw.

That is, she heard.

That is, simultaneously both saw and heard:

Milena (from the screen, still wearing crimson and her legs in the same victorious V): Give me more! More! More!

Husband (on the bed): I'm coming, Milena, hang on, love, hang on . . .

Milena (from the doorway): No! Get out! What are you doing? You're mine! He's mine! (Undecipherable from that point.)

Milena (from the screen): Well, look at that! Look! Now that's a turn-on! See? See? And now you do me, come up and do it, use your tongue, girl! Use your tongue, they all do me that way, all those cunts, and they all come from it, right there on the air, it's the highest-rated show, two million letters each month, more! More! Use your tongue, I said, your tongue, there's no other use for you anyway, come on! More!

(Milena moves from the doorway—she comes closer, takes the remote, and turns off the TV.)

Husband (rabid): What? Who? Who are you?

Milena: I am Milena. Your wife.

Husband: Fuck off! (Grabs the remote and turns on the TV.)

Milena (from the screen, sitting in a chair high up on the studio's podium): My beloved! My dearest, my sweetest viewers, and above all, my female viewers, my brothers and sisters, I turn to you once again, I, Milena! I am the one who comes into every home to remind you that there is no earthly woe that cannot be conquered by the great force of our coming together! I am with you, my sisters. Anyone who feels lonely and abandoned this evening, cheated and hurt, come to me and I'll satisfy you! I'll let you eat of my flesh and drink of my blood, my sweet flesh, and even sweeter blood, and your hearts will be filled with great joy, and you will be avenged on those who have hurt you, they will gnash their teeth and gnaw the earth in their impotent rage, for as long as they live they will never know the joy that is yours and mine, sisters! Here she is, my beloved sister who will be in the studio today with me and with you, here she comes now, come, my dove (a church hymn starts playing), come, my precious, my body is waiting for you, loving you, as no-one-has-loved-in-a-thousand-years, oh come!

141

But she has no body, the other Milena suddenly thought, and it seemed to her that she had cried out loud, "She has no body, do you hear me? This is all an illusion, a terrible fraud. This really used to be *my* body, and still is even now, and there is no other nor can there be." And, as if she were looking for proof for herself, she grabbed a knife, her husband's beautiful pocketknife, a Swiss Army Knife with a tiny pair of tweezers and a bone toothpick in the handle, which was lying open on the night table, or perhaps she was simply in great pain at that moment, realizing that she, too, had been jilted, the impossible had happened, what seemed unthinkable had come to pass, and she was finally united with the mob of all the countless women toward which she had been heading so unswervingly from the beginning, and she therefore had the instinct to block, outscream this pain with another, louder yet, but lighter, as people who thrust various objects into their bodies often do. The blade grinned blindingly in the teleblaze with its teeth poised sharp and ready above Milena's bared forearm, and then there was a stream from that arm, a steady drip of something inky dark, the color of a blank TV screen at night, and with a shine like that of a metallic, greyish oily film, which crackled with sparks sputtering out . . .

From that moment on, it becomes difficult for me to state with certainty what happened to Milena—it's like she's been cut off, our connection got interrupted, and the picture warped and began to flicker. I know she disappeared, because there was nothing else for her to do, but in what manner—in what order and sequence—I do not know, and if I don't know, you can consider it good and lost. Of course, there were no hospitals or morgues, nothing quite so, god forbid, morbid: I see, albeit out of focus, a frame in which Milena walks slowly down an empty street, at night, possibly supporting her left arm, bandaged awkwardly in a scarf or something like that, with her right hand—she is walking away from her extinguished apartment building with that single bluishly lit window and looks at other people's windows. In each, a TV glows. Milena moves her lips, but we hear no sound. She keeps walking. She turns the corner. And then she vanishes, meaning no one sees her after that. Never.

And what, I ask you now, am I supposed to do?

Naturally, with Milena's disappearance, her famous show lost its luster—it held on for a while, but out of pure momentum, it wasn't the same without the live wire of her energy—a dead woman's photo, a deflated ball, self-reference upon self-reference, beating on a dead horse, an utter loss of any credibility not to mention emotional power, so naturally, the viewers also grew distant and their feedback gradually went quiet somewhere in that distance. At the same time, the first voices of steel found their way into the reviews, and those were women's voices, saying, What is that girl doing, are you all nuts there on TV? The press rolled the piece of candy that was "Milena's phenomenon" in its mouth for a bit longer, but the candy dissolved as a result, and in one academic institution folks were forced to change one graduate student's all-but-approved dissertation topic that treated the show from some highfalutin sociopsychological angle, the committee suddenly declaring the topic as unscientific and really unseemly, so the poor student had to write about the viewer reception of the televised broadcasts of the parliament meetings by different demographic groups instead. Right about that time the studio finally canceled the show, quietly, without a fuss, and all I was left to do was haunt the sets without a particular purpose, dwell among the turned-off cameras and the dark spotlights, myself unplugged, colorless and weathered, like Milena the day she came to the studio, and just like her, no one here sees me, except that one time the night guard saw me rise full height during a thunderstorm—he now wears a little copper cross under his uniform. They still remember me, I'm sure, and will not forget me anytime soon, but they will forget—everyone is sooner or later forgotten, my brothers and sisters, I, for one, have already clear forgotten everyone who'd been brought to me, despite the fact that they still say, although usually with an awkward laugh, that it was an incredible spectacle to behold, the Roman Saturnalia and the feast of Astarte rolled into one! Actually, Milena is the only one I do remember—that's why I want to make sure I write everything down, the way things happened, stealing time on a studio PC someone left on for the night, while somewhere, in her empty apartment, Milena's mother is sitting alone in front of the TV, stubbornly expecting her daughter to appear again at the appointed hour, until the screen goes dark, day after day. I guess it is she and her vigil that stand between me and complete oblivion, because Milena's husband did buy a satellite dish, and cheaper than he expected, and turned himself off a long time ago, not to mention everyone else whose memory is so ephemeral and fragmented, so dot-pixelated, that if I had to survive on that alone, I'd have long ago turned into a sheaf of white sparks, like noise from the transmission signal.

AN ALBUM FOR GUSTAV

TRANSLATED BY NINA MURRAY

He: When people ask me what the hardest part was, back during those days on the Maidan—and it's usually foreigners who ask (Gustav is not the first), usually just to be polite, just to be asking something, because the only thing they remember from their press and cable news is that more than a million people (no one knew exactly how many anyway, and I bet no one will ever find out) came out into the streets of Kyiv and stood there, in the freezing cold and under snow—and you know they picture the Ukrainian winter as something out of the vast Asiatic steppes: birds frozen dead midflight, tongues stuck to metal spoons— so when they ask about the hardest thing, they are hoping to hear Hollywood-worthy horror tales of frostbitten cheeks and amputated limbs à la Jack London, and Manifest Destiny's Go West, my son, since a conquest of the West (and they are certain that's what we fought for—a piece of the West!) must need, in their mythology, be accompanied by purely masculine sacrifices; they ask in full anticipation of having you tell them what they have already imagined so that they can nod sympathetically and say, Wow. When people ask me this question and I try to answer, every time I feel like I come up against a solid wall inside myself, a profound lack of desire to explain anything, muddling in my inadequate English, to mutter that *hard* is not quite the right word, and it doesn't really fit what we experienced during those three weeks. That, actually, it was later that things got "hard," after everything was over, the rush was over, and we all had to go home, and become again anonymous strangers passing each other in the street, so that no matter how many times you clicked your busted lighter in the middle of the sidewalk in a hopeless attempt to light your cigarette, there would be no solicitous onslaught of helpful hands with ready flames offered to you from every direction. I remember how utterly lost I felt the first time this *did not* happen. After those three weeks I had forgotten completely what it was like to be alone in a mass of people, and this was only a few days later, and Khreshchatyk looked like the same street, and the people looked like the same people, only now they hurried along on their holiday errands and no one gave a damn if some loser could use a light—*that* was the moment when I, stunned for an instant by the chill of the sudden emptiness in the space that was only recently, days before, bubbling with thick familial, intimate warmth, a void not unlike the one left by the death of a loved one, understood finally and undeniably that it was all really over: we had begun to fall apart again, to segregate into the composite elements of a pedestrian mass, no different from a crowd in any city in the world, and one had to learn to live as before, as if one had never known a different life. *That* was really hard—it was like coming home from war, albeit victorious (for some reason, this particular metaphor strikes me as especially apt), like coming back from the front, Gustav, *you see?*

Gustav nods and grunts a low, respectful *ja*, he's all right, only, of course, he doesn't have a clue, this guy who looks in every way like a storybook Dutch skipper, with his red sideburns straight out of a cartoon; all he needs is a pipe. Sweetie, when she first saw him, cracked, "The Flying Dutchman!"—he really is a walking stereotype, but I'm sure there are tons of stereotypical-looking people in any nation, it's just our deeply inculcated distrust of national stereotypes that makes them seem like a rarity. Gustav has come for one thing and one thing only: pictures—and pictures are what he really understands, no arguing about that. He's got a good eye, instantly grabbing onto the shots he wants me to pull up to full screen, and really, I could very well shut up and not try to explain anything at all, because the pictures do speak for themselves, but I can't shake the suspicion that they are telling him something different from what they say to me. He wasn't in Kyiv back then, and all he's seeing now are untold numbers of people in the city streets, under the snow. A few angles are really nice (especially when I managed to climb a tree and take shots of Hrushevsky Street—a bright-orange human sea as far as the horizon, seen through the latticework of snow-covered tree limbs), and so are the wide angles, of course—the people's faces are beautiful, old, young, inspired, smiling, with happy tears in their eyes, with mouths open in joyful cries (Gustav skips over a grinning gap-toothed boy in a black stocking cap—that's taken from farther up the hill, next to the Supreme Council building; I got a few good shots there too. While I was hoisting myself into the tree, and my buddy Vovchik held my camera, the boy volunteered to guard my coat; the women standing around fussed over me, tutting that I'll freeze, that I can't go without a coat, Vovchik retorted sternly that it's nothing—the love of the motherland will keep me warm—and the boy, with his head tossed back, watched me from below, his face glowing with that spellbound grin that seemed fixed on so many people's faces in those days: the mouth beatifically stretched from ear to ear, the expression one gets standing on the top of a mountain or riding up a rushing wave on a surfboard—the awe inspired by the magnificence of a force greater than what can be accommodated by human imagination. That boy had come to Kyiv from Rivne, on the very first day, and told us what it was like: the highway was lit bright as daylight, all cars speeding to Kyiv, it seemed the whole of Ukraine had picked up and rushed to Kyiv, horns blaring, and along the road the villagers stood by the blazing fires and waved them on with flags and banners. "I won't have another night like that in my life," the boy said, and if I were to translate this for Gustav now, the Dutchman would probably think that's how men speak of a night with a woman, but we wouldn't have thought of it that way at the time because what the boy was talking about was also *our* night, belonging to all of us who listened, in a single oceanic wave that furled and crested for hundreds of kilometers around the capital and rushed through the darkness with the ascending thunder of an elemental force breaking through a dam, smashing anything stupid enough to stand in its way, and we were as proud of it as that boy, so I asked to take his picture and there it was: a common snapshot of a boy in a black stocking cap, with a beatific smile on his face, nondescript but for the orange ribbon, but then again, everyone had orange ribbons, so we move on).

Sweetie comes in to ask if we want coffee and, getting a no, makes herself scarce. I wish she'd stay and help me—she speaks English much better than I do—but she leaves me to suffer alone, with Gustav who says *ja* and doesn't get it. The only people who got us—really got us— were the Poles; with them we had a complete and utter *ja*, and didn't have to explain anything. The Poles lived it as their second youth, their second *Solidarność*. I knew it on the first day, when their parliamentarians came and I spotted one of the women on TV, the way she stood on the stage on the Maidan with the same expression as our older people, and held her hand in the air with two fingers in the sign of victory like a blessing for all of us. I knew right away the Poles were all right; even the young people, who were born after the Solidarity movement, knew how to recognize the same thing in what they saw in Kyiv; they had received a key from their parents, the score for this opera, and they knew how to read it. The Germans also sort of got it—they could rely on their own analogies: the year '89, the wall coming down, *Wir sind ein Volk*, but for them it was all more on the emotional level, without the grasp of the subtexts; all the others just hung out, wandering through the crowds, getting high on the pure scale of the human force around them, riding their own adrenaline rush—free thrills, a revolutionary vacation in the capital of a vaguely known ex-Soviet republic located somewhere on the Asiatic plains between Albania and Belarus. These other foreigners were sincerely thrilled with their ethnographic discoveries in this new territory ("Your city is really large," a British cameraman, with whom I spent half a day shooting shoulder to shoulder, kept saying in utter astonishment), such as the fact that we did not actually warm ourselves with vodka in the cold weather, and remained strictly alcohol-free for the entire three weeks of standing in the streets (that's what made it clear to these folks that we were different from Russians); that we did not break windows or windshields, and generally, against all odds, did not break or smash anything or anyone, and did not produce a single bloody nose that could be presented (exhibit A) to the powers that be in Moscow or Washington who insisted on alarming the wider world with predictions of a civil war in this obscure country between Albania and Belarus, the new Balkans. So, in the end, just by doing what we did and without any particular intention, we screwed things up for more constituencies than just the Russians—it's just that the Russians were as clumsy as a bear on a bicycle and couldn't get away fast enough, while the quick-witted American diplomats, who sat out the whole thing on the sidelines waiting to see who would win and did not leave their embassy even on that very tense night when our tent city expected to be attacked and asked all accredited missions in the city to let their personnel come out onto the Maidan and form a "sanitary barrier" around the protesters—the Americans, one must give them credit, fig-ured things out in a blink, and before Khreshchatyk even had a chance to cool down from the crowds, trumpeted to their press another success in their endeavors to teach us Albanian-Belarusians about democracy and the rule of law.

As I'm thinking this, Gustav scrolls past another picture that doesn't tell him anything: a shot of an apartment building window where one glimpses a hand holding up an orange teakettle. He'd have to zoom in to see that it is a very old and desiccated hand, resembling a chicken paw. It belonged to a very old little lady who couldn't even walk anymore, and had only this symbolic means of joining the column of protesters that passed under her window. I remember I heard people ahead of me (I was walking in that column) chanting a new slogan that turned out to be "Grandma! Grandma!"—someone had spotted that teakettle, and the feeble hand holding it, a shaky orange blot in the window, and heads began to turn one after another, people pointing—What's there? Look!—and I shouted too, "Grandma!" and pointed my camera, blinking off tears. Old ladies had a special power of bringing me to tears in those days; the little old ladies who shambled and tottered to the Maidan day and night, slipping on the steep hillside streets and carrying their treasured possessions, steeped in the smell of old-age poverty: knitted scarves and socks from their ancient dressers or a few hot boiled potatoes wrapped in a clean kerchief, which the tent city's wardens accepted almost reverently, many with a lump in their throats. Never mind that just a minute earlier those same wardens were practically begging women in mink coats and a French restaurant owner who drove in a Land Rover loaded to the gills with prepared dinners, "Please, don't bring any more food, we've got more than we could eat already!" Looking at these old ladies, at their stubborn, taciturn tenacity (I'll never forget the one who kept bringing tea in a tiny eighteen-ounce thermos. In the crowd, it took no more than three seconds to pour out the three cups of tea it contained, and the grandma would turn and crawl back home up the steep, iced-over Mykhailivska Street to brew another thermos full, and I wondered, How many trips does she make every day?), I was truly touched for the first time by their frightening, primordial almost, elemental life force that could not be cowed by starvation, wars, or labor camps—by any of the horrors, including the destitute old age that befell them, as if the inhuman labor of enduring through it all was a mere nightmare of history, a scam, a foolish bet, as folks would say, the devil wagering Job 'gainst the Lord—and the devil lost it all, because these little old ladies, who certainly could teach Job a thing or two, on their deathbeds, when they had no more hope of being themselves rewarded with the brooks of milk and honey, gathered their last strength and raised feeble hands to salute freedom through their windows. It occurred to me then that if one went looking for a single image of this revolution, for our own *Liberty Leading the People*, the young beauty with the orange carnation facing the shields of the riot police would not do no matter how awesome she looked on posters—it would have to be that hunched-over, inconceivably old, indestructible, and uncowed old lady from the Maidan, with her three cupfuls of hot tea—Here, children, warm yourselves, God bless you. Now, that would be the real truth about us, but who'd ever want that old flesh to be their revolution's allegory?

She: I can tell Sweetie's miffed at me for leaving him alone with that Dutch dude, but what can I do if I can't stand to talk about the same stuff for the millionth time! I just can't do it. The more you talk, the more you repeat yourself, and the next thing you know, you have lost any trace of your real experience of those days—you just have words, units of meaning, and they come out prerecorded, and then the entire conversation degrades back to politics, the talking heads on TV, oil prices, the government crisis, the fight against corruption, all that bullshit. Thank you, but no thank you. Mr. Gustav can shape his Eastern European album with its chapter on "Revolutionary Kyiv" however he sees fit. Without my help. I'm glad to see Sweetie's pictures put to use, else he wouldn't get around to doing anything with them for another year, but that doesn't mean I have to participate. You boys are on your own.

I have my own book of visions, but no one would ever want it. The world has determined to live exclusively in the present—for however long whatever is on TV stays there. Time has not sped up—it has simply disintegrated. The only reality is what can be touched. A problem of attention span, I think they call it. We have the attention span of a puppy, at best. Today there's a revolution in one country, tomorrow in another, on a different continent. And if it's not a revolution, it's a terrorist attack, or a hurricane, or another calamity, which we will forget about as soon as they switch to the next story on the newscast. We just want to make sure there's something new being beamed at us every minute, and we're not being asked to hold anything in our minds for any length of time at all. We don't want to go to the trouble of making connections between the past and the present because, you know, that requires *effort*. And we are not being encouraged to exert ourselves in any way; we are being taught to relax. Leaf through a photography book on the coffee table, at best, move your eyes left to right a few times, up and down. That's just a smidge better than channel surfing. Or the internet: snippets, tweets, fragments—*Where did I read that?*—screw it, who cares! Don't *worry* about it.

And here's the interesting part: I'm a historian by training, and what, I ask you, was all that training good for, inclusive of a graduate degree and a thesis on the Russian government's suppression of the Brotherhood of Saints Cyril and Methodius in 1847 (which was nothing less than our very first bourgeois-democratic revolution, nipped in the bud), and the hours spent in our gutted archives, and my trip to Moscow in pursuit of the documents the KGB, in their panic to cover up the tracks, culled from the Ukrainian archives back in the fall of 1991, in that short window of opportunity after Ukraine had already declared independence, but before the USSR officially fell apart—what was all this professional preparation good for, if it took even me until November, until the days of the Maidan, until the climax of the most significant Ukrainian political movement since the seventeenth century, to begin, laboriously, to realize, as if a heavy door was creaking slowly open on rusted hinges inside my brain, that *this is for real*— and to *recognize* it, incredulously. For the longest time, I simply could not believe that everything I had known through archival records and books was real, and very much alive, and happening to us—and none of us knew what it was. I actually needed a hint, a nudge, which I got from a German reporter, I think (there were so many of them, it feels like they had their own tent city in my head), the one we took along the front lines—from Institutska Street to Bankova, to the riot police detachments in front of the president's administration building, to Shovkovychna, and from there onto Luteranska Street and back to Khreshchatyk. We sat down to warm ourselves at one of the mobile canteens, and a man from the Sumy region told us how in their small town before the second round of elections, groups of shaved-headed men went from bar to bar, making everyone drink to the health of the ruling government's candidate and beating up whoever refused to do so with such violence that a friend of this man's ended up in intensive care. I interpreted, the excited German scribbled furiously in his notebook, and then later he said to me, delighted as a boy, Isn't it amazing, just think about it, your people never knew democracy or justice—they'd been ruled by despots the whole time, the Russian czars, with terror, persecutions, violence—and here the people have risen to defend their rights, *it's a miracle!*

I remember I all but choked with surprise: What do you mean, never knew democracy? Do you people not read? Andreas Kappeler, *Kleine Geschichte der Ukraine*—doesn't ring a bell? Were you not aware that the Ukrainian head of state, the hetman, was always an elected position, that was what gave it legitimacy? Or that we lived for three hundred years according to the Statutes of Lithuania, the most democratic code of law, if you'd care to remember, of its time? The Russian czar canceled it, of course, but not before 1840, and village courts continued to use it until the beginning of the twentieth century. There's even a special genre of charms in Ukrainian folk magic—judicial magic, spells to affect the outcome in court. Kyiv obtained the Magdeburg rights in 1494, and other Ukrainian cities had them too—so how do you figure, *your people never knew* the rule of law?

I blurted all that out in one gasping fit of patriotic outrage.

The German was a little surprised. He thought about it for a moment, and then said, Oh, was that when you were a part of Poland?

The Polish-Lithuanian Commonwealth, I corrected sternly, as if he were a C student in one of my classes. And we also had our own army—nothing to sneeze at, I assure you. And a mercantile middle class, we always had a strong middle class. A nation of small bourgeoisie, you know. Which is one of the reasons, by the way, that Stalin hated us as much as he did.

But all of this was a very long time ago, he objected, visibly disappointed: I think he really wanted to see a miracle and my academic prissiness was getting in the way. Today's generations don't remember it anyway, he said.

We were having this conversation while walking down Institutska Street, sucked into the massive, unanimous whirlpool of people around the Maidan: as one current carried us downhill toward the square, another ascended toward us; the sidewalks were filled with people, the street studded with myriad flickering lights. People carried candles set in plastic cups, and the whole scene looked like a vast vigil under the eternally dark December sky, lit up from below by the burning fires, flame-like orange clothes and pennants. I was shaky with lack of sleep, with exhaustion, tension, cold, and noise, and the answer slipped from my lips before I even realized what I was saying:

As you can see, I said, we very much do.

It came out very dramatic, like in a movie. My German just sort of stopped midsmile, stunned, and I realized—moments after I said those words—that I'd spoken the pure and holy truth. It was true: a sort of deeper, collective memory had come alive in us, even for those who weren't aware of it—a dam had burst open, our horizons fell back, and in one instant, millions of people discovered themselves to be in possession of knowledge and instincts they never suspected existed, of which they had never thought themselves capable. Perhaps *that* was the law of history: when a nation acts as a single collective soul, its collective memory, by some incomprehensible means, proves to be greater than the sum of its constituent parts. And everything then comes naturally and easily, as if people had known in advance how they ought to behave, and are, in fact, obeying the same centuries-old norms that had guided their ancestors. The warden at the tent city who, checking through the donated food, pulled out a bottle of vodka from a plaid bag with a trained motion said peaceably, "Didn't we ask you not to bring alcohol?" then opened it and poured the stuff into the nearest trash can, was doing exactly the same thing as his Kozak great-great-grandfather would have done on a boat setting out to sea. Except back in those days, they would've thrown the bringer of said vodka overboard too . . . But the point is, the warden's hand *knew* to grab the drink in that forgotten three-hundred-year-old motion all by itself, and the man *knew* he was doing the right thing. If you must have a miracle, then this was it: this ability to step into the current that flows beyond common time, through time, to be buoyed by it and to know that you are doing everything exactly right. And those kids who lined up in front of the cabinet building on the hill and stood there day in and day out, beating on steel drums—thump-thump-thump! thump-thump-thump! A signal, and the apocalyptic drumbeat scatters into a hail of quick, sharp bangs that get under your skin, and then shifts again, guttural, menacing—thump-thump-thump! thump-thump-thump! Those clueless undergrads, from the circus college, from all over, who found the discarded oil drums near Dynamo Stadium and decided to put them to *this* use, who stood on that hill for three weeks and never once stopped drumming, can be counted on to have been ignorant of the fact that this was exactly how the Kozak army used to be called together in the Sich, and the job they had taken upon themselves used to have a name—*dovbysh*—and that's exactly what those drummers would've done: they'd climb a hill, stand by a post, and begin sending their signal, with tympani and tambourines. And just as back then, these were the drums of war, war declared on those who'd secured themselves in the cabinet building—and everyone understood this, without a need for explanation, without the knowledge of historical facts, without textbooks, everyone knew it from the sound itself that had come from the ancient depths of memory and was recognized by all, and the drivers of the passing cars tooted their horns to the same beat. Things like this—they were every-where you looked. The law of the preservation of memory. A country that had previously existed only on yellowed medieval maps—*Ucraina terra Cosacorrum*—suddenly came to the surface. It hadn't disappeared at all, we realized—it was just hiding all this time, somewhere deep. Underground, but alive and invincible. There was no miracle at all; we just had to discover that countries do not disappear, no matter how many times the maps are redrawn, just as a person doesn't vanish just because his picture is destroyed.

Were I talking to Gustav about his book, I would tell him to put two maps next to each other on the frontispiece. In the morning after the first round of the election, when the TV showed the electoral map with the regions colored orange and blue and we were all calling each other with congratulations because we'd just glimpsed a real hope out there (in the streets of Kyiv, people began to smile again—the same people who days before had been glum and silent in the shops and on the metro), I got a call from my former department head. In the voice of a man on the verge of a great discovery, he said:

"You know, I was just looking at Coronelli's map—"

"Which map?"

"Vincenzo Maria Coronelli, the Italian who came through in 1657, you remember. The one with the embassy to the Hetman's government from Emperor Ferdinand III. The cartographer? He made a map of Ukraine?"

"I'm with you now. And?"

"You know, it matches. I'll have to check it against other sources, of course, but it looks like all the orange regions—that's what was Ukraine in 1657. Eastern Sarmatia. If you go further southeast, that's the Wild Fields, Piccola Tartaria, as Cornetti called it."

I hung up and checked the maps. They did match.

That's when I knew we'd won.

Two maps, Gustav. Just two maps: one from 1657, the other from 2004. Without them, your readers can't understand what all those millions of people in fire-colored scarves in the pictures are doing in the streets, and it's the easiest thing in the world to think it's all about the president they elected and whose name they are chanting. But that's not it, that's just a phantom, misdirection. What they are doing, in fact, is getting their country back—the one that sank to the bottom of history three hundred years earlier. And the amazing thing is—they know that's what they're doing, know it in their guts with a sudden and undeniable immediacy. That's why they are so happy.

He: Gustav takes a close look at almost every picture I took on Bankova Street, in front of the presidential administration (in the Soviet times, the building housed the Communist Party's Central Committee, I tell him, and he bats his copper-colored eyelashes at me, excited as a kid, Is that so? For him it must feel like glimpsing a dragon's lair straight out of a storybook and discovering that you could get a guided tour there), where the riot police stood in a solid wall behind their grey shields, and chooses many shots, almost all of them, to be copied to his discs, although, to my mind, they are not that interesting. But I know why he wants them, this show of naked force—government against its own people—it gives one pause. By virtue of physical presentation, Sweetie prompts in English (she came back, not with coffee, but with chips and nuts—she knows, my good girl, that I will chew anything when I'm nervous, like a demented rat, so I can't pout at her any longer). That's well said; I wouldn't have come up with that, if only things weren't as dire as Gustav must be thinking looking at the pictures now: turned out, my pal Vovchik went to school with a guy who was now one of the special forces officers; my fourth-floor neighbor's beloved nephew was also among those soldiers, and the woman went looking for him on Bankova, with sandwiches, because her sister had called and cried that the boys weren't getting any food, and didn't get to come off their shift, as they were supposed to, every hour, and stood there in the cold for four hours straight, and had to piss into their own boots. Gustav goes after a picture of an infantry colonel grabbing at the shields from the protesters' side: the colonel is square shouldered in a precise, disciplined way. You can see he's unaccustomed to bowing his fierce head as he had to do at the moment, to peer at the troops' faces under their visors—it's a good shot, a lucky one; everyone seemed to be snapping pictures of that colonel, as he spoke to the soldiers. "Sons," he pleaded in an utterly uncommanding voice that made all of our throats catch, "sons, boys, don't shoot, listen to me, don't shoot—I'll beg you on my knees." I know I wouldn't want to be one of those boys who sniffled wordlessly behind their visors, while the human sea in front of them chanted, "I'm brother to you, you're brother to me—lower your shield!" and the girls sang love songs and put sandwiches on the pavement before them. "What the fuck you think you're doing there? They're not dogs!" Vovchik's school pal the lieutenant yelled on the cell phone from the other side of the line, as if the sandwiches were Vovchik's personal fault, as if Vovchik personally managed the entire process of the sandwich offering or at least knew the person who did, as if anyone was managing anything at all, in those early days, when no one had a clue what they were supposed to do and just did whatever seemed necessary at any given moment, and things turned out splendidly—so Vovchik just came up as he was, camera in hand, to the teenagers who were prancing before the soldiers and passed on his pal's words, minus the obscenity, and in two minutes the sandwiches disappeared, never to be seen again.

The lieutenant called Vovchik again in the small hours of the night and told him, There are Russians standing behind us, inside the administration building, he said, like NKVD's antiretreat forces at Stalingrad. Others had spotted them too—the Russian special forces, gloried by their "cleanups" in Chechnya—and the suburbs and the city were abuzz on the internet following the route of their arrival: from a rural military airfield, the second or third where they requested landing (or so the rumor held, saying that the main base in Vasylkiv refused them, and the commander of that base did it early enough for the government to boot him off the job), through the base in Irpin, where they stopped god knows why (they could have been issued the Ukrainian uniforms to change into just as easily back in Moscow). Old-timers immediately recalled how much this resembled the Kremlin operation in '68 in Prague; we grabbed our cameras and rushed to where the internet reports had pinned these troops, but all we managed to catch was a string of large vans with blacked-out windows, parked in a side alley next to Mariinsky Park. Someone had incautiously leaned out the back door of one of them for a breath of air, and we took our shots of the open door and the inside of the van that looked more like a spaceship's cockpit, dense with control panels; then a few phrases were spoken, we heard an angry command—in Russian, as it is spoken by Russians, in hard, clipped syllables—the doors slammed shut, and that was that. There were unidentifiable black vans without license plates parked in an alley, and the very sight of them aroused unease; that's not something you can capture in a picture—the different feel you get from an empty van and a *muffled* van, full of people silently waiting for something. As we pointed our lenses, gaping like mouths opened in surprise, at the vans, it really felt like they pointed something back at us; they were watching us back, but only they were doing it through the optics of guns—I could feel it on my skin, and that was when, for the first time, I got really scared. Maybe it's because I've always been sort of, as Sweetie puts it, knuckleheaded, but I was never really scared throughout that entire autumn—the glum, hard, half-warlike autumn of my country when we all lived in a thickening fog of rumors, threats, raids, and demonstrations; I was not scared even though I photographed the blood on the pavement next to the Central Electoral Commission on the night of October 24 (and that was the first time I'd ever seen puddles of human blood on the asphalt, its spellbinding gleam in the streetlamp's light, silky and black like oil), and I'd seen plenty of similarly menacing caravans without license plates, brought to the city and tucked away on small streets—there were so many before the first and the second round of elections that I must've gotten five gigs' worth of pictures: sand-loaded dump trucks manned by immobile shadows and intercity buses with curtains drawn on their windows. The men who sat hidden in these buses sometimes came out to the stores to stock up on vodka and beer, and carried away several bottles at once, tucked under their arms with practiced skill, while opening beer cans with their teeth as they walked—churlish, brusque men with shaved heads, all dressed in track-suits under fake leather jackets, reeking of meanness and alcohol. They had come up from a darker underside of life, from prisons, people said, and were full of vengeful hatred of our comfortable, brightly lit city with all its cafés, young mothers, baby carriages, supermarkets, and orange ribbons tied to cars' antennas (and sure enough, the mere sight of a lens pointed at them was enough to throw them into a rage—once I almost lost my camera!). I bet they didn't do it just for the money, and the free drinks—I bet they enjoyed doing what they'd been brought here to do: slashing tires on those orange-beribboned cars, attacking polling stations at nights, smashing the ballot boxes and setting them on fire—I bet they got a vicious, deep pleasure from the shock they inspired in Kyiv's law-abiding citizens, who shied from them in supermarkets, snatching children out of the way. But when the revolution began and they ventured out into the light of the Maidan—tentatively, in small groups, instantly recognizable by the way they bristled all over like a hunting animal that wandered into someone else's territory—they were somehow instantly annihilated, disarmed like old warheads, dissolved without a trace like drops in an ocean. When people called out to them from the fires: "Hey, boys, come over, we'll get you something warm to eat!"; when people asked, "Where are you from, boys, do you have a place to sleep?" they retreated, squinting with suspicion and showing teeth, these nocturnal animals, used to people throwing rocks at them, not offering food, used to traps waiting for them behind kind words—and vanished back into the darkness, breathing their heavy breath, not finding any spoils at someone else's banquet. And unexpectedly a few peaceful souls emerged from their midst as well—those, who, instead of showing teeth, cracked open in the warmth, whose souls unburdened such depths of old injustices and rightlessness that I didn't have it in me to photograph them and lowered my camera. I have only this one picture of an old man, skinny as a bug, in a blue-and-white scarf, surrounded by the Maidan folks like a patient in a knot of concerned nurses. When they poured him a cup of tea and got him a sandwich, the man broke down crying; he just stood there and wept, shaking all over and unable to stop, and kept showing us, like some kind of exonerating evidence, his hands—a pair of black, gnarled wooden things, palms up. "All my life . . . ," he sobbed, in Russian, "all my life I worked in a mine . . . with these hands . . . and what for . . . for a piece of bread . . . The director promised a hundred hryvna . . . They brought us here, kept us in the railcar, haven't brought any food for three days . . . ," and kept thrusting those hands at people, with their unbending stubs of fingers, like proof of his clear background—the only thing he had to identify himself. No, not once did I get scared of anything, even when the city was full of troops, armed to the teeth (who started to take our side pretty much right away, battalion after battalion)—I only felt indignation boiling up in me, blood hammering angrily in my temples—Fuckers! They think they can do anything! But there, in the side alley next to the Mariinsky Park, for the first time, I saw death. It was there, and it was real. I couldn't ever tell Sweetie about this, or anyone else; I'd much rather not have learned this about myself at all: that there's something in me, deeper and larger than your basic physiological instinct of fear in the face of danger, something beyond the natural human fright that makes your mouth go dry and your muscles cramp—something else much more oppressive, a long, twisting spasm of memory. It was sickening, literally gut wrenching; it felt like I was recognizing something I had never experienced, something that had to come back to me from my Soviet childhood, back from the sight of my

old man using a pencil to dial a phone number because, for some reason, he believed that's how you blocked the "surveillance," or from my
mom's anxious shushing whenever I blurted out some especially inappropriate question while we stood in line in a store—all those unmarked
black cars, middle-of-the-night interrogations, floodlights aimed onto
one's face, fingers jammed in doors, genitals crushed under boots, everything that had gone on seventy years earlier right here, around the
corner, in the palatial building on Institutska Street, which was now
filled with protesters sleeping on the floor under the many warm blan-
kets donated by kindhearted Kyivites (and Sweetie was there, too, waiting in line to give a bag of warm clothes, and was so happy that she
remembered to bring her old winter boots that went to a big woman
from Polesia—the woman, on the first trip to the nation's capital in her
entire life, came dressed in her very best, and after spending a day in the
freezing cold shod in her fancy booties, was ready to schlep back to her
village, two hundred miles away, to get her old padded coat and a pair
of *valenki*). Seventy years ago, this was almost forty years before I was
born, and yet somehow I *knew* it, I recognized this apprehension that
was deeper than fear: like you're strapped to an operating table watching
a mad surgeon raise his knife above you (I recognize this "operating
table" look in a young kid from the Donetsk branch of the pro-oppo-
sition Pora! group; he'd been kidnapped before the first round of the
elections and the thugs who did it promised him they'd rape his sister
if he didn't quit—I remembered his face), and *this* version of myself—
an adult man who knows *this*—was not a version I could or wanted to
love, so there was no way I could share it with my precious Sweetie, my
all-seeing and all-understanding little hawk, because she wouldn't be
able to love this version of me either. Nor was there a chance I could
not live with that version of myself, and so, with one leg knee deep in
the snowdrift in front of that silent black convoy, I suddenly knew, clear
as day, that all I had left to do—all any of us had left to do—was to
stand our ground to the end, and do our men's work: to fight a good

YOUR AD COULD GO HERE

fight, and, when needed, to die an honest man, and that's that. I had no idea how one went about doing that, and none of us did; none of us had ever wielded anything more damaging than a camera, so we just walked from that alley to the hunting and fishing store, where they kindly told us, "You boys are a little late, we sold everything we had on the first day," and we marveled at that, and thought ourselves total losers, shaking our heads, swinging our snow-laden hats from side to side like a bunch of demented snowmen. The snow came down berserk, ran, melting, in rivulets down our faces, and we wandered away from the store arms-less but feeling initiated into an invisible warrior brotherhood whose presence we could feel vibrating all around us in the air, making us giddy, so we kept ribbing each other—Can you believe that? Sold out, you'd never thought of that, you're such a total nerd, it never occurred to you, did it? You fucking wimp . . .

This triggers another unphotographed moment from my memory. I think it happened in the same twenty-four-hour interval, or maybe the next day. It all ran together because I couldn't really tell you where and how we slept during that first week, but here it is: we're in the brightly lit, crowded fast-food restaurant in the underground mall below the Maidan, where we had staggered in to warm up after we ran out of tape and film and were frozen solid; the waitress, also semiconscious with fatigue but still smiling, said, "Boys, I'm out of everything except green tea, I'll pour you some, on the house, all right?" and that's when Vovchik's cell phone rang. It was his school buddy from SOF, calling to tell him that they—the officers—had made their decision: if they were ordered to open fire, they would turn their men around and face the Russian antiretreat troops, making themselves into a human shield to protect the people on the square—that's what they decided, our men, our officers and commanders who would lead us and whom we would follow to wherever they said, to take over armories and depots, to take our defiled country back—and on this note, while Vovchik, on his feet, delivered the word to the entire restaurant, which exploded in

163

triumphant cries and applause, I blacked out, face onto the table, next to my unfinished tea, for I don't know how long, a minute, a couple of minutes. When I came back, I found that someone had slipped a folded-up woolen scarf under my cheek, my own scarf that someone had carefully taken off my neck and placed onto the hard tabletop for me, all without me knowing it; the mug of tea, still steaming, stood right there, and I stared at the gleaming Formica top, at the woolly orange blob of my scarf and the white mug reflecting the bright overhead light as if I had become, all in one instant, this mug, and the light, and the scarf, and every single soul in that restaurant, and all of us at once who were outside, and everything and everyone that was around me, and I knew in my heavy, warming body that this—all of this together—this was *freedom*, and I would remember this moment for the rest of my life, because, as that boy from Rivne had said, "I won't have another one like it."

She: Our Dutchman is getting into it now, flashing his eyeglasses, pointing and nodding quick as a squirrel, and Sweetie's excited, too, a little flushed even; they can't point at the screen fast enough; they exclaim things; they jump up on the couch, a little like fans at a soccer match. They grab handfuls of nuts from the plate and then, forgetting, wipe their fingers on their trousers. They have a complete understanding, no words needed, intraverbal communication, that's what it's called. Like children. All men of the world are our children.

Except during wars, of course. Or popular uprisings. Also, revolutions. Then they are different. All visible history belongs to them, to men—they know how to band together.

I could see it: Sweetie would grab his camera and go to the Maidan every day like he was going to the front lines. They all banded together in what seemed like a single instant; they have the instinct of the pack, a boys' gang. Men's work. A man jumps off the bed, pulls on his pants, throws on a coat, blows you a kiss, I'll call, Sweetie, don't worry, and is out the door. On the very first day, when Liona's husband called—not

Liona herself, as always!—to say that the police had been ordered to prevent protesters from the regions from reaching the capital, there were roadblocks and checkpoints on the Odessa highway, and several thousand people were sitting there in their cars, unable to go forward, they sent word on the internet, my man—he, mind you, who commonly needs an hour to achieve consciousness in the mornings, with coffee and a shower, who would not be roused for any tea in China once he'd gone to bed at night—this man was at the door in three minutes, eager as a bird dog, car keys in hand: "I'm going, Sweets, get on the phone, call everyone we know with cars, we've got to get these people to the Maidan." In just over three hours, they got it done, he came home happy and fell asleep almost before he pulled off his clothes and threw them all over the floor. They made their strike, they got their people, they dispersed. Done.

There was something of the medieval chronicles in this lightning-fast banding-together, these instantly organized efforts that resembled military maneuvers, something from Samuil Velychko's seventeenth-century "Tale of the Kozak War," from Sarmatian tactics—something of the Haidamaks, of the Kozaks, something that belongs to our long line of rebels. Somehow, overnight, history ceased being the past, and I could see how things worked back then—exactly as they did now, except with different technologies. One no longer needed to light the fire atop the watchtower because we had satellite communications. On the second day: I hailed a cab to go to the Maidan, and dropped into the front seat with the first words that all of us had for any new person, "What do you hear?" The driver (orange flag stuck to the rearview mirror) had the radio turned to Era, and we both listened to the broadcast: they were reporting an attempt to break into the presidential administration building, and about the Russian Special Forces, and because Sweetie was also there somewhere, with his camera, I cried out, "Good god, what's next?"

"War is what's next," the driver said, sounding certain and game for it, words not so much spoken as bitten out of the air, and that's when I really looked at him. I looked and got even more scared—he meant it. The man was probably in his midthirties; olive skin, dark hair, a sharp profile fit to be cast in bronze, a hooked nose, a stubborn chin. All he needed was a pipe in his teeth and a Kozak haircut.

"War? God forbid, what are you saying," I fretted, but the man wasn't listening; he looked at the road ahead and spoke his mind— slowly, dropping words one by one like a miser who'd been saving them for three hundred years, like the words had ossified inside him and he had to chip them out—spoke hefty words of a man profoundly ill at ease with the intellectuals' endless blabbering:

"What've they got to do with us, huh? No, excuse *me* just a min- ute"—that was him preemptively shutting my peacemaking mouth that was ready to spew platitudes he didn't want to hear—he knew *his* answer. "Why are they bothering us? This is my home. I decide how I want to live here. What are they to do with it? They'll get what they deserve. All of it. We'll go to the woods if we have to. Fight a guerilla war."

I wanted to say, Don't!—but I didn't dare. The man's squinting Tatar eyes (his family was from the Kyiv region, he said, from Skvyra) gleamed with a menacing fire. I felt all the folk song romanticism of Kozak-Haidamak uprisings evaporate from me altogether with the quick-drying cold sweat of my fear. Of course, that's how it's always been: Sarmatian steppes, consecrated knives, woods and hideaways, the fierce, blood-chilling beauty and might that used to inspire such holy awe in our Romantic writers. *Who desires to suffer for the sake of our Christian faith, who wants to be impaled, quartered, and drawn, who yearns to be martyred for the holy cross, who's not afraid of death—join us!* Good god, indeed.

The driver's walkie-talkie sputtered on its own frequency, and I listened to the cabbies' chatter: "All right, Sanya, my shift's over, you gone to the Maidan yet?" They all did free runs to the Maidan at the end of their shifts—to take people home. They were our cavalry, the city's sleepless guard, like in the Middle Ages. You stop one of them, tell him you need help, and in fifteen minutes you've got half of Kyiv's motor pool there—and who will be our Velychko to write about them, what Dutchman, flying or otherwise, could fit them into the pages of a coffee-table book, this winged cavalry of our metropolis, Kyiv's triumphant cabbies of 2004? On the regular radio, meanwhile, the host asked a well-known poet to pick a song for them to play to help lift the tension a little, and the woman asked to please put on "Let My People Go." Yes, please, I agreed in my mind, riding toward the rising million-throated drone of the crowd, the lights, the thickening human mass in the flickering of orange—a whirl of faces like leaves tussled and spun in the November wind, lit by a magnificent, Rembrandtesque light, and I heard a voice say in my mind, clear as a bell, These are my people, and felt my breath catch in my throat—please—and Louis Armstrong's coarse voice on the radio was asking for the same thing, please, and the poet, and the radio show host in his studio, and the people who were walking toward the Maidan, candles in their hands, to join others in singing the national anthem, hands awkwardly placed on their heart, please, let my people go. Lead them out of Egypt. Lead them out of this darkness before the winter, the darkest time of the year. Lead them to the quiet waters, to clear skies. To the christened world, to the blessed land. A pizzicato note, a breaking voice, a sob.

He: Actually, he's a good soul, this Gustav, and he's got his head screwed on right. I'm beginning to see, from what he chose (and he's picked at least twice as many shots as he'll need), the narrative of the book that he's building in his mind—he is really interested in the Maidan itself, the people on the square and the streets around it, and not the Maidan's *stage*, populated by the politicians and rock stars. As an expert visual storyteller he grasps instinctively what has remained hopelessly beyond the reach of common, politics-obsessed journalists;

that there was never a direct, simple connection between the stage and the Maidan; that all those people there, whose number exceeded a million every single night, spent all those weeks living and organizing themselves independently, with their own centers of gravity and energy meridians, and the stage served as a sort of temporary center to which we looked for instruction, the symbolic capital of our temporary nation—yes, a country, I tell Gustav, a promised land, and Gustav doesn't laugh, doesn't take this as a joke but waits, eyes eager and curious, for further explanation. Well, I tell him, we basically lived for three months—how should I put it?—with a growing sense of brotherhood or something like it (I'm short of words again, where's Sweetie when I need her?). We all loved our neighbors as ourselves—and this started even before the elections, before the first round, when just the sight of a bravely displayed orange ribbon was enough to make your day, as if you'd seen the dearest old friend, and you walked down the street or drove literally awash in love, among people smiling kindly at you, people waving at you, honking their horns in greeting, and you felt yourself lifted above the earth, eager to hug and kiss everyone—they were all so dear, so good and beloved, and so beautiful—I've never seen so many beautiful people in the streets! I remember one day, in the middle of October, when the ribbons were still hard to find and people were just beginning to get orange scarves and stuff, I saw a young woman walking down Khreshchatyk: fire-red hair loose in the wind, she proudly carried in both hands a huge bunch of fire-colored leaves, like a lit torch, her own firebrand, and I kicked myself for not having the camera with me as I watched her march—this Nike, a priestess of freedom—and the rest of Khreshchatyk also watched, awed and instantly in love, and this unassailable force field of warmth, gratitude, and trust spread wider and wider—we were the City of God, we lived as men are supposed to live, as people should be living all over the world, all the time, you see? So when hundreds of thousands of people flooded the city from other towns and villages, the doors of our homes flew open like open arms, and we all marched down, in hundreds and thousands ourselves, to the Maidan, to the Trade Unions Building, which housed the organizers, and said, I have a room, and I have two, I have a country house that's sitting empty, I could put forty-fifty people there, I want to give money, and I have ten sacks of potatoes, and I have nothing so give me a broom to keep this place clean . . . The slogan "Love Will Overcome All!" appeared on walls and cars, and it did—and who would have thought we had so much love in all of us, all we needed was to be freed of fear, to break it, like a dam, and our love that was held back for who knows how long and dispensed in miserly trickles for the closest friends and family spilled out in an ocean of light, illuminating the darkest time of the year. After we won, this city of three million people functioned for an entire month without a single road accident, people fell over themselves to be solicitous of each other, crime went down tenfold, and folks smiled to each other in the streets as if we all lived in a village where everyone knows everyone and says hello to strangers; it lasted for weeks, this feeling—that you could say hello to anyone and he would respond happily, as if he'd been waiting to see you; there was so much love that for a while it seemed we could fill the entire world with it, never mind that horde of shaved-headed slaves under their different banners (which they shed, throwing them onto the ground, as soon as their slave drivers looked the other way). I'm just sorry I don't know how to communicate all of this in English, but it also seems that Gustav somehow understands anyway, he's on the same brain wave, so I say, Why? Because I can't hold it in anymore; I've been carrying this question inside me since that very day on Khreshchatyk when I stood there lost with the unlit cigarette in my mouth and realized it was all over. Why can't we live like this *all the time*, why is the world so fucked up that we cannot, and then again, if we had been able to live like that—for months!—and we weren't a handful of saintly Mother Teresas but millions of perfectly common, regularly stressed-out and busy people, then it must be possible at least in principle? Mustn't it? And it wasn't hard at all—it was as if you'd been drifting down your life year after year, working hard to shove the shit that's floating around away from you, to stay more or less clean, and then suddenly you hit this current, a massive underwater gulfstream, and it grabs you and carries you with impossible speed, with a thunderous, mighty roar (The sound! That's what's missing from these pictures, damn it! The round-the-clock hum of the crowd, the clapping thunder of chants that echoed from the buildings' walls and reverberated to the far shore of the Dnieper and, after several days of booming insomnia, began to rumble inside your own head; we all went around, especially during the first week, with that internal soundtrack, the thrill of ascension, as if your blood had been wired to a woofer and rolled down your veins with a growl, like the mass of people stomping down the streets and the metro tunnels, as if you yourself expanded to the size of the entire city, and all of this should have very well short-circuited and if it didn't, it was only because you yourself, with your separate, individual life, had temporarily ceased to exist—everything that belonged to you, and nobody else, had been pushed to the background, suspended like a piece of software waiting for an upgrade. There was no room left to hide in the face of the danger we were up against, neither at home, nor at work, so we came out, all together, not just into the streets from our individual apartments, but out of our individual lives, crossing the thresholds of our I's and there, once we had all stepped beyond our limits, it opened up and embraced us—the limitless ocean of love. We saw our promised land among its waves—we glimpsed it, real and tangible, for a few weeks, and then it began to fall apart, to grow distant again, sinking in the muddy political swirl of negotiations, agreements, bluffs, turf battles, the everyday pageant of human flaws). The thing is, I say, that all of this proved to be within our reach, only apparently separated from us, as if by a wall, as if it existed in a different dimension, but I now know it exists, it's reachable—our country of the possible—like an underwater current, a subterranean river. We had brought it to the surface; we had cracked its path open, with one titanic blow, and it had flowed through us, searing us with its living flame, only to fall from our sight again, like a myth, like that Sarmatia my Sweetie talks about, our ideal motherland, in which we were *supposed* to live and for which we were ready to die—so why can't we keep it forever? Why is it that the most we are capable of is to glimpse it once and then just keep telling stories of that one miraculous appearance, until the end of time, twisting our testimony, patching up the truth with lies, rewriting, repainting things, faking small details, photoshopping until we're left with something glossy and hard, like a piece of candy, that no one can believe, and we'll have to start all over again, looking for the promised land from scratch?

She: "Our culture has no fear," Gustav says. "No memory of fear."

Sweetie and I just sort of stare at him, startled by this apparent non sequitur.

"We're more open to manipulation," he explains. "We have no immunity. We don't know how to recognize real danger."

We stare.

"Take advertising," he says, "as an example. There's so much illicit violence in it: a girl throws her boyfriend out of a boat, a kid throws his parents out of a car—all to take possession of their potato chips. This is understood to be humorous. When you mention visual fascism, people look at you like you're crazy. They all believe that fascism, communism—that's all gone and forgotten. People don't see that they're being manipulated with the same methods. They don't see they're being herded into the prison of virtual reality. When something really happens, we are defenseless as children. Like those kids who get into an argument, fight, and kill their classmate and then stare at the body and cannot understand why he is not getting up, because in their computer games, you come back to life even if you'd been shot. There is no death, only simulacra. We are being trained to live in simulacra, and we are not afraid. We have no antidote."

We don't say anything; what could you say?

"That, of course, is a small example," Gustav says, apologetically.

I feel I'm beginning to understand.

He's looking for immunity, this dear soul. He's wandering the world, very much like the Flying Dutchman, shooting and publishing his Middle Eastern, Balkan, Eastern European, and who knows what other books—all in his quest for a way to find reality. He wants to juxtapose real sweat and blood, love and hate to the avalanche of simulacra. He wants to see for himself and to show others the world in the gaps and holes in the opaque sticky film of information, where the true, uncreated nature of things shows itself like raw flesh in a wound.

"You know," Sweetie says suddenly, "our former president, the one who sat out the revolution at his dacha, he, people say, also couldn't believe what he was looking at when he saw Maidan on TV. He was convinced it was CGI."

We laugh, all three of us, united in a shared impulse of wordless understanding and strange relief. It feels like we have accomplished something here tonight, like we have won a small victory. We've defended something, a patch of reality; we've washed a window clean—and are basking in the sunshine. "Boys," I say, "isn't it time we had a drink?" *"Tya-koo-yoo."* Gustav butchers the only Ukrainian word he'd learned, and we all laugh again.

The boys get up to wash their hands; I glance at the screen before shutting down the computer. The shot there, taken from a low vantage point looking up, shows the line of shields and below them flowers and burning candles, and it looks as if they are bursting straight from the earth itself, breaking through the asphalt and the tamped-down mass of millennial snow—small agglomerations of light surrounded in the picture with uncannily bright halos.

YOUR AD COULD GO HERE

TRANSLATED BY HALYNA HRYN

They were the most splendid leather gloves I had seen in my life: finished to the gossamer weight of a rose petal, with a dazzling, luminous bay hue that instantly brought to mind the Imperial horses and their silky croups at the Hofreitschule, delicately laced with a finely cut design at the wrist (all of it handmade, my goodness!), they immediately wrapped my hand in the firm loving grasp of a second skin, and one was compelled henceforth to stroke the hand thusly gloved with the same reverence as an Imperial steed. One wanted to stroke and admire the hand, spreading one's fingers against the light, making a fist and letting it go—Ah!—and never take such beauty off. In a word, walking away from those gloves was beyond my power.

They existed—as befits any work of art—as a singular artifact. Everything in that glove shop was singular, not one pair resembled another, each more fantastic than the next, but these—these caught my eye the second I walked through the door, like the glance of a dear fellow creature in a crowd. And they were exactly my size: I told the gentle old man in a knitted vest who sat behind the counter I wore a size six, but he just shook his head. No, he said in his slightly raspy Viennese English, you're not a six but a five and a half, here, try these. But I always buy sixes! You'll be telling me, miss, he laughed, I've been making these gloves for fifty years. Oh, you make these? And sell them? So you are the owner? Yes, he confirmed, with the quiet pride of a master craftsman who knows his worth. The tiny store on Mariahilferstraße, which I entered on a whim with a purely touristy I wonder what's here? transformed into a fairy-tale forest hut—the one to which the fleeing heroine stumbles at nightfall and where she meets the master of the underground kingdom who chops his own wood, carries his own water, and makes his own supper. I dearly wished I spoke better German—and the old man, better English—we could hardly talk about anything important with our tourist-minimum vocabularies. I adore such dapper gentlemen in vests—in my own country they were exterminated as a species fifty years ago, shipped out to Siberia in cattle cars, and their absence from the universe in which I grew up was still evident—as visible as silhouettes cut out of group pictures, with the names written underneath. It warms my heart every time I see what became of them in other, less chaotic lands. To spend fifty years sculpting such gloves, from tanning and cutting to the finishing stitches around the eyelet holes that would adorn imaginary hands—does this not mean becoming the Lord of Gloves, the one and only, not just in Vienna, but in the whole wide world?

I named them my sunshine gloves—they glowed. I could see their aura in the paper bag into which the Lord of Gloves packed them for me—with his name imprinted, and the address—Mariahilferstraße, 35—and the telephone numbers (landlines—everything about him was so Old Worldly, solid, with a distant nineteenth-century breeze of faith in an ordered world, a world in which things are made to last forever because the makers know that things outlast people and will one day serve for our descendants as the only tangible proof of our existence). Even through the paper bag, I could feel the silky softness of the rose-petal leather. I kept touching it and smiling. I had been entrusted with a treasure, in the fairy-tale forest hut—a talisman from a different age. Who today would labor over such gloves—every pair unique, every pair a single copy—to sell them for those same fifty euros they charge for the thick chunks of mitts in the mall across the street?

Later I got myself a special designer sweater to go with the gloves. A special jacket. A special pair of fine suede pants. I had the persistent feeling that my sunshine gloves stood out no matter what I wore, no matter how carefully I selected it, and they most certainly did: they demanded different lines—designed by someone *in love with their model*. With the gloves, I could tell the mood with which another item of clothing was conceived and made: they accepted some, but rejected other garments without any apparent logic, but irrevocably and at once. In the fall of 2004 they suddenly fell in love with a flamboyant fiery scarf, which I then wore throughout the entire Orange Revolution—never mind that the scarf did not come from a fashion designer and cost a third of what the gloves had. They were perfect together, and press photographers all to the man wanted my picture in that orange scarf and my sunshine gloves—No, no, don't take them off, just leave everything as is!

Here one rather expects a certain development of the plot: Julio Cortázar, for instance, or even Peter Haigh would have definitely written a story (and Taras Prokhasko would have told one in a pub, being too lazy to write it!) in which the gloves quietly move on from approving garments to approving—or disapproving—people and begin to rule the heroine's life, guiding her to the authentic and away from the fake, sweeping out from her life's wardrobe false friends, unnecessary obligations, and ultimately her own masques, stripping her down like a cabbage to her bare core, and then we might discover that there is no core, that the heroine herself does not pass the test of the magical gloves, so in the end she has to perish in a dramatic fashion, to disappear, be disposed of, and the gloves, fine as a rose petal, will remain gloving in their silky-chestnut splendor on a desk, waiting for their new owner. Something along those lines.

What actually happened was different. What happens is always different from what we read about later. In May of 2005 I did what I had never, in my recollection, which begins more or less at the age of three, done: I lost a glove.

Maybe I lost it getting out of a cab. At least, it was not anywhere on the sidewalk—I retraced my steps along the entire length of my route, where I could have, theoretically, dropped it, looking hungrily into every single trash can. All in vain: the glove was gone. Evaporated. Vanished. Rose up to the sky and flew away. Took off and flew into the wide blue sky. Burned to a crisp like the Frog Princess's skin. My sunshine glove from my left hand. The hand was left naked.

And I don't think I wept like that since the age of three. I mean, of course, I'd cried countless times, and had abundant occasions and much weightier reasons to do so in my more or less coherently remembered forty years since I was three—but weeping like this, truly, never. I wept like the child who discovers for the first time the injustice of the world, which she had begun to believe to be orderly and safe. Adults call it a life crisis—and instead of weeping, they usually climb into a noose or call a therapist. Or look for other ways to glue together the shattered self, because the older you get, the more you see that really life can be put back together somehow, made bearable, although it will never be the way it was before, but that's okay, it's going to be all right, really, things have a way of fixing themselves, as long as you're okay. That, specifically, is what everyone at home told me: Stop being a child, you have the other glove, you have the address, you have a book coming out in Austria, you're going to Vienna anyway—stop by the store and just ask them to make you a new one! You could even send them the right one by mail, my husband said, call them, make the order, and have the left one ready for pickup when you're there. There was no way I was doing that, though, no mailing—for me, that was somehow out of the question. To pass the surviving glove into unknown hands, to entrust its fate to a faceless tracking system felt like a betrayal to me, as if I would be confirming I deserved to have been abandoned by the lost glove, as the folk song goes, "You knew not how to honor us . . ." No, I had to do it in person, I had to face the Lord of Gloves in his forest hut at Mariahilferstraße. One step into a side street off the busy shopping thoroughfare, push the right door—and I will be again in that cozy, draping silence, green colored, as if tinged with the virgin forest outside the windows but in fact because of the green lining the display case, filled with the gorgeous, one-of-a-kind pairs of gloves in liver-bay, black, buckskin and roan. Perhaps the Lord of Gloves will offer me tea and we will have a chance to converse a bit, about important things—such as pursuing his craft for fifty years, despite the rising flood of Mariahilferstraße outside his windows. I memorized several particularly difficult phrases in German, in case he couldn't understand my English.

The prospect truly made me nervous.

On that trip, I barely had an hour to spare in Vienna and had to fit in the trip from Hotel Mercure, near the Westbahnhof, to Mariahilferstraße and back. So I started dialing the numbers listed on my paper bag (in which I carried the right glove) as soon as I landed and kept calling until the cab came to pick me up at the hotel. There was no answer on either line. I felt a sick knot in my throat; my heart hammered. In forty minutes, I was due for an interview with a reporter from a popular weekly, back in my hotel's lobby. At least I long memorized everything one says to a reporter about one's book, in well-polished blocks of text, like an audio guide—please press ten now. It was fall, the air beaded with moisture, and early lights glowed along the inappropriately festive Mariahilferstraße. I wore the same tweed coat I had on the day I lost the left glove. Here? the driver asked. Here, I said: at least the door was where it should be, I was looking straight at it.

Nothing else, however, was there.

It was like coming home at night, opening the door with your key, and seeing someone else's apartment, with entirely different furniture, long inhabited by strangers who, disturbed, turn to face you in alarm. There were scarves, and belts, and some high-tech home decor, plastic, not wood. Different lighting, vertical cubical display windows, everything a sterile white, a crowd of people, and a completely different smell. Instead of entering a magical parallel world, I was standing in the accessories section of a large department store. *Grüß Gott, darf ich Ihnen helfen?* asked a glamorous young woman with a smart haircut and fluorescent fingernails. Stammering in my English, I pulled out my paper bag, the talisman that would let me be recognized at the entrance to the other world. (What if, I'd desperately thought, there's still another room here, and the forest hut is now there?) Desperately looking in all directions in search of a secret door (maybe behind that curtain? No, that looks like a closet . . .), I tried to explain: I had one glove, which I bought here two years ago, and I lost the other. Please, over here, the woman pointed with her blinking nails—the gloves are here! Faceless chunks of grey hung from clothes pegs like carcasses in a butcher shop. No, you don't understand, I want one exactly like this . . . This is Roeckl, the woman repeated, and the brand name sounded piercing, like the cawing of the carrion-feeding crow—Here are our gloves! Mine appeared to irritate her, like a piece of evidence testifying to a covert misdeed in which she, too, had a part: she kept saying *Roeckl, Roeckl,* as if she meant Shoo, shoo! Where is the older gentleman who used to have a store here, a glove maker? I asked and Miss Crow screeched as if stung by a wasp, in German, *Er ist tot!* Slamming that word like a door into my face. Then, in a nicer voice, she repeated in English: The elderly gentleman has died, Roeckl bought the place.

When did that happen? I made an effort to keep down the trembling in my knees—I already knew the answer.

In the spring, Miss Crow said, sometime in May.

In May, wasn't it. It was pointless to ask for the exact date, everything was clear: he took his glove as he was leaving, the dead sometimes do that—when they want to leave the living something to remember them by. Something more reliable than mere words.

Doors swung open and closed, a plump lady in a down jacket was asking to see a wallet, behind me a pair of Russian women chatted loudly about scarves. Passersby looked into the windows. A cell phone rang. Nothing was left, nothing to remind me. He died—he's been disposed of. Gone to be recycled. And what about the gloves? My sunshine gloves and other, moonlight gloves (Mars gloves, Jupiter gloves, Venus gloves, Saturn gloves?)—gloves for love, gloves for mourning, liver-bay, black, buckskin and roan, that had inhabited this space so recently, what became of them? Were they disposed of at a garage sale?

Aloud I asked, trying to sound more or less composed, Wasn't there anyone to inherit the business? Miss Crow made a face that simultaneously expressed the appropriate respect for the deceased and a barely indulgent sympathy for the total unsustainability of his business model—meaning, well, you must understand. Yes, I understood. Understanding, in fact, is my job, that's what writers are for—to try to understand everyone and everything and put this understanding into words, finished to the gossamer fineness of a rose petal, words made supple and obedient, words cut to hold the reader's mind like a well-made glove that fits like second skin. One can't do this without understanding, no matter how regularly our kind appears on official paperwork under the rubric of "Entertainer" and gets paid not so much for the hours of labor but for the brand. *Roeckl.* The old store's location smack in the middle of the main shopping street must've cost a fortune. I can imagine the bidding war that broke out after the Lord of Gloves died, the space is practically a mansion. But can anyone tell me: Is there no one left in Vienna who makes gloves like these? Is there anyone left even still alive who knows how to make gloves like these? Can it possibly be that I became witness to the death of an entire art—like one of those Pacific Island languages that disappears from linguistic atlases every year, sealing off for us, like treasure caves, the parallel worlds they give expression to?

Why didn't he pass his craft to anyone? Why wasn't there the right person to pass it to, another slightly crazy, bearded nerd in love with women's hands, or simply with a girl to whom he wanted to give the most beautiful gloves in the world? One doesn't even have to be all that crazy for this—the Lord of Gloves probably himself started there, and the girl refused him, most likely, and for the next fifty years he touched women's hands with all his unrequited tenderness but all of us who bought his gloves dragged off, bit off a bit of it for ourselves, like hungry geese, and before we knew it, it was all gone. How could it be that no one stopped, no one asked to be taught this language? Every great master has to have students—and he was a great master, I still have proof I could show you, look at this chestnut glove I have, look how delicate and sensitive it is, like a living thing, don't you want to try it on?

Try it! Please, girls, don't be afraid . . . don't run away!

No, this last line is me making things up, that didn't happen. I didn't stand there brandishing the master's last surviving piece in front of the alarmed saleswoman and did not deliver a fiery oration that would scare the customers (although we could have yet another short story here, in which the heroine is taken away by the police, a little Hollywood, a little homage to Woody Allen, but squarely in a feminine sensibility—why not, the sixties are coming back, female rebellion is trending). Instead, I politely purchased from Miss Crow a pair of her mass-produced mitts in a less-than-acidic color (and never wore them): it was my way of paying her for the information. Then I walked, without seeing where, along Mariahilferstraße, stumbling—*Entschuldigen!*—into other pedestrians' bodies and thought, swallowing tears mixed with rain, I could write a story! Oh, what a story I could write—winged and sure footed, as if dictated by heaven itself, I could go lock myself in my hotel room right now, and write it—if I didn't have the interview to go to, and then my reading in the city library, and then a dinner with the organizers, and my flight at the crack of dawn—the usual schedule of our literary marketplace. I, too, work regular retail. The Lord of Gloves was mistaken to trust in me.

And you, too, should forget everything just read here. One day, someone will erase all of our scrupulously crafted words from their electronic depositories in order to save some space, and on the white screen of the new and improved supergadget of fall 2063 we will see the flashing slogan that already so often covers up the vacant spaces of bricked-up doors:

YOUR AD COULD GO HERE.

III

THE TENNIS INSTRUCTOR

TRANSLATED BY HALYNA HRYN

I irritate him, it's obvious. Nothing surprising—when I think of how I must look, a veritable cow, legs awkwardly spread and tennis racket clenched convulsively in my fist (how in the world is one supposed to look graceful in this unnatural pose?—like those two young things on the next court, some fat cat's daughters, no doubt: the blonde Barbie on the right keeps tossing her long, loose, picture-perfect hair held back by a white headband—she knows, the bitch, she's gorgeous!—I experience my own arms as poorly fit artificial limbs, and the legs too), I make myself sick at this tragicomic spectacle and feel genuinely sorry for the dude. It can't be fun, can it, for this athletic bro to be running drills with a gawk like me—and he must think I'm a moron!—for ten bucks an hour—I know I couldn't do it even for a hundred! But there's nothing I can do to help him, except maybe try and explain that I'm really not as dumb as I look on the court. Like that's going to make him feel better.

"Wrist tight, fingers loose," he repeats patiently, catching me for the umpteenth time with a deadly stiff palm and authoritatively unwrapping my rigor mortis clasp. "The *racquet* should move freely."

(His *racquet*, which he pronounces pretentiously as *racquette*, grates my ear much the same as I grate his with my irreverent *racket*, which he corrects every time with a shade of disgust: every trade has its pride.)

"I know," I mumble like the class dunce, and really, I do know, I catch everything he says perfectly the first time (I stick to *racket* not because I don't know better, but because I physically cannot make myself utter the pompous *racquette*, my whole sense of language rises up in revolt!) and there really is no need to repeat the same thing for the hundredth time, and to what end, when the information received becomes hopelessly stuck in my brain and in no way can be transmitted to my limbs—I'll bet paraplegics endure this same agony of humiliation. When I was four, my father bought me a bicycle. He must have had the day off and decided to sacrifice all of it on the altar of paternal duty, and by the end of it, I could be said to have grasped the concept of pushing the pedals with my feet and steering with my hands at the same time, but the only thing I recall from that entire day—one of the scariest days of my life—is the mute terror of my body, rigid with the desperate longing for the torment to end. The spectacle of me on a bicycle brought kids running from all over the block to stand around and offer, loudly and for several hours straight, advice and commentary to assist my father in his task. He probably enjoyed being at the center of such unanimous attention—I, on the other hand, crushed and helpless under the collective pressure like a kitten hurled out into the middle of a roaring stadium, was as good as electrocuted—the wires connecting the first and second signal systems were resolutely cut, leaving the ability to understand instructions and the ability to reproduce movement forever separated, and thus for the whole afternoon my father, not noticing a thing, faithfully wheeled a victim of catalepsy around the yard—a tiny, frightened, motionless body curled up on a bicycle seat. Maybe if I'd burst into tears then, my whole life would have turned out differently. Or if my parents had divorced earlier. As a weekends-and-holidays parent, a role that demands no pedagogical skill (or ability to understand another human being), my father was as sublime as an inventive lover, and from the time I was eight, our excursions to the zoo, to theaters and museums, with the obligatory concluding ritual of ice cream in the café, most resembled amorous rendezvous, especially in the sweet and anxious anticipation they engendered beforehand. In terms of intellectual maturity, I think we may have been peers already, and the game excited us equally: my father, may he rest in peace, knew how to play much better than he knew how to live. As do most men, for that matter.

Like this one here telling me, with a note of scarcely discernable superiority: "Relax now, you're not at work! This is supposed to be fun."

Hmm, but *you* are supposedly at work, mister, aren't you—or have you purposely found a job where you can play and get paid for it too? This "fun" of his he is eager to manifest at all times—when he takes the racket from me for a demonstration (I mean, *racquette* of course—I wonder if he addresses it as *vous* in his mind—a pretty expensive toy actually, almost 350 euros, I practically blew my whole honorarium on it at the Reebok store in downtown Stockholm: I thought it would make a nice present for Oleh because I was feeling guilty about something I no longer remember, which has been happening more and more recently, and when Oleh, after a long lecture on account of Reebok—because why didn't I talk to him first, there are even better, more exclusive stores in Sweden—sent me off with my own gift to these idiotic lessons, I went feeling even more guilty, which raises the question, Is this what my better half was after in the first place?).

"See heere, ma'am," he says (dear Lord, what a way with words he has, see *wheere*? but, unlike him, when I say *racket*, I don't frown, not a single muscle in my face moves, I'm a veritable tobacco-store Indian!) and slows down his movements deliberately, for instructional purpose, a film in slow motion, and I can't shake the feeling that he's showing off a little in front of me—he is easy on the eyes, and I do enjoy looking at him, he's good at this: the racket sweeps up as an extension of his arm and then connects with the trajectory of the tennis ball, there's even a hint of infinity here, of a projection of oneself into the universe with its own mathematical function and limit (the limit in this case being the ground, or else the wall, which the ball meets with a dull thud that sounds a little bit like a moan—if not for this wall, it would fly on and on to eternity). It is only at such moments, when I am watching him,

that I relax: what can I say, it's a pretty sight, and he would make a
Hollywood-ready couple with that blonde hussy working her hips on
the next court, him dark haired and all, but I definitely see no place for
myself here—I will never be able to do this, you can point a gun at me
and I still won't be able to move like that. Any situation that requires
me to go through the process of acquiring a physical skill in public
instantly throws me thirty years back, to that same little bike—I go
deaf, blind, enter a stupor, and wait for it all to end so that I can be set
free again. My greatest nightmare in high school was gym class, from
which, despite my best efforts (I even pretended to faint once and succeeded in falling quite convincingly, but still lightly enough not hurt
myself) I never did manage to get exempted. In high school I figure
they must have suspected me of permanent uterine bleeding, like that
poor woman with the issue of blood for twelve years that Jesus cured. To
swim, at least, I learned on my own—in a deserted spot, risking death
by drowning countless times. I never did learn to dance properly—
waltzing with me would be something like whisking the Motherland
Monument up on the slopes of the Caves monastery in Kyiv, minus the
sword—but dancing, fortunately, always contains a sexual element, and
that's what saves me, sex being the only sphere where I can compensate
for my otherwise total physical cretinism. Well enough not to have been
found out yet.

And my poor instructor, too, suspects nothing. In his naive mind,
the explanation for my unnatural awkwardness is that I spent too much
time at my computer—"Yours is a sedentary profession," he says with
a hint of respect and advises me earnestly, the dear boy, to go for some
kind of special massage because at this rate I'll earn myself a herniated
disk, and I promise him that I will definitely schedule some, just as soon
as I finish my article for the *Atlantic Monthly*, and the conversation ends
there until the next lesson, when the whole story repeats itself. How can
I explain to him that there is no way to relax me short of knocking me
out? A good pint of cognac would do it, to be sure—then I could dance

whatever, wherever, put me on a catwalk, a bar, or a float, like a carnival queen, it's been known to happen. My body becomes Play-Doh, responding to the rhythm of the music alone, dissolving in it before soaring to absolute freedom, but those movements are all instinctive, as in sex, but once I'm sober again, teaching me any moves, however simple, is not something anyone has ever done, there are no methods for it. If this guy succeeds, he could write a dissertation about me. Put a patent on it. Why not—at least there'd be some benefit from all this.

But instead he flashes his eyes boyishly, hands the racket back to me—now you do it. In other words, have fun. Hell no, brother: you can drill me like a circus bear, but there'll be no fun in it, neither for the bear nor for me. There'll never be freedom in my conditioned tricks.

"I have a blister," I say, and think to myself, Oh my god, I'm like Mavka the forest nymph in that classic play when she says, I cut my hand, because she can't bring herself to cut down the wheat. He's going to ask me, like Mavka's prospective mother-in-law, Doing what? and he'll be absolutely right! Nonetheless, there really is a small blister at the base of my thumb next to the groove rubbed red by the racket handle: I'll have something to show Oleh for my efforts, let him see! And if *he* doesn't feel guilty after this . . .

"That's because you're not holding it right," my instructor answers indifferently: my boo-boo obviously makes no impression on him, typical male insensitivity (but when it comes to their own boo-boos, heavens help us, they all turn into the same mewling baby). Something else draws him in, though: he holds my hand a moment longer, studying it as if he's going to read my fortune, and lets go in response to my quizzical look—flushing, if only just a touch!

"You have such delicate hands," he explains, as if trying to justify himself. My laugh is loud and exaggerated—mainly from the relief of finally landing on my own turf: "Is that a diagnosis or a compliment?"

The instructor is flustered like a kid: word games are my Wimbledon, now the best he can do is follow the mean slice of my serve with his eyes—clearly he's not in the habit of returning balls like these, and I have no good reason to make the guy blush this way. I fell for Oleh precisely because almost from the minute we met, he rushed fearlessly to meet my every serve, showing himself to be a true partner, capable of staying the course. Having let his mind go inert at monotonous office dealings, he clearly savored exercising those stiff, inactive parts of the brain, returning most of my balls with growing enjoyment, and responding with an unselfish and sincere admiration to those he'd miss, pushed far off the court—almost like he was about to applaud me, the way I want to when I watch my tennis instructor play from the bleachers: there's an ecstatic, quasi-religious awe in the face of pure artistry. It was precisely during one such moment that Oleh burst out with a confession of his love—I still remember his mesmerized gaze in the moment just before he spoke—it was only later that I realized that was probably the most spontaneous act of his life, which was otherwise rather rigidly planned and controlled, but at that time we were still genuinely happy. You have to give him credit, he's got that athlete's staying power: Oleh's been playing tennis since childhood, hasn't he, and it gave him an education. And in this case, too, he'll get his way: after many hours, this poor fellow here will manage to drill "Mrs. Martha" (as he addresses me, although this form obviously makes him uncomfortable, he's not used to it, it feels foreign, but he doesn't dare simply switch to the first name, and so both of us, by silent agreement, teeter politely on the impersonal Mr. and Mrs.) into a state where she will be capable, albeit without particular relish, of accompanying her very own husband to the tennis courts in the role of a rather useless partner, but a hitting partner nonetheless, a squire. They say it's good for the marriage. It strengthens the family, they say, when the husband gets the opportunity to demonstrate to you, to the fullest extent, how pathetic you really are. What a hopeless squid of a klutz you are, for example—and he still loves you: you may not be much, but you're all his. I can see it now: In six months or so, come early fall, I'll be scrambling in confusion all over this court, unable to return Oleh's fierce, merciless serves—he can be vengeful, he can derive real pleasure from someone else's humiliation. I'll run after the ball when it's hit out of the court like a puppy and dive into the bushes to retrieve it while Oleh assumes an Olympian pose on the other side of the net and waits, slapping his thigh with the racket and smiling indulgently. And then we'll drive to a restaurant where he will clear his plates like a ravenous teenager and observe, before dessert, as he wipes his mouth with a napkin, that I smoke far too much, which will be true, I'll be smoking like a chimney. We'll talk little, because what's there to talk about anyway?

As God is my witness, I am always happy to play along, to deliver, in the course of any shared venture, a small, inconspicuous blow job to his erect ego, to underscore deliberately, occasionally with a touch of outright grotesque, my own ineptitude in all things in which he indeed surpasses me—to present myself, for example, as an oh-so-impractical scatterbrain with two left hands who can't even set the table properly and before the arrival of guests gladly turns herself into her jack-of-all-trades husband's gopher who brings him this, and gets him that, *That's beautifully done, Oleh darling, where do you want me to put the flowers?* I gladly delegate to him matters of personal management, as if I were indeed so frightfully disorganized that without him I literally wouldn't be able to catch a single flight (never mind that I lived alone for the four years that proved crucial to my career and managed perfectly to keep every appointment and meet every deadline), and that's fine, I don't mind, why should I care, after all this is the usual system of worked-out compromises, like a set of mutually interlocking gears, inevitable and unavoidable if you want to have a man for more than your bed, because victories in bed are never enough for them. So okay, fine, but goddamn it, I *told* him about my little bicycle, and about my torments in the school gym, I explained how horrible it is for me (Do you hear me? Is this really so hard to grasp?) to be anywhere, anytime someone is telling me how I'm supposed to hold my arms, my legs, what to do with them and in which order, it's like being gangbanged, if that's an analogy you can understand, or pick something equally traumatic, *just for God's sake, leave me alone!* I told him this, or rather I screamed it at him—screaming being the last weapon of the weak—all in a single breath, passionate and inspired, and my entire raging torrent, that fully constituted summer thunderstorm of emotion, crashed against Oleh's imperturbably and victorious smile like Comrade Stalin's on an old official portrait. "So here's a chance to overcome your problem," he said, and it sounded so persuasive coming from him, just like from the wise Father of All Nations who knows for certain which medicine his people need even if the people, like foolish children, think they are bitter (the Gulag, for instance), that I hesitated for just a moment, and it's because of that moment of hesitation that I'm stuck here now like a leper in the town square—What if, I thought, he's right? Oleh plainly enjoyed this setup—he was tickled by the feeling of his power over me, real, for once, achieved without me playing along. That his power was real he sensed instantly, and it revved his instinct, absorbed once and for all from his business world, not to let anything, once won, out of his hands. Never loosen his grip, so to speak. In fact, his bulldog-like grip used to excite me—as long as other people were caught in it, and I could stand back and watch.

It's my own fault: you can affect helplessness all you want, but under no circumstances can a woman reveal her real weaknesses to a man—sooner or later, he is certain to use them as a step stool to his own pedestal. You'll not get much pleasure from it, unless you're a masochist. And I, sorry to say, am not.

The only thing I do enjoy about these lessons is the courts themselves first thing in the morning, their scent of dampness and fresh paint and the surrounding stillness of the park disturbed only by the chirping of the birds, which, for some reason, is especially resonant in these old alleys between the trees, like a child's water whistle, and by the nearby thump of a tennis ball: someone got here even earlier and is already practicing, and, by the sound of things, is much better at it than I am. I would love to just sit on the bench and watch my instructor play, absorbing nothing and remembering nothing, mind blank, relaxed, like watching the waves roll in at the seashore until they lull you to sleep— it's especially nice to see how deftly he uses the tip of the racket to roll the tennis ball up his leg and into his hand: his motion is so balletic—it makes me wonder how many beautiful things there are in the world indeed and what superhuman effort we put into spoiling them all as soon as possible. Whenever I try to pick up the ball without bending, I only succeed in scratching the racket. In the short moments of respite from my torture—when I have to run to get the ball—I can feel the eyes of my instructor fixed on the exact shape of my legs and my buttocks, and for a spell, this returns me to my disrupted sense of composure, like the reliable trick I always pull when I'm feeling down: apply the radical makeup, one-two-three, with the firm hand of a master, a few avant-garde brushstrokes, march out defiantly into the street—and, by the time you click-clack your way to the subway with your proudly pursed lips, catching half a dozen looks from the male bystanders, you decide that things are not as bad as they seemed at home or in the car next to your dear husband, and in another ten minutes you are restored in your appreciation of your own professional accomplishments, and you tell yourself that you, damn it, earn your own living, and not a bad living at that, and that you are valued, sometimes even highly, for more than your legs and buttocks! And once everything falls thus back into place, your inner bitch is ready to go again—meaning, in this case, that the racket is in your right hand, the ball firmly in the fingers of the left, the left foot is parallel to the racket, and you're putting your weight on the right leg. Whatever the coach says, if it's right, let it be right, although I think the only thing I'll get for sure is being sore in that one thigh only, and won't that be a hoot.

"Let's try one more time."

He's practically begging me.

Nodding obediently, I freeze in the preordained pose, ready to stand for a hundred years like a character from *Sleeping Beauty*, as the instructor walks to the other side of the net—a well-made man, light footed as a mountain lion—and then stops, assesses the mise-en-scène in a split second (so, maybe my deliberate surreptitious-hunter's crouch doesn't look so bad after all), flashes his teeth in an affirmative smile, and waves to me: Go ahead!

Unexpectedly, the ball shoots into the sky like a slender candle—at the same time with a war cry from my instructor—"Yeah!"—who, with an extrawide swing straight from the shoulder (did my serve make him do that?) slams the ball back to me with hearty delight. But I'm not ready for it: I'm standing still, stunned, contemplating what I've just witnessed, processing the intoxicating taste of connecting to the ball with my right hand, feeling the resonant quiver of the racket's tight strings as a sympathetic tremor of my arm muscles—so this is what they mean when they tell you the racket is an extension of your arm! This is it! The phrase runs through my brain over and over. So that's how you do it. This is *it*.

And, just like that, I know it—clear as in a flash of lightning: I will beat Oleh at tennis. By September it will be me, not him, who will run the opponent ragged. No matter that the experience and expertise are on his side—I'm quicker than he is, more agile, and I don't carry extra weight while he's been getting rounder as fast as and as suddenly as he's been going bald, and that's why he's begun losing against his regular partners and hoped to replace them with me. And finally, I'm also stubborn, no less than he is, especially when it comes to defending myself.

"There, you see! You can do it." I hear the instructor's voice over my head as though he's overheard my thoughts, a gentle, soothing voice, the way you speak to a child. "Just don't get so tense, it's not like someone's after you, you know."

Suddenly my vision is cloaked with tears, an undulating translucent shroud that I must blink to remove instantly, I must turn my head away and hold my breath and not burst out crying here and now, while a heavy tear makes its way down my cheek slow and willful as a snail— and while a man's heavy arm envelops my shoulders and muffles my hearing with thick, soft, warm, mumbling cotton:

"It's okay. It's okay."

And so they come, these tears, making the world and my face lose shape. I bury my head in the tennis instructor's shoulder, with one convulsive sob, ready to cry all at once for all the wrongs done me throughout my whole life, as if it were perfectly natural to be standing on the court in broad daylight in the arms of a stranger and crying the way I could not all those thirty years ago. He gently strokes my hair, then draws me toward him firmly, in one swift tug, so I know right away how long he'd been wanting to do just that, and in response I gratefully press my whole body against his, feeling his lust through the thin fabric of his T-shirt, like I have no man closer to me in the whole wide world right now, and that, quite likely, is the case indeed. We kiss greedily, like schoolkids, swallowing the salty taste of my tears, which he then wipes away, carefully passing his finger over my cheek and smiling, his lips trembling slightly, and then again presses the full length of my torso against his until it hurts and he lets out a muffled groan, and that same subterranean groan echoes from me as well—the sound of cavernous depths bursting open to reveal the path to my complete and ultimate freedom.

I wonder if those two girls on the next court can see us.

"Well?"

His arms slide slowly down my back, he pulls away slightly and looks at me attentively, full of his man's privilege of expecting something to come next, but also adoringly, as at something he has created. "What shall we do?"

What indeed.

I sniffle guiltily, unable, nonetheless, to take my guiltless eyes off him: we touch each other with our eyes as physically, as clearly felt as if

195

we were naked. No, we are more intimate yet, like a pair of conspirators who just sealed a secret pact against the world. That pact has already come into effect, it is valid, so I draw a blissful, postlovemaking breath, deeply, so as to slow my racing heart, and mean it when I say: "I'd like to give it another try. I think this time I'll be able to do it."

NO ENTRY TO THE PERFORMANCE HALL AFTER THE THIRD BELL

TRANSLATED BY HALYNA HRYN

From the smallest thing, it always begins with the smallest thing—with a speck of dust in your eye, a crappy mood, a suddenly remembered insult from one screwed-up Gavrilo Princip (you really shouldn't have made fun of the little shrimp), and before you know it, bam! there's a cosmic catastrophe on your hands and just you try to stop it now. Would you mind rolling up your window? was all she said to the kid as the car turned up Saksahansky Street—she remembered her words as precisely as one remembers the pattern of the wallpaper on the wall the moment said wall came crashing down on one's head, as she remembered every detail of that instant: the leady breath of the street through that window, and the sudden whip of the draft that lashed her ear, and how just before that moment she was looking to her left, where two women with identically windblown blonde hair stood at the crosswalk, one older and the other younger, gesticulating with great abandon—as seen in a film with the sound turned off: she couldn't hear them through her own rolled-up window—but it was clear they were a mother and daughter and that they were happy together, and perhaps it was this last part that prompted her to call out from her back seat to her own daughter in the front—okay, maybe a touch more tensely than was necessary, but still with plenty of self-control, Would you mind rolling up your window? She remembered the way she said it, and would admit honestly, yes, the words were a release of long-simmering irritation, an undisguised reproach that communicated, You don't give a moment's thought to your mother, do you, you wouldn't care a bit if I caught a cold and lost my voice, never mind that my voice is what puts bread on the table, I feed you with it like a pelican with the flesh of her breast, and it's about time you stopped taking that for granted and showed some apprecia-tion, you're not a baby anymore! Yes, that's what she really wanted to convey to her pouting child, who stubbornly treated her only to the view of her delicate newly cropped crown and hadn't turned to face her once during the whole trip—a child with whom she could no longer imagine standing just like that in the middle of the street, both of them waving their arms and laughing (the young woman was imitating someone to her mother, she wondered if it was, perhaps, her boyfriend?)—and that reproach was meant to ricochet and reach her husband as well, at the wheel, in his favored position of radical noninterference, for whom both of them, at that particular moment, were no more than precious cargo, chattering about their things, it's nice, like a radio, classical or jazz lounge. Yes, there's no denying it: at that moment, she was feeling truly lonely and neglected, a stranger to the two people in the front—it felt like they had written her off long ago and now merely exploited her, each in their own way, what a nasty feeling, a truly childish sense of grievance, an injury with no one to tell, an orphan-like, little-girl-crying-in-the-bathroom-like hurt—although, come to think about it, how would she know how orphan girls cry in bathrooms?

Maybe it was all because of the war, she thought later. Maybe the war was to blame for everything, and it was the *irritation* of the three years of this war, accumulated under the skin, that was beginning to show itself. Like we all silently agreed that there are people among us who are fated to be killed by Russian bullets so that the rest of us could go on drinking mojitos after dinner while watching soccer on TV—and we'd just pay them for dying. And their families, too, once they'd been killed. Because we are not doing anything else, are we, no matter how often we tell ourselves we are "supporting our troops." Over hill, over dale, Helpful Billy hits the trail. A whole country of such helpful Billys, and each of them finding it harder and harder to respect themselves. Her husband has made it a habit of beginning each day by checking the Facebook page where they publish pictures of children who lost a parent in the Anti-Terrorist Operation, as the government euphemistically called it (Olha herself could never look at them, she'd burst into tears at the first one and then have to go to the kitchen to pour herself a drink)—he'd copy the banking information for donations into a spreadsheet and regularly wire small donations, tens of dollars, to benefit each—Taxes on our conscience, Olha would think but never say aloud. There was much they had stopped saying aloud to each other over these three years, the war taught them that, too: that words could destroy things much easier than bullets did, so it was better to treat them gingerly and not to waste them. And that's why all she said to the kid was, Would you mind rolling up your window, one sentence, and look what came out of it.

True, in addition to words, there was also her tone. Tone is music, and she, of all people, knew very well what a terrible force it can be—the human voice.

Ulyanka reacted as could have been expected—like something bit her: she huffed, puffed, snorted, and squealed that it was hard to breathe in the car already, that Olha's perfume was making her sick (meaning, it is she and not her mother who is the little girl here who needs to be taken care of), which annoyed Olha all over again, a degree worse this time (every one of their fights went in waves like this, like a multiple orgasm), all the more so because her husband remained silent rather than speaking up in her defense, saying, for instance, he enjoyed the perfume, and thus putting the kid firmly in her place, because, consciously or not, Ulyanka took aim straight at her mother's *pre*eminence as a woman. For the first time, Olha wondered if she had somehow missed the moment when she stopped being a style icon for her daughter—and the idea made her stomach flip, like on a plane flying through turbulence, which was unpleasant and humiliating in its own right, as if her body obediently, against her will, reacted to Ulyanka's *It makes me carsick* with a fit of solidarity, the same as it used to leak milk at the sound of her baby's crying. Except now Ulyanka was becoming *more powerful* and was testing her new power on her mother the way she used to bang on the piano keys while simultaneously trying to reach and hold down the right pedal, and that's why Olha raised her voice—she did it instinctively, just someone trying to regain control, Quit it right now! as she would've commanded at the piano, that's what her tone meant. It was unpedagogical, yes, she was ready to admit that, she should have taken an entirely different key, her confidential one, lower by a third, the one that worked without fail on men, and with a few smart, well-aimed phrases squish the nasty little frog so she'd shut up and spend the rest of the trip thinking about how young and foolish she was—but alas, everyone makes mistakes, especially with a creature that is closer to you than anyone else in the world, and thus knows perfectly, by ways of blood and womb, where your weak spots are—where to poke the needle so it will hurt for sure. And it did hurt, no point denying it. She was ashamed to remember the stupid, intense way it hurt, how it nicked the nerve of her female vulnerability—she'd never have expected that.

Later, as she prepared herself for the Big Talk, Olha wondered if perhaps Ulyanka really wasn't feeling that well at the time—it was the first day of her period, and at seventeen, a period is still an event that requires special attention—or is it, anymore? On this score, Olha was lost because she couldn't remember anything about herself in this regard, she remembered little about herself being seventeen, and that prompted her to realize another thing: that Ulyanka had, without her noticing it, pulled a curtain across her own memory of herself. Family stories involving one or the other of them were getting mixed together, like their makeup in the bathroom; she could no longer immediately tell if an event happened in her own childhood or in Ulyanka's, the way sometimes reality and dreams merge in one's memory. And of course, like every mother, she liked this: she liked the fact that her daughter grew up to resemble her, she liked it when strangers mixed them up from a distance, or mistook their voices, or thought they were sisters—just last summer, when Olha had suddenly lost a lot of weight, it happened all the time, and they had such fun with it, as if they really were the same age, a pair of coltish teens, two fluffy-headed dandelions in identical jeans. At that point they would still trade tops (only the bust size was different, and she'd say to the kid, Don't you worry, just wait till you have your own baby, you'll be a C cup in no time), and Ulyanka, mouth open, absorbed her mother's unwritten rules of heritable stylishness, and bragged about her to her friends while Olha would sneak at night onto teen-oriented websites to keep up her street cred (and bite her lips anxiously at the fashion videos she and her husband called "a pedophile's banquet"—but it's not like you can pack your child into a burka, and besides, Olha, back in high school, herself wore skirts so short she could not bend down, only squat, and nothing terrible happened to her, and what did happen came later and had nothing to do with the skirt). That was a happy time in their relationship, heady and euphoric, as if spiked with spices that quicken the blood, and make a small anthill explode in the hollow at the base of your skull, sending invisible insects down your spine. They did not discuss this at home—Olha knew she had her husband's tacit understanding; it was during that summer that he began to trawl the internet in search of war orphans, and Olha made several trips to the front to sing in morale-boosting concerts (and locked herself in the bedroom to cry every time she came back—as if the tears could wash out the sight of those young soldiers, boys with velvety skin and small blue veins on their necks, just like Ulyanka's classmates)—at night, after Ulyanka went to bed, the two of them would sit around the kitchen drinking cognac or whiskey, not a lot, a few drinks to relax because no one could stand being under that much stress twenty-four hours a day—and sometimes after this they would make love like they used to when they were young, with a renewed thirst for the process itself (and sometimes, her husband would come back into her, as she was sleeping, in the middle of the night, like an animal doubling its tracks, and after that they would fall asleep in each other's arms, and in the morning the pillow would be wet with tears). Neither one of them would give voice to it, but against the background of all those horrific rumors and news stories that went straight as a loaded needle to that groove at the base of your skull, and Olha's weeping over the pictures of the men killed in combat, and the unremitting dread lodged under their skin—that was the summer they were all afraid the Russians would take Mariupol, that's all anyone could talk about, that boring grey industrial city that never had anything going for it except its location on the seashore—secretly, they both *rejoiced*, gloried in the fact they had a daughter and not a son, that no matter how many waves of mobilization came, none could bring a draft notice to *their* home, ever.

They would never have to face the choice Olha sometimes allowed herself to imagine, inwardly shutting her eyes in horror at the very conjecture: to call in every favor with everyone they could think of to get your child a safe job at headquarters or to send her, together with all the other people's children, to face the bullets at the front. It's better not to know some things about yourself, Olha learned a long time ago, better not to end up in situations where such choices need to be made. Of all her friends whose children were drafted, only the Nazarenkos' son served at the front ("mile zero," they called it): the boy never said a word to his parents, on purpose, and called them when he was already on the bus to boot camp, said, "Hi, Mom, everything's okay, I got drafted," and his poor mother spent the next year explaining to everyone that the boy lost a friend in the Battle of Ilovaisk, and just had his heart set on going after that—well, thank god, he came back already, alive and well, and Olha heard he was about to get married. Every once in a while Olha would remind herself that she really should go visit the Nazarenkos, but at heart she knew she didn't have the courage to do it—that she wouldn't be able to hit the right key with that boy, it was as if their generation had swapped places, and in front of him, *she* was the clueless teen and he the adult she'd rather not face.

For the prom they bought Ulyanka a gown from Lilia Poustovit, for almost two thousand euros—red silk, lace bodice. Ulyanka, with her delicate neck and lovely arms, was so beautiful in that dress that Olha couldn't hold back tears and spent the whole evening, again, bawling. Of course, they could have been less extravagant, could have saved the money—Ulyanka would have been just as gorgeous in a dress not made by a famous designer—but their smutty, secret joy at the fact that they, thank the merciful Lord, had a daughter and not a son also demanded to be expressed, needed its own celebration—a legitimation, a recognition, and an absolution. The knowledge that other people's sons were dying, and some other people's daughters, as the Nazarenkos' son told his mother, from the villages near the front would sleep with a soldier for a can of beef stew gave Olha's vision of her daughter walking across the stage, in her crimson gown, a yet more poignant, marvelously painful intensity, an ecstatic, rock-hard booming in her blood, the triumphant chorus from *Carmina Burana*, as she felt again the sting of fire at the base of her skull and the familiar ant-footed, acidic languor flow down her arms, prompting her eyes to fill with tears. Never had she felt so alive as that second summer of war. Never, not even when she was young.

Not even when she was in love. Not even when in love with Odainyk.

Not even that night he asked her to dance, and she had wanted him so badly that her teeth clattered and she could barely control her shaking.

You wee pesky gnat, you nit, she spoke to her daughter in her mind, marveling at her grandma Hanna's voice that unexpectedly resurrected itself in her head, What do you know? How dare you? What have you done?

She wasn't letting herself off the hook, of course not: *she* could have stopped that fight, could have prevented it from unraveling. Could have doused it at the spark—but that's the point, isn't it: she *didn't want* to quell it: that would have meant giving in to the kid, tacitly acknowledging her new, alien, condescending separateness, her adult right to evaluate and judge her mother according to her own criteria no longer known to Olha, even when the judgment concerned only her perfume—which was, incidentally, exquisite, perhaps just a touch too musky, a little bitter, with a hint of incense, but it was not meant for you, you little monkey, was it? Not to suppress the fight— to take it, and win it, that was the point! To rub the kid's face once again in her inappropriate behavior, to make her repent and become, once again, the way she was a year ago. That was the casus belli. All their fights that shook the house like the reverberations of mortar fire in Donbass had essentially one reason: it was a war for *territory*—that narrow strip of solid ground on which until recently they had been sisters, girlfriends wearing the same jeans, one *already* and the other *still* a woman, who could scarf down ice cream together at outdoor terraces and gossip about someone's pierced lip, and loll on the couch at home, talking, so Olha could thread her life into words and dangle it for the kid like a pearl necklace—Here, hold it, cherish it, it's yours now. She heard her first bell—a holler, actually, a vulgar prison-guard bark to head for the exit—at the endocrinologist's office, but she knew how to take a hit, not for nothing did she spend all her years onstage, and gave no sign of the news at home, and a thing not named does not really exist. That Ulyanka herself soon began edging her out of their shared space, like a maturing pup growling at the old loose-titted bitch at the food bowl—Just give me a break, Mom! followed by the door slamming (when couples begin treating each other this way, it means love has come to an end, and people who have even a tiny bit of sense part ways at this very moment so as not to torment each other—but what do you do with your own child?)—did not deter Olha from defending her right to the ground that was slipping from under her feet (a fight in which her husband was of no help because he, like all men in such times, understood jack shit); she wanted the impossible, of course—to hold back time, to hold it like a note perched beneath a fermata symbol, to stuff it back, hammer it back, scream it back if necessary. Why not, she could always hear her own voice and control the sound, even when she was screaming, so after that last peaceful turn where she said, Would you mind rolling up your window, the two of them went at it for real, racing up the crescendo as the car climbed Saksahansky Street, outpacing each other, a twelve-tone composition for a rabid violin duet that the good-natured interjection of her husband's voice, like a double bass, could not hope to overturn. Olha, enraged as she was, registered, at the edge of her awareness, how similar her daughter's voice was to her own, only a bit higher, more shrill, it's a shame the girl refused to take up singing, just had to go all preppy with her law degree, didn't she?—and all of it, all of it could have been stopped, she could have cut herself off midsentence and laugh, change her tone, speak confidentially and gently, or, by contrast, firmly, and everything would have turned out okay, if only Ulyanka had controlled herself also, and hadn't said, half turning to face her mother (finally!) with all the vileness and contempt she could (or so it seemed to Olha at the time) muster, that last sentence of hers, like the last blow of a sledgehammer that knocks down a cracked-up wall:

"You're just menopausal!"

All sound ceased in Olha's head. The world was quiet as an aquarium.

Shocked, she inhaled deeply (and noisily). Next, instead of saying something mature and rational (all she had in her head was a tinny bleat, You're such an idiot!), she reached awkwardly, and like a cat with her paw, slapped the kid on her conveniently turned cheek.

Every time she thought of that singeing contact of hand with face—each time the memory of the slap returned—Olha wanted to curl up and hide, not just under a blanket, like she did as a child, but way deeper, somewhere beneath the earth. Her fingers remembered they slipped—Ulyanka jerked her head back and Olha was afraid that she might have scratched her with her false nails—and what if, god forbid, she'd caught the girl in the eye? Her husband yelled at them (finally!): they were stopped at a traffic light, stuck in traffic, in the middle lane, and that whole horrible scene lasted less than a minute, wasn't nearly as long and slow as it felt to Olha in her aquarium, and yet, somehow she missed the moment that came right after the slap—as if a computer in her brain froze up for a second—when Ulyanka opened her door and jumped out of the car. It must be, Olha thought later, that we really do perceive the world in chunks, in discrete frames, because in her next frame Ulyanka was already running down the middle of the street, between the cars, her fashionable little turquoise coat flapping. For some reason, she was not running for the sidewalk but in the same direction as the traffic, like a rabbit caught in the headlights at night; the cars were beginning to move as the light changed, and one after the other hit the horn hysterically at the blinded girl in the turquoise coat (a perfect soundtrack for the end of the world)—and in the next instant (another memory gap)

Olha too was running after her, tripping in her high heels, through the sound storm of car horns and the rumble of disaffected drivers that rose up around her like a forest, herself shouting full throat, at the top of her powerful lungs: Ulyanka, stop! Come back! Ulyaaanka!— seeing nothing before her but the turquoise coat, which finally did turn and skip across the street to the sidewalk just as traffic revved up and surged ahead, projecting into Olha's mind, with command-ing clarity, the most horrific product of her imagination: a vision of Ulyanka being hit by a black SUV, several tons of dense metal, how she goes flying out of her coat and jeans like a rag doll, and hits her head—splat!—on the hood of the grey Toyota in the right lane, the blood and brains on the asphalt, and one of her shoes (she'd seen this in a police newscast) resting sixty feet away at the curb. She had no awareness of it, but for the duration of time it took for Ulyanka to reach the sidewalk, she, Olha, stood shock-still among the moving cars in her stupid goddamn heels and shrieked after her daughter like an air-raid siren, like she meant to hold all those cars away from her child, as a prehistoric human must have shrieked to ward off predators in the primeval forest, like a whole women's battalion in the Finnish Winter War whose battle call, at a perfect fifth, scattered the Soviet Army lines—and like those women, Olha won: she shrieked that whole intersection of Saksahansky and Tarasivka to a halt, she stopped all those crouched rows of cars like a herd of walruses with their tusks—she stopped them and cleared the path for her child to reach safety. Spit three times at that horrible vision, never tell anyone, let it blow away like dust.

Except she could not sing that night. That's where they were driving—to her show (meaning, she and her husband were going to her performance, and Ulyanka asked for a ride to meet up with her friends—long gone were the days she followed her mother to every show like a puppy).

That same day, or rather night, after it was all over, when Olha, like a deflated tire, lay in bed with a migraine, and the muffled, insistent beat of her husband's and daughter's voices in the kitchen assaulted her like the heaving of waves, and knew they were conspiring against her in the kitchen (So she did come home, the little brat!), her husband slipped silently into the room (the drumbeat in her head did not stop, though), stood over her in the dark for a moment, and then sat down beside her. He asked how she was feeling. He asked about her headache. He asked about her throat. She almost expected him to ask when her last period was.

She knew there were more questions coming. Her husband was good at questioning people—he had thirty years of experience as a lawyer plus his acute, far above the average, sense of fairness, it was from him the kid got it, she was *his* daughter, too, much more than hers, really, Olha thought with blazing clarity, Oh, this blazing clarity of pain, and marveled weakly that the thought evoked no emotions in her.

Instead, what her husband said was completely unexpected—otherworldly:

"Your ex died . . . Odainyk. She knows."

"I don't understand . . . ," Olha's voice a rustle in the darkness.

Something was coming at her, like that entire street of cars at the stoplight, but she no longer had the voice to stop it. Odainyk? Dead? Why, how? And, wait a minute, what does this have to do with her child?

"She says she knows his daughter," her husband said simply, in response to her unspoken question, as he often did lately. "They met in a club, she said the girl approached her." He paused, then added, "Don't be mad at her. She's quite shaken."

That's when Olha's voice came back.

"Fuck," the voice said, coming from the bottom of a barrel, clear and low, from the bottom of her diaphragm. "Fuck. Fucking goddamn it."

Apparently, she knew no other strong language that she could say out loud, and this, for some reason, made her feel as small, helpless, and unable to move as earlier in the middle of the street on those high heels.

At this, she finally cried—this time really like an orphaned child. She lay there with her head squeezed in a steel band of pain, slapped the bed with her hand, and kept saying as she wept, "Fuck, fuck, fuck . . ."

Tiffany—the word popped up in her head like a jeering clown: that was the name of Ulyanka's trendy raincoat's color. She had forgotten this word during the day, and now it came back: a word that had suddenly slipped from her memory, yet another symptom of aging. Hello, menopause!

❖

Nobody knew of what Odainyk died, and there seemed to be no way to find out: after three years of war, a death from disease, even if it befell a public figure, had ceased being an event worth talking about. Anyway, Olha did not have anyone to talk to about it: the old circle of friends they hung out with in the nineties had long fallen apart, and when she did happen to see one of them—and there had been a few times when friends from her youth popped up at her shows and came backstage afterward (to network, she always thought, suspicious) they, of course, acted like old friends, exchanging telephone numbers and old resuscitated jokes that had long since stopped being funny, but no one dialed those numbers afterward. Olha did not like to think of herself as a woman who, in the course of climbing the ladder of success—for example, after her successful marriage (after an initial period of doubt, she decided to view her marriage as a success, even before Ulyanka was born), or after her solo album (how many Ukrainian musicians in those prewar years could put out a solo album?)—discards her old friends at each successive rung like worn-out shoes, that wasn't true about her at all, she hated throwing anything out (as she had once told her husband's friends and realized right away that wealthy people did not brag about things like that), and in fact she still had friends from her music school, from kindergarten, and from the neighborhood where she grew up, she was even godmother to some of their children, so the problem, she finally convinced herself, did not reside with her: simply, that whole crowd was infected with Odainyk, and everything that was infected with Odainyk was sooner or later meant to fall apart—the way he himself fell apart over the years. She was no longer obligated to watch it happen.

Kyiv was a damn big city, and unless you belonged to the same professional circle, you could go for years without running into each other and without knowing about each other. Olha knew that Odainyk had gotten married, that he had a daughter, in fact had the daughter first, and then got married, "shotgun-style" as whoever of their friends who told her the news joked (even back then it was not funny)—it wasn't someone from the core group, their nucleus, but one of those electrons that gravitate toward every strong social group with powerful men and beautiful women, who flicker on the outside orbit for a while, doing favors, going to big parties, until they break away or, conversely, get pulled into the denser layers of connection—so Olha did not remember the person's name, and their conversation left her with an awkward feeling, like a tight shoe, mainly because of the need to avoid addressing the man by name, and given that she was completely absorbed in her own family at the time, all she retained was: Huh, so Odainyk also has a daughter, as if he were aping her life. In other words, she felt a scratch but no pain—water under the bridge, good riddance, and so on.

That the water, in fact, had not gone under the bridge at all she learned that night at the opera, at the concert in honor of the king of Sweden. Olha remembered neither the king nor the queen (of far greater interest to the womenfolk), and she even had trouble remembering the program after the intermission, even though it featured her conservatory classmate who procured an invitation for her in the first place. What stuck in her mind from that evening was the smell of sweat—the heavy, homeless, railway-station stench of unwashed women's armpits that followed her in the foyer and in her box, so much so that in the second half of the evening she snuck out a perfume sample from her clutch purse and kept it by her nose, until it suddenly occurred to her that the source of the smell might be her. But she didn't remember breaking into a sweat. She could have sworn that at first she did not even recognize the unpleasant burly man with a big gut with a sharp penetrating look when he approached her husband during the intermission together with a few other expensively cologned men to exchange business cards and exploratory pleasantries—this was exactly the kind of event where people went to make connections, set up meetings, and demonstrate their proximity to power, and the entire opera house, from the orchestra seats to the third balcony, truly stank of money, dirty and putrid like a used menstrual pad, money from the meat markets, illicit card tables, and security services' conference rooms, from "sperm, oil, and blood," as a poet wrote—and was right, bull's-eye right, it just took Olha a while to learn about the oil and blood parts. The sperm, though—that smell was obvious, like on Odainyk's old briefs, which she, mad with love, once stole and kept in her lingerie drawer unlaundered; later, of course, she threw them out, maybe even burned them, but looking at that beer-gutted man was like having those sperm-stained briefs turn up after all this time, after she'd forgotten all about them, and make her cringe—What *is* this? Who is this? The face seemed familiar, where could she have seen him? The look the man gave her when they

211

were introduced—like a handful of spiders—was deliberately indifferent, a see-nothing, hear-nothing, say-nothing kind of look, like in Mafia movies, but at the same time self-congratulatory in that implied way a man has of showing a woman he hasn't forgotten what she's like in bed. Olha, in her best black sequined gown, splendid and statuesque, like a monument to her own bust (forget the queen!), dug into her dear husband's elbow while he kept nodding at that bastard, Yes, please stop by . . . I'd be happy to . . . (so the man needed *him*, and not the other way around!) and suffered feeling that all her carefully constructed armor, all the defenses that she spent years raising and was so proud of, could no longer protect her—unless she remembered who this man was, and what evil thing transpired between them that he dared look at her like that.

She remembered him when he laughed. A sparse, beady laugh, a little staccato, strangely incongruous with his size. That must have been when she broke out in a sweat. Twelve years ago he had the same laugh.

The second man she ever had sex with in her life. And he didn't have to be; the choice was hers to make. He did not rape her—though in fact he did, she was the only one who knew this, and she never told anyone, she wouldn't know how. Theoretically, she could have said no when she realized what was happening, realized that this predatory-eyed gangster (without the belly back then) whom Odainyk introduced to her as his business partner and her future record producer was telling the truth, and Odainyk indeed had *made an arrangement* with him, wherein Odainyk let him have the apartment with her in it, and vanished—she could have said no, packed her things, and left. (She would have many months to consider why she hadn't done precisely that, and those indeed were the worst months of her life.) She knew everything about Odainyk's debt, or so she thought; she was the first to suspect he had been set up, deliberately, in such a way that he would have no other option but to sell his business—and sobbing, on her knees (she remembered the sound her knees made when she dropped on the freshly laid oak floors), she begged him not to get involved with those people, who were dragging him deeper and deeper into the heart of an incomprehensible dark forest, but Odainyk was growing distant, alien right before her eyes: the new evil thing that came into him together with the big money grew like rapidly progressing schizophrenia. For an entire year she watched, with a sick emptiness in her stomach, as he struggled like a fly in a spiderweb, no longer even attempting to repay the loan, but at least to push it back a bit so that it wouldn't topple over and crush him with its full weight immediately. One by one he sold off, for next to nothing, the office space he'd bought with the loaned money, and the brand-new car he'd fawned over, saying he had no need for them, or he would suddenly throw a raucous party, with her singing the blues and everyone else smoking throat-scratching Crimean weed that made your mouth go numb, or he would take her off to Austria to ski, which she didn't know how to do and spent half the trip at the hotel crying—looking back, it seemed like she was constantly crying back then, that entire year, even more bitterly than the year before, when her mom died, although of course this couldn't be true, it was just the way she remembered herself—a helpless, weepy hen who was some-how to blame for the fact that her man went bankrupt because how could a dumb hen like her bring anybody good luck? One depressing night back then, she said to him, desperate and earnest as in church (they never did get wed as they had planned to do), I will do anything for you! so that he would know that she would not abandon him in poverty, nor in sickness, until death do them part, and that he could always rely on her—and he said nothing, she remembered *that*—he stayed quiet: as though what she said no longer mattered. As if she were nothing and could not fill the abyss into which he was tumbling. Only when she was being raped by that man—a rape to which she, no denying it, *consented* because it's like war, either you fight or you surrender, you give or you don't, there is no I-don't-care-what-you-do-to-me-because-I'm-already-dead option, especially since, as it turns out, it matters very much—it was only when she, motionless and hard as a rock, shook, rocklike, from the shoving of the hateful alien appendage inside her, knowing at the same time, with clinical clarity like at the dentist's, that with each shove he was *shoving Odainyk out of her*, erasing, physically eradicating their love and intimacy, sending them to the irretrievable past—it was only then that it dawned on her, under the (quite literal) pressure of this new experience, that Odainyk, who was incapable of thinking about anything other than his debt, interpreted her puppy love I will do anything for you! to mean exactly this, an offer to pay off his creditor with sex (because, what else could she do for him—sing?), and that's why he didn't say anything right away, he had to consider her offer. So, again, the fault, as always, was hers, her incompetence at communication—and thus she had to take it, simply endure it, like standing in a downpour without an umbrella (it's funny, it seemed important to her in the moment that she'd made no motion to aid her rapist)—silently, obediently, like a clump of food under the masher at the bottom of a feeding trough, not entirely comprehending what exactly was being squished out of her, up to and including smeared shit and vomit on the sheets, to the several months of disgust and hatred of her own body, which tolerated and accepted all that. Her morbid rigidity did not cool or discourage Mr. Corpse-Fucker, as she named him in her mind—on the contrary, it seemed to be precisely what aroused him, her lack of resistance and the knowledge of his full power over her; until then she could not fathom something like this, although she'd read about it, and here was a man from another reality, straight out of that dark forest that dragged in and devoured her beloved, so perhaps she ought to have been scared—she couldn't have lost *all* the instincts that enable a woman to survive!—and have done something, found within her a motion she could make, a maneuver that might have at least abbreviated her physical suffering, if it weren't for one clinical detail, which turned out to be the single thing she remembered about Mr. Corpse-Fucker twelve years later: he had a small dick—about half the size of Odainyk's, judging from the sensation, and its swishing about inside her, like a swizzle stick in a cocktail shaker, completely eliminated in her any feeling of danger. She felt endlessly disgusted (and suffered fits of dry-heaving for weeks after), especially when after everything he said to her, "Good job!"—in Russian, of course—and laughed his bleating, staccato laugh. She threw up then.

Olha had time to recall all this—as if buttoning up her clothes—before the bell that rang the end of the intermission (since she was a child, she had a deeply anxious response to the grave notice, like a storm warning—"After the third bell there is no entry to the performance hall"—in her worst nightmares she was late for her own concerts and left standing in front of the locked door, trying to peer in). The men were still exchanging business cards and the hot sweat on her body was cooling down, because this time, twelve years later, she did get scared—scared that the same dark forest she managed to evade once (barely!) caught up with her again in order to claim her husband, the *true* one, the father of her child—and forgetting, erasing from her memory the face of Odainyk's creditor did not in itself protect her, and did not cancel the past. In that half minute when everyone said their goodbyes before going back to their seats, she instinctively grasped for the only advantage her body had in regard to this beer-bellied animal: she *looked back* at him—with the calm, open, mocking gaze of a woman who can see the tiny dick under his clothes, and dismissed this deficient male like a doctor sending home an athlete that has had his day, go on, take it easy, button up your pants, Godspeed.

To her surprise he turned away. Put away his spiders. And never again showed up at her husband's office, disappeared without a trace. Did not need the business card after all.

215

She warned her husband to be careful—told him she thought the man may have been Odainyk's creditor, the one to whom Odainyk planned to give her in repayment of his debt. Her husband knew the story up to that point, and that she packed up and left, not waiting for the "audition" she'd been promised; this was enough to orient him in her past. The rest—what happened *before* she left—she did not tell him, and it sat petrified inside her into a solid layer of immovable rock. Olha cherished her husband: in that most difficult period of her life, when she was learning how to live alone—how to support herself, how to love herself, how to decide for herself when to say yes or no— he restored her sense of physical freedom, gave her back the sense of her own body as a source of joy, and in that way seemed to rehabilitate her, purge her of the evil. This was more important than if he had been her first man and in and of itself sufficient cause for the eternal warmth of quiet gratitude that burned steadily in her heart year after year. Aside from that, what drew them close in the beginning was that as an attorney he knew loads of much more terrible tales of debt: with murders, trafficking into slavery, and not just of the sexual kind, but whole families sold into indenture—she had no idea what kind of medieval barbarity roiled all around under the guise of outward normalcy, and thanks to her husband was able to look at what happened to her, for the first time, from the vantage point of an outsider, like stepping out from dirty clothing and leaving it on the floor, and honestly appreciate how much worse things could have turned out, and how relatively easily she got away, thank god! Her husband felt it was her achievement, and Olha wanted him to continue to be proud of her. Inside, of course, she knew there wasn't much to be proud of: she was Odainyk's *accomplice*—from the very moment he asked her to dance, and seeing her tremble, held her close and whispered, What's the matter, baby? and she was ready to faint from the idea that he could release her from his embrace, and what would she do then, what would she be good for? until that night almost six years later, when she obediently, like a beaten-down whore, allowed herself to be fucked by devil knows who, because a sliver of her submissive self still *did what Odainyk told her* and continued to believe, like a fool, that he *knew better*, that he knew *how things should be done*, even when that meant throwing her into another man's bed—she spent her youth infected with Odainyk, and decayed together with him, and the fact that she was able to keep her balance on the edge of the abyss, into which she was ready to fall headfirst together with him without a second thought, was nothing short of a miracle. She just was lucky that Odainyk let her go.

And now, after his death, when she honestly tried to retune herself to a lyrical key and recall *what* exactly was so wonderful about that relationship that she had pined for him so much (she remembered most strongly her girlish, roof-blowing sense of bliss when she already knew for certain that he would make love to her, she just didn't know yet where and when) what her memory summoned, repeatedly, was his false confused grin and guiltily shifting eyes with which he presented himself to her after Mr. Corpse-Fucker—not to apologize, not to explain or justify himself, not to console her, but to pretend that *none of it had happened* and to persuade her to accept this version of events, which would require her to pretend that *he* knew nothing, and that overall nothing exceptional had happened to her, nothing worth telling him about. That's what she couldn't take. Perhaps, if he had behaved differently—if he had returned drunk and fallen to her feet, if he'd said it was all a mistake, smashed dishes and screamed, if he had had the guts, the wits, or the cynicism to behave differently, given her anything but his backstabber's shifty eyes (not once during that conversation did he look into her eyes) and his cowardly hope—no, faith!—that she would indeed be silent and thus relieve him of the burden of what he'd done—perhaps then, Olha thought, shuddering at the idea, as if her body again rehearsed the dry heaves, she still might have forgiven him. She might have forgotten that mobster, and his two used condoms that she personally threw down the garbage chute (and dreamed about for years) and would have gone back to Odainyk's bed as he had hoped she would. Like that dirty joke: "And then the husband came and fucked everything back the way he liked it." It's been known to happen. Whores live with their pimps; it's a version of family harmony. She simply didn't know, didn't have an answer to the question of how her life would have turned out if he hadn't, in effect, broken his embrace. If he had kept holding on to her—as from that first moment of their first dance, all those years that she was "his little girl" and would have gladly danced not only as her beloved Cohen sang (and as she too sang, brought the house down at every party with that song) "to the end of love"—but further, *over the edge* of love, into the dark forest full of beasts, into the world of big money and little dicks where the invisible majority of Ukrainian musicians had already drunk and drugged themselves to death, and only the freshest new meat from the visible minority were made "stars," to be rented out by their Moscow producers to their sponsors' beds at hourly rates.

Had Odainyk behaved differently, he might have still had enough power over her to persuade her to remain with him and pursue precisely this kind of a career, but he left her no choice. She was as disgusted as she had been with Mr. Corpse-Fucker. She wanted to hit him. But all she did was ask, in her new voice, calm and mocking, how much that little favor shaved off his debt—You didn't charge too little, did you, dear?

She remembered very clearly his tone when he screamed at her, "Do you want to say I left the two of you alone on purpose? You think I could do that? You think that's what I'm capable of, and you're telling me just like that?"—his rage so rehearsed, and the sound of it so false it made her embarrassed, not for him, but for herself, for listening to this pathetic, community-theater production. That's when she started packing, after she said, "Fail!" over her shoulder, in Russian, the language Mr. Corpse-Fucker spoke, as if she'd contracted it from him, like crabs, and was now giving Odainyk back his due share—please sign upon receipt.

And now it had been twenty years, and Odainyk had left this world, and yet his voice lived on inside her, as if recorded on a nineties tape that you couldn't listen to for lack of equipment, it was still there, it existed—Olha remembered him but couldn't produce the sound. This surprised her; it was as if someone told her that she'd kept Odainyk's sperm alive inside her all these years.

It was not a pleasant thing to realize that his beautiful, muscular male body (although, let's be honest, it ceased to be so a long time ago), with his horseman's powerful torso and strong legs, the body she once embraced with her entire self, whose salty sweat she picked up with her tongue, the body she knew so thoroughly and was delighted with that knowledge, now lies and rots, what's left of it, in a wooden box somewhere underground—no death had ever evoked in her such a creepy feeling and such a strong urge not to have anything to do with it. Secretly, Olha hoped that Odainyk's new wife had the good sense to have him cremated. She understood how the news might have affected Ulyanka: she had never told her daughter she'd lived with another man for five years, before she met her father—she had only told her, half in jest, how as a student, bored in class, she'd practice signing her future married name (she made sure this sounded like typical postpuberty silliness, girlish fancies, trying on boys like outfits—what if it's this one? or that one?) and made sure Ulyanka would never know how intimate of a memory this was for her—many years later, going through her old notebooks when she found those pages, curlicued with versions of *Olha Odainyk, Olhaodainyk, Olya Odainyk, O. Odainyk*—the name of a new, unfamiliar woman she wanted to be, tore those pieces of paper to shreds, as if they bit her, and burned the shreds in an ashtray. And she certainly would never have told Ulyanka about how once, about a year or so after the breakup, she was watching a children's choir on TV and burst out sobbing: the children diligently moved their mouths like little fish following the conductor as she bawled uncontrollably, with a fist in her mouth, because she could have given Odainyk three, four, or five such children that looked like him, she could have gone with him to the ends of the earth, lived in a hut in the forest, lived on bread and water if need be, as she once had offered—where nobody could find them, and everything could have been completely, completely different.

That was the last time that she spoke to him in her mind, reproaching him as if he were standing in front of her—or on the TV—the way she didn't have a chance to do in real life. In fact, that was her real goodbye to him—the final spasms, delayed in time, with which one expels the placenta after a stillbirth. For years, Olha believed that was it, and with that came an end to her turmoil. When her husband, after the encounter at the opera, made his own inquiries and told Olha more about Odainyk, she felt neither sick nor wounded at the news, despite its violent force, which, she guessed, now also rocked Ulyanka's world; what he told her robbed her of her entire youth, and to stay whole, she now had to squeeze all of it out of her, like a worm from a healthy apple. According to her husband's sources, Odainyk did lose his business, but went into politics instead of slavery: he hung around campaign offices for dubious errands, was passed from hand to hand, from project to project, and most recently was seen at the very bottom, at those preposterous staged pro-Russian demonstrations— with priests swinging incense and men wearing Stalin-style cavalry pants and astrakhan hats—which occurred with odd regularity in Crimea and along the Black Sea coast and that no one took seriously. No one suspected that the freak shows with the local riffraff were a cover for rehearsing the Russian invasion. Her husband showed her a photo of one such protest, somewhere in Odessa or Kherson—they all looked alike, like a grotesquely Russified Tolkien production, with Baba Yagas and orcs, plus a dash of military style—and there, behind

YOUR AD COULD GO HERE

toothless old women with accordions, skinny tattooed alcoholics fit for a herbarium, and bullnecked jocks in striped navy-issue undershirts, Olha, aflame with shame, spotted the object of her youthful ardor. True, Odainyk had aged, and not in a good way—his face sort of lost structure and sagged in search of its new shape ("Beastly," Grandma Hanna would call it)—but it was him, without a doubt, peeking from behind the zombies, with a cell phone pressed against his ear, like an anxious overseer. The very same one to whom Olha used to sing Leonard Cohen's songs from the stage, publicly declaring her love. Olha's cheeks burned.

"It's quite likely that he's the stage manager there," her husband confirmed and pointed out a few more men in similar attitudes spread among the crowd (which, when you took a closer look at it, was actually a pretty thin crowd): they were running that whole gathering. Olha liked that he didn't put down her ex in any obvious way as most men in his place could not have resisted doing—he spared her even greater humiliation—but rather approached the matter in a purely professional way. That's what she remembered, taking the rest, the dirty backstage of political spectacles in the convoluted Russian-Ukrainian war for oil—or was it the pipelines?—that her husband explained to her the way she always received his explanations: she gasped, nodded, and made her eyes round as appropriate while assessing all the time what this might mean for her and for her family, and as the answer to this key question typically seemed elusive at best, she let the rest of it slip by as background noise, a parallel tonality in a secondary musical part, and soon forgot it—Olha could hear the same thing again as if for the first time. It's not that it was too complicated for her to grasp; it merely seemed unnecessary. Olha let her ear be her guide in public affairs as much as she relied on it in private: she listened for false notes in a voice, focused much more on *how* people said things rather than what they said, on laughter and timbre, on the harmony between appearance and behavior, on the *vibration*, as she would say—that was how she judged political groups and individuals, and was rarely, if ever, wrong. This also made it easy for her to carry on impeccably with her husband's colleagues, and none of them ever thought of her as stupid. A woman like that could never have been in love with the man in that picture—even when she was very young, even at seventeen. She wasn't supposed to have even met him.

The worst thing after this discovery was that Olha lost confidence in her own past, in that entire period of time she was with Odainyk. She no longer knew how to think about what she had considered facts: for example, when Odainyk told her (and she always did as he said) that they could not afford to have a child just yet—did he really, as he told her, care about her stage career or was it possible he never intended to marry her, and simply let himself enjoy being the object of a much younger woman's love, which gave him the opportunity not to look like a loser at least in his own eyes? Or, that skiing trip to Austria—was he fooling her, or himself? Did he already know he was bankrupt and wanted to have one last fling, or was he, good god, already running Russian secret service errands for his creditors and needing to keep her in the dark? Each piece of her youth she touched fell apart, as if rotten from within—everything could turn out to be not what she had believed it to be, and the only thing she could be sure about was that back then she was dumb as a bag of hammers. Not exactly a great achievement on which to build and, of course, not something you want to share with your own child. So Olha pushed that whole period of her life into the furthest room of her mind, locked the door, and broke the key in the lock. By the time Ulyanka grew old enough to have women's conversations, she found no traces of Odainyk in her mother's life. And thank god, Olha thought—she knew her husband agreed.

At the beginning of the war she once again thought of Odainyk: when it became known that, following Yanukovych, hundreds of Russian sleeper agents in government agencies, and even some musicians, who would have thought, fled to Russia. Olha pictured them as a murder of crows, a huge black cloud, disappearing on the far side of the national border. For some reason she decided that Odainyk must be among them. This would have been logical, given his political past, and—more importantly—it would have been a fitting end to a secondary theme in her life: the last and final purification, the extraction, the surgery, the distancing from the man in physical space, the separation visible like the parting of light from darkness, the good from the evil . . . let him go, far, far into Mordor, beyond the moat filled with crocodiles, beyond the border, beyond the front.

But Odainyk did not go anywhere. And now Olha felt as if he spent all those twenty years hiding, lying in wait, biding his time until her not-his-daughter grew up in order to thrust himself into Ulyanka's life at exactly the same point at which he'd broken into her mother's: at the age of seventeen. Alive or dead.

It was at that age that Olha first saw him. Age seventeen: first year of university, second semester, exactly like Ulyanka.

My god, Olha thought, suddenly lucid, was I as beautiful as she is now? And it still didn't save anyone?

⁂

Olha prepared for the conversation meticulously. First, she had to apologize to Ulyanka for losing her temper and slapping her, and this, in turn, required her to introduce and lay out several incredibly difficult topics, among them the one most obvious to her, which was still unknown to everyone else. Before visiting the doctor, Olha went to her dentist—because in addition to losing weight that summer, her teeth came loose like they did when she was pregnant, and that was the first thing the doctor asked, whether she was pregnant.

Olha tried out what she thought was a good tone: Kiddo, one day you will understand. No, that's not right—for Ulyanka the age of

223

forty-five is the same as seventy, light-years away, the whole you'll-get-it-when-you're-my-age is not going to play, she has to try something else.

Kiddo, remember when I talked to you about menstruation and taught you to use a tampon? So, about that—you know jack squat, and no one does, until it hits you personally what it's like to lose a part of your own body, something that's always been yours—and to have to learn to live *without* it, knowing that it will be forever. In fact, we spend our entire lives losing pieces, running along on the goddamn treadmill, training to accept loss—to drop bits that won't grow back and not regret it—but we always resist, and you know why? Because we refuse to believe we are mortal, that's the thing, every loss is a microrehearsal of death, a tiny little bell that we do not want to hear. First it's the glow of your skin, this golden softness of yours, like an ear of corn—that will dim and dimple in just three or four years, just so you know, and the first lines, if everything goes well, will come in about ten, depends on your sexual life, too, but that's a separate conversation. Shit, no, forget that part. And then our babies carve the calcium out of our bones and teeth and suck out our breasts—remember how you told me not to button the top button on my shirt? So it would drape over my breasts just so? Well, no dice, honey, your mom can still manage a fashionable just-rolled-out-of-bed haircut, and keep her hips, stomach, and shoulders in respectable shape so as not to fear the swimsuit, but after nursing you, the combat-ready position of nipples up that these pedophile-bait shirts are cut for is quite beyond her, and the veins on her arms and legs, after the double duty on the heart, won't be chased or massaged into disappearing, and that's how it's going to be for the rest of my life, just think of that, but not a single woman ever regretted it, do you understand the point here? These are all medals that we carry on our bodies, like scars earned in victorious battles: the red capillaries of stretch marks on the sunken drum of the stomach, the scary brown tracks after a caesarian, shreds of blue lace of veins on our thighs—we show these off to each other whenever we take our clothes off, never mind that pop culture screams at us to shut up at billion-dollar volume and every surface around features a fifteen-year-old model airbrushed to the smoothness of a greenhouse vegetable. We know what those models—what you—don't know: that all of our physical flaws and injuries, acquired from you, all these blemishes we are ordered to hide like something shameful, only make *you* more precious—this is the tax that we paid for the fact that someday you will survive us and will be better than us. This is not a reminder to us that we are mortal, but just the opposite: the marks of immortality. Do you understand? She will understand, she will have to understand this, as long as the delivery is right, the passion not too much . . .

So that's that. And there's only one physical loss, my dear child, that women avoid talking about, as if it were indeed shameful, and that, just so you know, is menopause, the word that you let fly so easily. You must think it's something like PMS, don't you? You noticed you are the only one taking tampons out of our box over the past four months (damn, I should have stolen a few . . .), you put two and two together, you clever girl, and gave your mother a drive-by diagnosis? No, Ulyanka, it's not the same at all, especially at forty-five. At forty-five, just so you know, it's too goddamn soon, and it comes down on you like the lid of a coffin. You come out of the doctor's office with this idiotic grin plastered onto your face, as if there's a crowd with paparazzi waiting for you, and you must not let them suspect anything, and you just keep carrying that grin along the street as if someone had slapped you in that office, and no one must find out. The loneliest experience in a woman's life. Never mind every one of us goes through it sooner or later—and each one wants it to be later, as late as possible, so you have women on the far side of fifty bragging about their periods like schoolgirls, with eye-rolling, stomach-grasping complaining about the irregular schedules and asking their younger girlfriends for tampons so that everyone would know that they've still *got it,* even though they understand that the younger ones can see exactly what they are doing and are secretly laughing at them—just as you laugh at your own mother now, until your time comes, and you hear that coffin lid coming down: only then does it become clear why nobody wants this particular experience and thus doesn't want to admit to it, because this, my friend, is the bell you can neither ignore nor protest, no matter how long you still have to live.

Just think: for thirty-five or forty years, or more, depending on your luck—that's twice as long as your present age—there is this idea alive in your body, on the cellular level, unknown to you, and all this time it acts as its conductor's baton: Do I or do I not want—right now, without delay, at this very point in my life—a child? And the rest of your body's orchestration, the monthly bubbling up and flooding, despite your will, is built according to this idea: it decides how to live to avoid a pregnancy, or how to acquire one, and you are like an instrument in an orchestra, you are plugged into all the secret rhythms, vibrations of the universe, pheromone choirs, weather patterns, magnetic storms, Mayan calendars, phases of the moon, ocean tides, all those things that you, my little friend, are only beginning to discover and make your own—now imagine they snatch that baton away from you—poof, it's gone! From this point on all your days run together, indistinguishable, as if you have been transported from spectacular mountain country onto an endless flatland covered in grey ash, and you lose your bearings—only your body continues to writhe like an animal that doesn't understand why it's been punished: it lows mutely, it fights, it struggles to get out of its own skin that's become a prison. Until it grows quiet and succumbs, because, in the end, we all go quiet. People still ask you if you happen to be pregnant, and you yourself are unsure of what's going on with you, until you find out it's menopause, very funny. Yesterday a maid, tomorrow a hag. A classic comedy of errors. A menopausal woman is such a comic figure:

men fall over themselves to pay her back for the power she used to have over them while she went around stinking to high heaven with pheromones, and the women, too, are not far behind, that whole fertile full-blooded herd is only too happy to expel the one who is no longer their *sister*. The one kissed by death. So that's whom you decided you want to join, daughter dearest. And that's why your silly ole mom lost control and slapped you. She is very sorry.

Olha was herself moved by her decisiveness. It was important that Ulyanka understand her as one woman understands another, for them to delineate a common territory—the one where she would always be needed by her daughter, because she, Olha, would have something to tell her about that which lies ahead for her. Ulyanka is a smart girl, she will understand. And from this territory, Olha's dead antediluvian lover, who passed through her life long before Ulyanka was even born, will appear, as Grandma Hanna would put it, a speck in the eye—as seen through the wrong end of the telescope. Regardless of what she might have been told by Odainyk's daughter. Somehow, Olha repeatedly failed to ask her husband, who shuttled between her and Ulyanka like an envoy between warring nations, to find out from Ulyanka what the name of that girl was. Who, obviously, is not to blame here, but who has become, for all intents and purposes, Olha's main adversary.

❖

The girl's name was Hanka—the first surprise thrown at Olha by the newly departed. In those times immemorial when she and Odainyk dreamed about their future, Olha confided in him that if they were ever to have a daughter, she would like to name her in honor of her grandmother Hanna—Hafia, in full. It's beautiful name, isn't it—Hafia: Hanka, Hasia. It has been ridiculed and spoiled, mocked as a hillbilly anachronism, so no one chooses it anymore, but it's so melodious, like a chord on a harp. And why, for example, is Sofia fine, and Hafia is not?

When Ulyanka was born, her father chose her name; Olha never thought of her as Hafia, not once during her whole pregnancy—as though her old fondness for the name was also infected by Odainyk, as if he crawled into her head, took it away from Grandma Hanna in there, and kept it for himself. And now we see that's exactly what he did, Olha's instincts did not betray her. Even from a distance he was eating and drinking up that which nourished her and gave her strength. *Her* roots, *her* resources.

"Probably Agafia, then?" she asked Ulyanka, her brow in a sarcastic arch while her heart quickened its beat: the conversation was going in a totally different direction from what she expected, but it had begun, Ulyanka was talking to her. "You know, don't you, that her father was working for the Russians? Did she tell you that?"

Ulyanka shook her head (gosh, it hasn't been that long since she braided her hair and the braids swung back and forth comically when she did that).

"No, Dad told me."

She paused, then said roughly, as if she'd had to find the courage to do it: "Is that why you broke up with him?"

Olha licked her suddenly dry lips. She doesn't know! Thank you, dear sweet Jesus, she doesn't know anything. To conceal her joy, which spontaneously spread across her face, she turned her back to Ulyanka and opened the fridge. Should she make them cocktails? Same size, like equals?

"That, too, among other things," she muttered, addressing the cheese. "That was the final blow, the last drop. He just wasn't the right man for me, not a match. Not like your dad. Would you like a mojito?"

"I'd like a martini, please."

Olha was struck by the automatic response—it revealed a habit: that's how you reply to a waiter who's getting in the way of an important conversation. Who's Ulyanka been going to bars with? With Hanka Odainyk?

She must be very lonely, that girl, if she came seeking Ulyanka's intimacy. Trying to become friends on the basis of "my father once had an affair with your mother" did not strike Olha as a normal thing to do; clearly this Hanka, be she Hafia or Agafia (or even just plain old Anna—the name is still stolen, stolen from her, Olha!) must suffer from neurosis and identity issues—Ulyanka told her dad that Odainyk left his family several years earlier and they, too, found out about his death from someone else and not immediately, and were told it was his heart, or maybe a stroke. Of course, to a seventeen-year-old it all sounds the same, Olha smirked, heart attack or stroke, they think fifty years old is one foot in the grave. She did not like the idea of Odainyk dying of a heart condition—it implied he had a heart, not just anatomically, and somehow catapulted him into being "one of us," one of the Kyivites who, after the troops opened fire at the Maidan protesters, suffered from posttraumatic stress for months, aggravated by the shock of war, and were so easy to pick out from the crowd because they spoke quietly and reacted violently to sudden noises—some froze if a spoon was dropped, clattering, to the floor in a restaurant, some couldn't swallow solid food because they had a lump in their throats, some had their hair fall out or nails break, the women had their cycles off kilter. Olha herself interpreted her physiological changes as delayed reactions to the stress of war and even humbly bragged about them sometimes, as in, there's always a silver lining—lost twelve pounds without even trying. At her concerts, people thanked her for her civic engagement, she felt electrified at all times, plugged into the national grief, and friends asked her to take good care of herself and not to take everything so much to heart, because cardiologists and neurologists were reporting an exponential leap in complaints and a shortage of in-patient beds—a collateral effect of any war that usually goes unnoticed, they talked a lot about this. And then she has to find out that the joke's on her, her civic engagement is plain old menopause, and it's Odainyk who gets to die of a broken heart. It's always like that, no sooner do you get used to a certain way of seeing things, you have to give it up, and how are you supposed to hold it together? The kid wants a martini now. Sometimes Olha could understand people who were nostalgic for the old Soviet days: at least nothing ever changed back then. You didn't have to make any choices.

"We're out of olives for the martini."

"I'll take a lemon, then."

"Do you, by chance, have a picture of her? On your phone?"

"Of Hanka?"

"Uh-huh." Olha energetically mashed mint leaves with a wooden pestle in a glass, sucking in the smell with her nostrils, like ozone after a storm. She would win, she would definitely win this duel with her daughter, she no longer doubted it.

"I don't know. I'd have to look. But you've seen her."

"I have? Where? When?" Forgetting her face, Olha turned back to Ulyanka, who sat slumped at the table—like a guest, Olha thought, She won't get up and come fuss in here with me. Must still be mad, then. "She's been to one of your shows—at the Docker, maybe. Or the Last Barricade."

Olha knew the kid wasn't being vague on purpose—she truly didn't keep track. Which hurt even more.

"Do you think I get so few people at my shows I remember them all? And I've never sung at the Last Barricade."

"Well, I don't know then. Hanka said it was a small place. She kind of dug you, by the way. She said you were okay."

"She did?"

"Yup." Ulyanka missed Olha's irony. "She said that all women do a terrible job with 'Day Goes, Night Goes,' but yours was pretty good.

And your jazz cover of 'Dance Me to the End of Love' sounded even better than Madeleine Peyroux's."

"I'll have you know I covered it way before she did." Olha took a deep breath, feeling her cheeks flush with inspired outrage. "Back in the nineties. I owned that song. And if people like Hanka's father hadn't taken the country apart and sold it to the Russians, who flooded all our airwaves with their dreadful pop, and drove us to begging, my albums would be selling hundreds of thousands today, have no doubt!" For a moment Ulyanka had that bored blah-blah-blah, heard-it-all-before look that was usually followed by a shadow crossing over Ulyanka's face, which was usually followed by, Just let me be, Mom! and Olha worried that her outburst had severed the contact she had barely established with her daughter—but Ulyanka was about to practice her deposition skills.

"That's not what Hanka said. She said her father paid for you to be auditioned by some big-deal producers, and they turned you down. Like your range wasn't good enough for the big stage, or your breathing, something like that. Basically, you didn't cut it—you were no Billie Holiday, they said."

"Is that really what she told you?"

Olha suddenly remembered the girl. She remembered the table at which she sat, how she was dressed—in green, like a troll, hair in dreadlocks, a dragon on one bare shoulder, a tattoo or a sticker. Someone like this would indeed attract Ulyanka as an antithesis to all the glamorous rich kids who drove their own Mercedes to class. She felt alone among them. The hip Hanka was awkwardly tall, with broad shoulders and large hands, altogether ill fitted, as if she hadn't learned how to inhabit her own body yet, or the body itself wasn't done coming together for her. It took Olha a while to notice the girl's fine features—she was quite beautiful when she sat still and stopped making faces—but Olha had noticed her not because of her appearance (although yes, the girl's profile plucked at a forgotten poignant string, made her wish, during the instrumental intervals, for the girl to turn around, let Olha see that profile), but because the girl *insisted* on being noticed no matter what and thus became a real bother for the musicians: she laughed loudly, talked at the wrong time, made things clatter, until even her friends began hushing at her, and Olha was left with an anxious aftertaste following that performance, unsure whether that girl was drunk, or high, or intentionally came to mock her. Olha dismissed the last thought outright—she could drive herself paranoid with that. And now it comes out.

Turn, girl, do turn around. Let me see your profile.

Again the dark forest came for her, sneaking up, entangling her legs in the dense brushwood, drawing her into the thickets. Setting its sights on her own child.

Oh no, that won't do. You'll get squat.

Maybe this is the girl's way of looking for a relationship with me, Olha thought in a flash of rage-powered insight. What if she wants me to adopt her, metaphorically? To tell her about her daddy—what a great catch he was, handsome and fun? I'm not such a heartless bitch that I would begrudge an orphan a few good words about her father; he was, in fact, good looking once and a fun time, so why shouldn't we talk about such a great guy? Like in that Lemkos folk song—"Let's drink for Yanichko, who has loved us four . . ." A gorgeous song, by the way, just begging for a jazz cover . . . She should invite her and Ulyanka, the two of them, for drinks—not for ice cream, mind you, they are grown women!—for drinks, for martinis, for double and triple martinis, let's drink, drink, ladies, so we could bring that little bumpkin, apple off a certain tree, into the fold of the family, talk to her about her daddy, may he have what he deserves wherever he is now—share the good memories, leave all the shit outside the frame, of course, the children don't need to know all that, neither his nor mine, I'm not a bitch, I am a mom, my job is to defend the little ones, and the one in dreadlocks knows this no worse than Putin and acts

accordingly—"Our troops will stand behind women and children"—
she set herself up behind Ulyanka and is coming at me like a tank.
Aren't you a clever one, Hanka! I wonder, is it nature or nurture—did
Odainyk have a chance to teach her how to live like this or did she follow her own nose to the same path? Because the strategy is the same:
worm your way into someone else's life, worm right into their weak
spots, get them to feed you, to give to you from their own heart (just
close your eyes and think of England, is that really so hard?), to feed
you as much as you want, as much as you need to grow and mature.
No, girl, you'll get squat. Wrong door. The only good thing I can tell
you about your daddy is to thank him for biting off less of me than
he could have, so that today I find myself neither in a ditch nor under
a fence somewhere—and I could have been!—that I didn't become
a whore, a drunk, a junkie, and most important, that nothing, you
hear me, you little shit, *nothing* binds me to him today—that I did
not give birth to *my* Hafia Odainyk with the full panoply of her dad's
characteristics that she'd have to spend her whole life spitting out of
her—now there's something that's indeed worth drinking to, every
single day, to celebrate to my dying day how lucky I am not to be *your*
mother. Is this what you'd like to hear from me?

Olha put the drinks on the table and let her hand rest, for a
moment, on the glass: the cold touch soothed like a cool towel on a
burning forehead. Don't look at me that way, she begged Ulyanka in
her mind. I am not your enemy, daughter dear. It's not me you have
to worry about.

She saw quite clearly, as is only possible among blood relatives—
as though she were looking at the world from inside Ulyanka's head—
why Ulyanka, who had already outgrown teenage rebellion, had
changed so much toward her recently, and had grown so much closer
with her father: for all these months the poor child measured herself
against Hanka Odainyk, as in a mirror—measured herself against a
girl who she, in her mind, *might* have been had she had a different

233

father, had her mom stayed with Odainyk. At seventeen this must take its toll, this constant measuring up—especially when the alternative father is dead and can't interfere with the workings of your imagination. Olha urgently felt she needed to hug the kid and hold her head against her chest, but the fear, deep in her stomach, that Ulyanka would tear herself loose, the way she'd been breaking away from any physical contact with her—cruelly, as if fighting off a rapist—brought Olha back to her senses and stopped her.

"You see, honey," Olha felt she finally found the right tone, "there's this thing called the revenge of a scorned man. Men, just so you know, hold grudges much worse than women. Once you leave him, he'll be making up shit about you for the next twenty years, and tell his children too. What I mean is you can tell your Hanka that at the time her father could barely afford cat food, let alone pay someone to audition me. He was almost half a million dollars in debt."

Olha was pleased to see Ulyanka's jaw drop at this, which instantly made her look like her eighteen-month-old self, a funny round-eyed toddler who saw a turtle for the first time, they took a picture.

"Of course, if this girl believes that her father was a gas oligarch and this is a part of her identity, then perhaps you shouldn't traumatize her, let her keep believing it—just please, not at my expense, because this is fake news . . . so, cheers?"

Ulyanka lowered her head over her glass. Then she turned away abruptly, and Olha, with that same prick of satisfaction, realized the girl was hiding tears—easy to tear up, just like her mom!

"Don't cry, kiddo," she said, gently. "It's not worth crying over. Just a burst illusion—that's not a loss."

Now, now was the time, Olha thought, flexing her muscles like a cougar before a leap, to pivot to her losses. And menopause, now the kid will understand. Cheers. She took a gulp from her glass, and the alcohol rolled down her throat like garland of happy lights coming on one by one. The invisible corpse of Odainyk that had been raised for a moment from under the floorboards went up in flames in her mind's eye, its final sparks circling around the kitchen and disintegrating into dust. Now she'll be able to mention him to Ulyanka in the future. Or not. It did not matter—she was free. Free.

A fat tear ran down Ulyanka's cheek and dropped on the table. Oh, baby—Olha felt a moist squeeze inside and a tickle in her nose, but the last thing she needed was to dissolve herself. It was probably because of this swell of sentiment that she didn't immediately hear the words Ulyanka half sobbed:

"You are such . . . you are all such . . . you all lie."

"Who do you mean—all?" Olha asked, stumped.

"You! The grown-ups!"

This came so unexpectedly childlike and pitiful from the mouth of her intelligent daughter, straight-A student, who, in conversations with her father, easily deployed words already quite obscure for her mother, that Olha almost laughed out loud—but then realized what Ulyanka said.

"Who's lying to you?"

"You are!" Ulyanka sniveled. "Why didn't you tell me any of this? You think I'm stupid, don't you? No, you don't even think that, because you just don't think about other people! You only think about yourself."

That's her slapping me back, flashed through Olha's mind: That's how she must have felt in the car when I hit her.

"*I* don't think about *you*, do I?" she repeated quietly, voice lowered by a third, into her deep-chest velvety timbre. She hesitated whether to add something more biting (If you're so unjust toward your own mother, how do you expect to judge other people one day?) but decided it would be too much; Ulyanka's sense of justice kicked in by itself—the girl blew her nose into a paper napkin and continued more calmly:

235

"You only think of how to keep me from *getting in your way*. That's the way you treat all people, not just me. Like everyone's doing backup vocals for you or something. You seem like you are onstage *all the time*, Mom. You want one thing from people, including me, and Dad—for us to harmonize with you. To hit the key, *your* key. That's why you don't have any friends of your own, it's only Dad's friends that ever come over here. You just don't see things that don't fit your narrative and you want me not to see them either. But I don't want to live like that."

"That's not fair." Olha felt helpless; she felt she was about to burst into tears—this time not in solidarity of feeling but entirely on her own.

"What's fair is not always something you like," Ulyanka recited something she obviously learned from someone else. "You want everything to be *perfect*. For everyone around you to say what a brilliant singer you are, what a passionate patriot, what a model family you have—heck, if I'd have gotten up onstage and sung with you—you'd be in heaven!"

"Just you wait—live a little, see how other people live, and you'll understand that you did, thank god, grow up in a model family. I can only hope you can build one as good for yourself one day."

"There won't be any liars in *my* family!" Ulyanka shot back with cold precision, and Olha felt like slapping her again. "You—everything about the way you live seems fake, Mom. Like it's all for show. Like you're forever trying to prove something to I don't know who, I don't know who'd gotten to you—but you have to keep showing how cool you are and how cool your life is. There can be nothing not cool in your life. If I'd been born with cerebral palsy or something, you'd have hidden me and never mentioned me to anyone, am I wrong?"

Is it, Olha desperately grasped at a new idea, that Ulyanka sees that Hanka girl this way—as a handicapped person, or something like that? She's always been such a sensitive girl.

"Or what if," Ulyanka continued, "I quit school and enlisted? Straight to the front, imagine that! Scary, isn't it, can you do that? You'd be hysterical for days until Daddy brought me back—go ahead, tell me I'm wrong?"

"What the hell are you talking about?" Olha's voice was muffled, a piano with the left pedal pressed. She felt a jolt of fear—a migraine?—Anything but that, I can endure anything, but why is the child being so cruel?

"Am I wrong? You just don't want to hear the kind of truth you don't like! You run away from it! Andriy told me his mom made dinner several times expecting you, because you promised her you and Dad would visit—but all for naught, because you did not come, you found something more important every time, a rehearsal, or some other bullshit. You don't want to see a cripple, do you? Well, you'll just have to!"

"Wait!" Olha pleaded. "I don't understand anything. What cripple? Who's Andriy?"

"Mine!" Ulyanka's voice welled with tears again, and Olha instantly realized—there it was, the real thing Ulyanka had been keeping down this whole time, *her* thing. "My Andriy!"

"I don't know anything about any Andriy. You haven't told me."

"Oh, this is rich! Talk about fake news. You don't know the Nazarenkos now?"

"The Nazarenkos?" Of course, Olha remembered, their boy's name was Andriy. "You mean their son? The one who came back from combat? So, are you . . . dating?"

Dear god, how old is he, that Andriy, he's an adult, he was in tenth grade when Ulyanka started school, no, wait, she was in second grade then, they went to a birthday party at the Nazarenkos', and he played with her, the good teenager with the little girl, told her stories, god, he's a veteran, a grown-up man, a year at war is like ten at peace, they say it takes months to get the grime out from under their fingernails, the things he must have seen out there, they say PTSD lasts years, oh Ulyanka-baby, you little duckling, a homebody girl with delicate hands, wait a minute, Mrs. Nazarenko said—so is it her he is planning to marry?

"We love each other!" Ulyanka exclaimed pathetically, and Olha thought—under different circumstances, she would smile: the declaration was so unnatural, as if in a foreign language; Ulyanka sounded like a child invited onto a chair to declaim a poem. But she did not smile. The Nazarenkos' son was older than Ulyanka by exactly the same number of years as Odainyk was compared to her, and there was something inexplicably horrible about this—something that shot heat into the base of her skull, like a signal flare, goose bumps running down her arms and legs, while Ulyanka, guessing nothing, kept plowing through her speech—clearly prepared and rehearsed with diligence to rival her mother's.

"And do not think for a second that you can talk me out of it, I know all your arguments in advance! I'm not afraid of his stump; I've seen him without his prosthesis, and we'll be ordering a new one, they make very good ones now, with sensors and stuff, not like the old hook, it's like an artificial hand, really cool, like a cyborg, and I told him, you're Freddy Krueger now, but you'll be Luke Skywalker."

Ulyanka giggled, and Olha, going numb, saw her daughter's face, wet eyelashes stuck together, lit from inside by the memory of that conversation—who she was talking to, who she was looking at at that moment—it filled with misty tenderness, aglow, as if it had finally found a source of light. So it's true, then—Olha believed her daughter, believed everything at once, in one leap, it was only her physical inertia that begged for one more minute, just two more clarifications, a reprieve, like the last cigarette for a man at the gallows.

"His hand?" she asked blankly.

Ulyanka rapidly—presto, presto, drumming on the keys—chattered about muscle engagement and the prosthesis's twelve functions—or was it twenty-four? Olha stopped understanding the words; she only saw Ulyanka's thumb held perpendicular to her hand—she was showing how it bends, then took the martini glass and held it, to make a point. Olha felt her forearms ache as though she grabbed and lifted an apartment building.

"So he . . . doesn't have an arm?"

"Only the hand," Ulyanka showed. "A grenade went off in it when he was tossing it away."

"But they said," Olha recalled, as if through deep water, "that he was fine."

"He *is fine*, Mom. He *only* lost his right hand. Things like that happen at war, it's normal." Jesus Christ, Olha thought, normal? "That's what prostheses are for."

And there I was, wanting to tell her all about loss. Olha hid her face in her hands. The sense of guilt that powered her shrieking among the cars on Saksahansky Street while the Tiffany-colored raincoat drew away from her, zigzagging through the traffic, came over her now with such force that she plummeted into it without a sound, like a rock to the bottom of a sea. Didn't look to it, popped up the forgotten expression in her head—what Grandma Hanna said about letting dough rise for too long. Seriously, how could she not have noticed, when she loaded the washing machine, that the sweat on Ulyanka's T-shirts started to smell different, a woman's sweat—sharp, musky, seductive? But no, she did notice it, she just stopped herself from thinking beyond this fact, was afraid to think forward, and blocked it. She was afraid of a lot of things in this life, that was the problem.

That's what Ulyanka, without even knowing it, is rebelling against—and her Andriy too. Something they'll never understand, and I can't explain to them: what it means to live in fear. To live *with* fear, like a member of your own family. I can't even explain it to Hanka Odainyk: that this was her father's greatest mistake—above all else, he wanted everything to *look* good, he bet on it, and was terrified of missing the mark. He listened to his own fear, and that's why in the end everything turned out so ugly for him, as only could happen to a man at his time and in his place. But this is something that his daughter will have to discover for herself—after she repeats, in a different key, a different arrangement, the main theme of his mistakes in her own life.

They have no fear, these children, Olha thought with an unbearable surge of tenderness—of her Ulyanka, and at once, through her, of the Nazarenkos' Andriy, and of other invisible children, myriad of them, who have suddenly stopped being children. When something frightens them, they do not run but go to face it. They take up arms and go to the front. They are not afraid to live, and to die, too, if they have to: they already know that, too, is a part of life. My girl, my dear little baby girl.

Tears streamed down her cheeks like from a poorly shut-off tap: as soon as one rolled down, another one took its place. There's nothing I can warn her against, Olha thought, as she automatically licked the tears off her lips, like salty raindrops. She'll go through everything I went through, but in her own way. My experience is of no help to her. I can't help her. She simply won't recognize it, she won't see when she is walking in my steps—at least not until she reaches my age. Until she catches up to me at precisely this point—but I'll no longer be there.

But then—there's still a chance then: as long as I'm alive, and in possession of my faculties, like Grandma Hanna, lucid till the end, we will be able to meet up again as equals, and in that narrow strip of time (a narrow beach, a sandy spit) speak to one another, and hear each other. Then we'll have lots to talk about—in just thirty years, it's not that long to wait. And that will be our last time, kiddo. We had one such time, we were lucky. With more luck, we might have another one. But we won't have the third—no one has the third chance while alive.

Olha raised her head and looked at her daughter through all her tears at once.

"To the end of love," she uttered, in a voice heavy and moist as a soaked quilt. "That's what it is." She wanted to sing a bar from Cohen's tango, but her moist voice faltered, and she was afraid that she'd start weeping for real, knocking head against table. "You are right. At your age, I'm afraid I wouldn't have had it in me to love a cripple. You are very brave."

Ulyanka made a confused noise:

"There's a war on now, Mom. You can't compare . . ."

"I know. That changes a lot. But not everything."

"Come on, give me your glass, it's long been empty."

"I could use another drink," Olha said.

"I'll make you one."

"Make one for yourself, too, as long as you're up there."

"I will."

Ulyanka got up, a dazzling wavering shape in the tears still perched between her mother's eyelids.

"Just don't cry, okay, Mom?"

Olha smiled. A child is always scared when Mom is crying; a mother is not supposed to cry. Mom can do anything—yell, curse, nag, grow old, grow strange—but not cry. No child should be afraid, not at any age.

"I won't," she said. "You know what I just thought of? Why don't you invite Andriy over on Sunday? And I'll sing Cohen for you? Would he like that?"

ABOUT THE AUTHOR

Oksana Zabuzhko is one of Ukraine's most celebrated contemporary writers and the author of more than twenty books. She graduated from the Department of Philosophy of Kiev's Shevchenko University and obtained her PhD in philosophy of arts. Since publishing her influential novel *Fieldwork in Ukrainian Sex* (1996, published in 2011 in English translation by Halyna Hryn), she has been working as a freelance author.

Zabuzhko lives in Kiev, where she and her partner, artist Rostyslav Luzhetskyy, operate a small publishing house.

Zabuzhko's books have been translated into fifteen languages. Among her numerous acknowledgments are a MacArthur Grant (2002), the Antonovych International Foundation Prize (2008), the Order of Princess Olga (2009), and the Shevchenko National Prize of Ukraine (2019). Her magnum opus, *The Museum of Abandoned Secrets* (2010, published in 2012 in English translation by Nina Murray, won the Angelus Central European Literary Prize (2013) for the best novel of Eastern and Central Europe.